Nuclear Knights

Nuclear Knights

Jesse Wilson

Published 2021 by Next Chapter
Cover art by Cover Mint

Chapter One

The dust blew across the land, the same as it had done for ages. Ryan sighed as he watched the deep yellow sun just start to break the horizon through the small opening in his wall he called a window. Another day in the wasteland, another day trying to live. Ryan rubbed an old injury on his arm, long since healed but that phantom pain still persisted. He did his best to ignore it.

He walked through his house that looked like it was going to fall over at any minute to his clothes of which he didn't have many. An old black shirt, jeans and a worn-out pair of shoes that had seen better days. It only took a few minutes to get dressed and a bit longer to fasten his gun belt.

The shack was nothing more than rusty sheet metal attached together in the shape of living quarters. The walls were much the same. Brown, rusted metal separating him from the outside. On the shelves were cans of food and bottles of water and he moved to the equally excuse he had for a door to his shack.

He shut the patchwork door behind him, turned and tied it shut with his frayed rope. Security around here was all for show, the only thing of value he owned was the blaster in the old leather holster on his hip. He took a breath of fresh air, at least as fresh as it got. There was always a slight metallic scent on the air. It was the best way Ryan could ever describe it. In a life of constant change and potential for it, this was one thing that never changed. It comforted him, he almost smiled.

Ryan walked down the path to the side of his shack, this early in the morning was the best time to be out and about. The heat didn't get bad for a few more hours and he needed to do his part to refill the town's water supply. It was a job, everyone had one if they wanted to live anywhere. Thankfully he happened to like his after about five years of doing it.

He walked to the side of his house and picked up the end of a net that was filled with gallon buckets. With a grunt he dragged the end of the net on to a metal trailer and quickly fastened the ends down on the side with the same old cable he'd been using for a couple of years now.

Then he walked to the front, picked up the dust covered cable and hooked it around the hitch on the back of his small hoverbike. It only took a few seconds to make sure it was secure before getting on the bike. He flipped a switch and the old machine hummed to life, lifted off the ground. Ryan put on his goggles and eased the thing away from his stitched together shelter.

There were other people here in town and most of them didn't bother getting up before the sun came up. Ryan didn't care if the hum of his bike was going to wake anyone up or not. He got to the wall in just a few minutes and slowed to a stop at the gates.

"Why are you going on a water run this early?" a man on the wall asked him. He was wearing brown pants and a white shirt, both covered in dust and frayed around the edges. "I don't know, I just want to beat the crowd is all I suppose," Ryan replied and there was a second of silence. "We haven't had a report of a beast in weeks, so I guess it's okay to go out," the man said, put his tattered glove around the metal switch and pulled it. Ryan nodded at the information.

"You don't say? I haven't seen one of those things in almost a year now, and D-class don't count," he replied. No one counted the D-class as a threat. Matt just laughed in response as the gates slowly started to open.

The lights on the metal gate flashed green then swung open with a slow squeak. "Hey, if you find a box of Twinkies in the city, can you bring one back?" Matt asked and Ryan sighed. "I'm not going to the city, the place has been picked clean, you know this," he replied and Matt laughed.

"I know, I just had a dream about them last night is all," Matt replied and Ryan tilted his head. As far as he was aware, the only time either of them had ever seen a Twinkie, was in an ancient advertisement that a trader caravan brought on the rare occasions. He shook his head and got to the task at hand and the realization of what Matt just said.

"You're on the night watch, you're not supposed to be dreaming about anything," Ryan said as the gate finished opening. Matt just nodded, smiled and motioned him to go through. "Yeah, yeah, just come back in one piece and if you meet one of those things out there, please don't lead it back here, please," Matt said and Ryan shook his head. "I live here, so yeah, not a problem," he replied sarcastically and moved through the gate into the desert beyond.

He pushed his hoverbike down the dirt path and into the desert towards the river. Ryan heard tales of the before time. The older people often told tales of green lands, water and paradise that were passed down to them from generations past. Ryan couldn't imagine that much green could ever exist in one place, or water, or anything else like it.

He was born in this wasteland and this was all he knew. The quiet was always relaxing. The way the old timers described the world in the before days always sounded like noise and constant chaos. Ryan liked this world, it was his world. Dangerous, but fair, usually.

It wasn't long before he made his final turn and saw the bright green river flowed in front of him. the rays of the sun glinting across its water. This river might have had a name once, but now everyone just called it the river. No one he knew had ever seen where it started, or where it ended. All anyone knew was that it was constant and if it ever went away, they would too.

He pulled up to the muddy shore and turned his bike off, it slowly moved down to the sand and he got off the bike. He walked to the back, untied the net to bring his plastic jugs to the water. He looked up and down the shore. Sometimes predators liked to hang out in the early morning hours like this and being too careful was never a bad idea.

Today, nothing. Maybe they had a good night eating, he didn't worry about them and he hoped they didn't want to eat him. It worked out fine so far. He started to pull the jugs out of the net and started to kneel near the edge of the river when suddenly he heard a deep noise but he felt it in his chest. The ground beneath him shifted a little.

"No," he whispered to himself and stood up. This was the telltale sign of a beast. Every kid was taught that from the beginning. Shaking earth, silence and the smell of ozone. That last one wasn't always reliable. The earth shifted again, this time he was sure something was close, but he still didn't see anything.

Then in the middle of the river, the green water bulged up. "Oh," he said and backed off. The thing rose out of the river and stared blankly ahead. It had long floppy ears, a brown shell on its back. Its skin was dark green and it stood on two stocky legs, its arms were just long enough to be useful. They ended in long claws. The thing stood one hundred feet tall. Ryan sighed with relief and a smile.

"You're just a D class," he said and knew he was relatively safe. D class beasts were big doofs, harmless mostly. It took a special kind of stupid to get killed by a D class. "You must be my good luck charm for today," he said to the beast in the middle of the river. He was sure it saw him, too, but neither one was a threat to another.

Ryan kept an eye on the beast as he continued to unload his plastic jugs on the shore when the thing turned its head in his direction and its pale green eyes went wide. Ryan wasn't sure what he did to anger the nameless thing, but a second past and it was easy to realize that it wasn't looking at him at all, but past him, towards where he lived. With a high pitched bark of fright, the D class beast wasted no time in diving into river in a panic.

"No," Ryan said in a hurry and ran to his hover bike as the large wave of water created by the sudden diving thing threatened to destroy the second most valuable thing he had. He turned it on as the wall of water was getting closer. The machine came to life, the second it lifted from the ground Ryan spun the bike around. He floored it seconds before the water washed over the shore line.

He sped away and didn't care about the jugs, they could be replaced. Something spooked that thing and the only thing capable of doing that, was a higher-class beast. He sped down the dirt path and stopped after that last turn. The sight he was seeing, it didn't make any sense. Mere minutes ago, the place was fine. Now a three hundred foot beast was wading through the center of town. He could hear the alarms still blaring in the distance.

The thing had dark purple skin and like most of the beasts wandered blindly ahead on two, thick and powerful legs. It had one row of black spines running down its back. Its arms were long, thick and powerful, but they were bent with its hands hanging limp. Ryan looked up at the thing's dinosaur head. The first thing he noticed were the eyes, they were closed.

"What in the hell?" he asked himself. He'd never seen anything like it, but then again, the last time he was in an attack, he didn't have time to study the monster from a distance either. These days monster attacks like this rarely happened, not since the knights took down the last walking nightmare five years ago.

Ryan looked ahead of the beast and he could see the crowd of people fleeing from the monster as it slowly lumbered through the village with no effort at all. Then he looked to his left and on a hill, in the increasing light, he saw a someone dressed in silver and it looked as if they were holding a strange device in his hands. There was no way the two events weren't connected. He spun his hoverbike around in the stranger's direction and rode as fast as he could.

He didn't really think about what he was doing rather than thinking that this was something that had to be done. If someone was somehow using the monster to attack where he lived. He needed to figure out how, why. So many questions and things that didn't make any sense.

The stranger lowered the device as Ryan sped in his direction and looked right at him. Ryan knew there was no running, he was going to find out who this was. Then the silver figure disappeared right before his eyes in a flash of green light before he was close enough to see anything else about them. "Damn it," he said and stopped the bike.

Just another thing that didn't make sense. He'd never seen anyone disappear before.

Ryan turned around and watched. The beast in the middle of town stopped in its tracks. It shook its head as if it was just waking up from a dream. Not only from a dream but the eyes opened, it looked around at where it was. The beast was clearly confused, maybe even nervous. The expression changed at once and it turned around as slowly as it could, as if to not do any more damage than it already had and began to walk away.

He'd never seen a beast do that before, usually they were, well, much more vicious. Then he looked to the opposite end and thankfully there was a crowd of people evacuating town. He accelerated the bike in their direction kicking up a trail of dust behind him.

Chapter Two

Ryan slowed down as he got to the crowd. The thunderous footsteps of the beast fading as it left town. He saw Matt towards the back making sure people were alright. "What in the hell happened here?" Ryan asked him and Matt shook his head. "I don't know, it, well, it just came out of nowhere. I swear one minute everything was fine and then it just was right there," Matt said and that didn't make any sense to Ryan.

"How could it sneak up on you. It wasn't a ground dweller C-class or something. It was a B class beast. You can't exactly just not see it, you know?" Ryan asked again and Matt shrugged. "I am telling you, it just appeared out of the dark," Matt replied and as much sense as it didn't make, it was just another thing on the list of things that didn't make sense today.

"Well, it's gone now, we got lucky. I need to check to see if the water purification center is smashed or not. If it is we'll need to spend a few days in Hadoth until we can get it fixed," Ryan replied and Matt looked into the wreckage of the city. "It's smashed, I don't need to go in there to check to know that. I think the thing just stepped on it," Matt replied and Ryan was about to agree when another voice began to speak over the crowd and the various voices quieted. Matt and Ryan turned to pay attention as well.

"Well, that's one hell of a wakeup call," the man said and the crowd had a slight laugh. He was wearing a tan shirt with faded green pants. He stood at the front of the crowd.

"Alright, me and a couple of others are going to go to Hadoth to get a new water unit. The rest of you are going to stay here. The damage is contained and I don't see too much fire, most of it can be repaired by what we have on hand. We have two days' worth of clean water saved up, three if you ration it out," he said and tossed a ring of keys to a man beside him who caught it.

The man looked over the crowd and saw Ryan who still had a bike, and the man responsible for not warning them in advance right next to him. He knew that they'd eventually blame him Matt for this so it was right then he decided who was coming with him. "Ryan, Matt, you're coming with me," he said to them. This attracted the attention of the others. Matt was on part of the night watch and the beast walked from his direction. The pieces were starting to come together.

"You're lucky he picked you, these people might get mad and kill you once the shock passes," Ryan said and continued. "Get on my trailer and I'll get you away from the crowd," Ryan said under his breath and Matt didn't have to think twice about that. People were already starting to look in their direction. Matt quickly jumped on and Ryan took off towards the leader of the village.

"Thanks," Matt said the second they pulled up to him. "Don't thank me. I'm just saving you from being hanged. If I find out you were sleeping on the job, well, you won't be so lucky," Joppo said and Matt looked at the crowd, then at the destruction behind them.

"Joppo, man, you've got to believe me. I swear. It just appeared out of nowhere. There is no way it could have snuck up on me. Or anyone, the thing was a B-class, they aren't known for their stealth," Matt said but Joppo wasn't interested in stories.

"Don't worry. The cameras will let me know what's up. You two wait here. I'm going to get my pack and we'll start going to Hadoth in twenty minutes," Joppo said and Ryan nodded. "I need to get mine too, if it's not crushed," Ryan said and shut the bike off, it settled to the ground.

"You stay here with my bike, I need to get mine too. If yours isn't flattened I'll pick it up. If it is, you're going without. I'm pretty sure you were sleeping on the job," Ryan finished and he got off the bike and started to walk back to the village.

"Thanks," Matt said and sat down on the trailer, the crowd began to leave and Joppo and Ryan disappeared into it. Matt crossed his arms and looked around. Something about being out here alone was making him nervous. If that thing could appear out of nowhere, nothing was stopping it from happening again. The sun was barely up this morning, but it was already getting hot. Right now, all he really wanted to do was go home and go to sleep. He wasn't even sure if he had a home left.

Chapter Three

"Joppo, I saw something strange during the attack," Ryan said as they walked behind the crowd. "What?" Joppo asked. "Someone in silver, it, well, it looked like it was controlling the monster. I tried to chase them down but whoever it was disappeared," Ryan said and Joppo shrugged.

"I've got no idea what that could be, I've never heard of anything like that. Maybe the Hadoth people will know something," he replied and continued. "Why would you run after someone like that?" Joppo asked. Ryan wasn't sure and didn't have an answer.

"Well, if you see any more weird people in silver, maybe it's best to just steer clear of them for now," Joppo added as they walked. Ryan wasn't okay with that, but figured it was the best course of action, at least for now.

They got into the village and the place was a mess the farther they walked. The crowd ahead of them started to wail. Houses were smashed into rubble and smoke rose up into the sky. Thankfully no major fires had broken out yet.

The beast's stroll through town could have been worse, Joppo supposed. He had a sigh of relief and thanked the universe for small favors. His hut was intact besides a large wooden beam sticking through the side of the wall.

"Alright, I'll meet you out at your bike in twenty minutes. I need to talk to Lisa while I'm gone. I hope your place is still standing, good luck," Joppo said and walked towards his house. Ryan could only hope for the best at this point.

Ryan broke away from the crowd and made his way back to his house, thankfully the creature didn't get this far into the town. His simple place was just like he left it. He walked to the door and unlocked it, stepped inside.

"Sorry about this, but I had to test out my theory," a voice said in the dark and Ryan pulled his blaster immediately in the direction of the voice. A woman walked out of the dark, dressed in the silver clothes as before. He noticed right away that her eyes were dark purple.

"I, well, I have some questions," he said and she crossed her arms. "No one has ever seen me work before. I just wanted to meet the person who did before I killed you," she said with a smile and lifted a strange looking weapon in his direction. Ryan fired and the green blaster beam hit her silver clothes and dissolved harmlessly into green sparks.

She pulled the trigger on her weapon and a blue beam hit Ryan in the stomach and knocked him straight back through the door, tearing it off its weak hinges in the process. Ryan landed on the ground and his wound sizzled. He heard footsteps coming towards him. "I know you're not dead, also I know you're not willing to talk but I need to know. Did you happen to tell anyone else you saw me? Because that would be really inconvenient," she asked him.

Ryan opened his eyes. "I'm not going to—" she pointed her weapon at his head. "You tell me who you told or I'll bring my pet back and kill everyone. No one is going to miss this garbage fire of a village, but I'd rather not attract any unneeded attention until the time is right. One more time, who did you tell?" she asked again and narrowed her purple eyes at him.

"Joppo, Matt. That's all. I swear, that's all," Ryan said between breaths. She smiled, nodded and sighed. "I have no idea who they are. You're going to have to show them to me," she said knelt down, pulled a syringe filled with bright red liquid and injected him with it. Ryan's pain faded just a few seconds after she pulled the needle out.

"What in the hell did you do to me?" he asked and sat up. "First aid kit, you wouldn't understand and you're not going to live long enough to care anyway," she said and put the syringe back where she got it. Then she tossed him two tiny metal spheres and they landed on his chest. "Put one on each of the people you told and don't tell anyone. Remember, everything you see here is one monster attack away from obliteration," she said to him with a smile.

"How did you even find me?" Ryan asked as he sat up. "You're going to be dead in ten minutes. Who cares," she replied and disappeared before his eyes. Ryan looked around and was really surprised no one was around to see any of this. "Damn it," he said to himself and had no idea what to do next. He supposed he was being watched, too. He picked himself up and was still sore from the experience but glad to be breathing, at least for now.

He walked back to his now damaged place and went inside. Then he found his travel pack. In a world like this you had to always keep a thing like this on hand. He picked it up and put the strap over his shoulder. None of this seemed real, but the fading pain was a good reminder that he needed to think of something to prevent the disaster that was coming.

There was no reason to trust the stranger. If she really could control the beasts, nothing was stopping her from unleashing the monster on the town again even if he did what she wanted. Ryan looked at the trackers in his hands and knew what he had to do. There was no choice and it was worth the risk. He squeezed the metal orbs in his hand and walked away from his house and started to make his way back to his hoverbike.

Chapter Four

"What did you do?" he asked just after he appeared behind her. "Lam, I have it under control. These peasants are idiots," she replied. Lam crossed his arms and stepped beside her. They were overlooking the wrecked village. "You call sending in a B-class beast to a small town smart? This was stupid. I assume that you didn't finish the job because the device failed?" Lam asked her and she shook her head. "No, one of the locals saw me, then he told two of his buddies. I'm just waiting for him to place the trackers on them so I can kill the three of them," she said and smiled.

"That's the dumbest plan I've ever heard. No one is going to believe them, even if they believe him and, wait, trackers?" Lam asked and he didn't like where this was going. "Yeah, I did the old teleport into his house bit and threatened him with a shot to the stomach," she replied and smiled.

"First, how did you know what house was his, secondly, why would you do that?" Lam asked her and he was annoyed. All of this was just getting worse. "She isn't going to like this, and you know I have to report this, right?" he asked and she sighed. "Yeah, I know," she replied and he shook his head. "Nyogyth, listen. I know you think this plan is going to work, but you need stop rushing it. Controlling the monsters is genius, but you need to slow down," Lam said to her and she grunted, crossed her arms.

"What's the point of going slow. There isn't going to be anything left of the world at this rate. These people can't fix anything. All of humanity is hanging by a thread. I mean look at this dump. People call this home," Nyogyth said in frustration. Lam shook his head. "It's been like this for over a hundred and fifty years. I am sure the world will be fine for a little while longer," he replied and continued.

"Go home, give me the tracker frequencies and I'll follow your mistakes and see what happens. I'm sure it'll be fine. You're not in the right mind for this right now," Lam said and Nyogyth shook her head. "Fine, the trackers are on the beta frequency, good luck," she said, pushed a button on her wrist and disappeared in green light.

Lam took the scanner off his belt and adjusted it to track the beta frequency. Sure, enough there were three trackers and they were all still in the same place. "Damn it, woman. Everything was going so nice too," Lam said and hated being on this monster infested, burned out planet. Lam thought about just going back home and he almost did it too. For now, he would wait for the three of them to be a little more isolated.

Joppo made it to his house. It wasn't much more impressive than any other in this village. "Lisa, are you in there?" he asked and for a second, there wasn't an answer. He walked to the door and went inside. "Hey, I need to go to Hadoth, where are you at?" he asked, the silence was starting to make him feel uncomfortable.

"Yeah, I'm out back, I can barely hear you," she yelled from outside and all of his tension went away. She sounded fine at least. He walked through the house and through the back door. She was just getting finished moving debris off the hoverbike in the back. "It's not broke is it?" he asked. "Nah, just buried a little. Not a problem," she replied.

"Good, and thanks. I need to go do Hadoth and report the damage, and we need a new water purification unit," he said and she nodded. "Yeah, I know. I heard you tell everyone. I know what to do. Don't worry about this place. I'm sure the monster won't come back," she said, he had no idea how she could be so sure about that.

"Well, keep the people busy, you know what to do. I just wanted to say goodbye before I left. We should only be gone a couple of days," he said and she smiled. "Yeah, you know I hate it when you go, but just be careful, okay?" she said and he nodded. "Of course, you know I will," he replied and looked at his bike. "The last thing I wanted to do today was take a road trip, I really hate road trips," he said.

"I got the pack ready, it's behind you. You can leave at any time," she said and smiled and he nodded. "The sooner I leave the faster I get to come back," Joppo said as he turned around, walked to his pack and picked it up. He looked at it the way he always did, a brown leather bag that was always the only line of defense against death outside of the walls of this place. He hated it as much as he needed it. "Well, Lisa, thanks a lot, again. I love you and I'll see you soon," he said and she smiled.

"Love you too, now get out of there. I'll have this place as good as new by the time you get back," she replied and he walked towards the bike, as he did, she grabbed him and kissed him as he walked by, surprising him. He returned it and did it the same as he did every time, like it was the last time. Neither of them ever talked about it, but they and everyone else knew that every day out here in the wasteland could be their last, today almost was.

He drew back with a smile. "I can't wait to get back home," he said and she let him go. "Me either," she replied and looked at the mess. Realizing other people had it so much worse right now.

With that Joppo moved to his bike, got on it. He was hoping it wouldn't start, he didn't really want to go anywhere but as he flipped the switch the thing hummed to life and lifted off the ground. "Good, it still works," he said with a heavy amount of sarcasm.

She laughed and watched as he slowly started to go down the path and quickly disappear around a corner. Lisa knew each time he disappeared like this, might be the last time she, or anyone else ever saw him again.

Chapter Five

Joppo made his way out of town and back to where he expected the others to be. Matt was sleeping on the trailer and Ryan was leaning against his bike. "No pack for Matt?" Joppo asked him. In all the things that just happened, he forgot all about it. "Uh, no, but we have a problem," Ryan replied, held out his hand and showed the trackers. "What are those?" Joppo asked, these metal things didn't mean anything to him.

"Trackers, remember that person I told you about, they found me. Joppo, we're going to die out here," Ryan said and had panic in his eyes. Joppo rubbed his chin and thought about it for a few seconds. "Here, I have an idea," he said and continued. "Throw them on the ground," he said and Ryan looked at him like he was crazy.

"You don't know these people, I don't know these people, but this lady, she shot me, then made me better with something," Ryan said and was beginning to panic, he wasn't listening to Joppo as the panic inside him rose. "Ryan, put the trackers on the ground," Joppo said again calmly. Ryan shook his head and dropped the two orbs onto the sand. Joppo took his blaster off of his side, pointed, and pulled the trigger. His green beam hit the metal and melted them instantly. Ryan jumped back in surprise.

"There, problem solved," Joppo said and put his blaster back. Ryan looked around, he expected an assassin to jump out at any moment to kill them all. Nothing happened, however, Ryan didn't feel like he was safe at all, less than usual. "Come on, let's get going. Once we get to the city we get what need we can get back. This is just a milk run if anything. Let's not over complicate it," Joppo said and Ryan was confused.

"You don't seem too worried about the crazy invincible assassin. If I didn't mention it, I shot her and nothing happened. Your blaster is about the same as mine and it did nothing," Ryan said and Joppo just shrugged. "I guess if she shows up we'll have to go low tech, then. If blasters don't work, I'm sure this will," he said and moved his vest just enough to reveal a black pistol in a holster under it. Ryan didn't know he had one of them. He'd heard stories but never saw one before.

"Just uh, keep this to yourself, alright?" Joppo said and smiled. Ryan was impressed, he wasn't convinced it would work. Ryan got on his hover bike and switched it on. "Is he going to fall off?" Joppo asked looking at Matt passed out in the trailer. "I guess we'll find out," Ryan said and was relieved that the trackers were gone. He felt as If he was forgetting something, however.

Joppo took one last look at the village then turned back to the open road that pushed through the hills and started to move forward. Ryan quickly did the same thing and they were on their way. Hoverbikes were the main mode of transportation, but they were slow. Ryan looked at his speedometer and it was topping out at forty-five miles an hour already. "Can you believe the stories we used to hear as kids. Things that could go hundreds of miles an hour?" Joppo said and laughed.

"Yeah, I can, we could use some of that right now," Ryan replied. He didn't like talking and driving at the same time or going on road trips. Ryan also was still worried that at any moment now someone was going to be standing in the road ready to kill them. "What we really need is to just get to where we are going. That crazy silver woman could still come back," he said and Joppo shook his head.

"She won't be coming back. They always pull stuff like this. The outlanders and the knights have been, say, abrasive towards one another since the fall, they'll ignore and forget about you. I promise," Joppo said and Ryan looked at him, taking his eyes off the road.

"Joppo. The knights haven't been seen in five years. Are you telling me the silver woman was a real outsider?" Ryan asked. Joppo nodded. "Yes, they aren't just stories you know. Just not talked about a lot or seen often," Joppo replied to him. Ryan wasn't all that surprised. He'd never seen one before but now that he thought of it, the silver people, the description matched some of the stories he's heard in the past. Those stories were always the same. People see them in the distance, shiny clothes and only for a few seconds.

Joppo smiled. "Yeah, I guess so. I mean. The elders of the villages know about it. It's kind of a secret that we all share. We don't know much more than you do, but it's the main reason we haven't all been overrun by the beasts. The knights keep them in check like they always have since the fall. The outlanders, well, they are just weird," Joppo said as much as he knew.

Then it occurred to him that Joppo was telling him all of this without hesitation. "And keep your eyes on the road," Joppo added. Ryan realized that he was distracted and put his eyes back in front of him. Nothing was there, however, just miles of empty desert.

"Ryan, I'm thirty six years old. I'm not going to live forever. Today's attack made me realize that someone should be ready to be in charge. You've been the water man since you were fifteen years old. You're reliable and the people depend on you. So, why not you take over when I'm gone?" Joppo asked him and Ryan's eyes went wide. "What about Lisa?" he asked quickly.

"She hates it. She hates it that I'm the leader most of the time. She says constantly that when I get stepped on or sick and die that she's giving all of the stuff up. You're what, twenty-one now. I mean I don't plan on dying anytime soon but, you know, good to be prepared and all that," Joppo said as they took a curve on the road. "I'll think about it. No promises," Ryan replied. Joppo smiled.

"There never are any promised things in this world, but if you could keep what I told you to yourself, that'd be good. I don't plan on checking out yet," Joppo said to him. Ryan nodded. "I understand. I'll think about it. Right now, we should just focus on getting to the city," Ryan replied.

The two of them drove on the lonely road. Ryan was about to say something else but as soon as he started to open his mouth, there standing in the road was a silver figure. They were standing in the distance right in the middle of it.

"Oh, damn it, look. I told you she'd show up again. How did she find us, you melted the trackers," Ryan said and began to slow down. "No idea, maybe we can talk some sense into her. She must have put a tracker on you while you were injured," Joppo said and slowed down with him.

Ryan put his hand into his left pocket and sure enough was a tiny orb. He pulled it out and saw a similar tracker. "Damn it, why didn't I check?" he asked himself and tossed it off to the side in a hurry, feeling really disappointed himself for not knowing better, he was sure that he'd never figure out how that got there.

"Don't worry about it, just stay calm," Joppo said as the two of them approached the silver figure and slowed down and came to a stop just before they met with the figure. To both of their surprise it was a man. Ryan didn't know what was going on. The man in the silver suit had his hands behind his back and began to walk forward.

Chapter Six

"Hello, wasteland people. My name is Lam. I believe one of you met an associate of mine?" he said to them in a cold, almost robotic voice. Ryan's eyes shifted nervously, Lam caught it. "It must have been you. I would, well, like to apologize for any threats she might have made," Lam said and shook his head. "She gets a little too motivated in her mission. So, if we can agree to keep that, and this little encounter a secret I think everything will work out nicely. What do you say?" Lam asked the both of them.

Joppo studied the Outlander carefully. Lam was aware of Joppo's eyes but it didn't bother him. Ryan swallowed and felt like he couldn't breathe. Everything felt like it was closing in around him. "Yeah. I can keep a secret," he said weakly and wasn't sure if it was just in his head or not.

"Excellent, I'm glad we came to an understanding," Lam said and leaned to the left. Matt was still sleeping in the trailer. He didn't need any more people knowing anything. "I'll expect you both to be quiet," he said then he disappeared in a white flash of light with the noise of a small explosion.

Matt woke up at the sudden noise with a start. "What, why are you stopped, what happened?" he said trying to get his bearings. "Joppo's old bike just had a loose compressor, you know how it is," Ryan said quickly. "I didn't know they could get that loud," Matt said and laid back down. "Alright, let's go to Hodath," Joppo said and started moving forward again. Ryan did the same thing. His anxiety was going away, but not much.

Matt passed out again and Ryan looked back briefly to make sure. "Does that happen a lot?" he asked and Joppo just shrugged. "Not really. They usually keep to themselves. None of the elders know where they come from or where they go. That was the first time I've ever seen one in real life. It has only been pictures up until now," he replied. "They are much shinier than I remember the picture I saw," he added and wasn't sure what to think.

"I guess secret keeping is part of the job when you're the leader. Besides no one is going to believe us anyway that we saw one anyway," Ryan supposed that was true, but he didn't want to break his world to the shiny person.

Hours on the dirt road past, the two of them didn't have anything to add on to the situation. Then the road took a final right turn and revealed to them the broken city. For miles in all directions all they could see were burned out and broken skyscrapers, hundreds of years old. A scar from the past that endured. The wasteland was filled with such reminders of how the Earth used to be before the fall.

"Every time I see this place it gives me chills," Joppo said and took it all in. He could only imagine the beasts that ruined this place and the terror people felt seeing them for the first time. They could still smell a faint whiff of smoke, nothing to do with the past, however.

The broken cities were lawless places where the sand raiders like to live. To get to Hadoth, you had to get through here. "What do you think, should we go through here or go around?" Joppo asked him and Ryan didn't know what was worse. Meeting a potential beast on the outside roads or meeting a gang of cannibals in the city.

Ryan knew this was a test. It was obvious to him that it was nothing else. "We need to get back home so we can't waste time trying to go around," Ryan replied and Joppo nodded. "You got that right. It's only a couple days through the city but I think we can make it," he replied and Ryan took a deep breath. The ocean of wreckage lay out endlessly before them. "Alright, let's go," Ryan said.

Ryan and Joppo started pushing their hoverbikes down the beaten dirt path. The dirt beneath them slowly gave way to shattered and broken asphalt that had been warped with heat, radioactive fire from days gone past. The first building they passed had faded red letters on a blue sign, tilted to the right. The remaining letters only spelled out half a word Walma, it read.

"You know, I've been that by that sign a hundred times I bet and I can't figure out for the life of what a Walma could have been. The before people sure were weird," Joppo said as they drove by. "It's too bad all this had to happen, but if it didn't, we likely wouldn't exist," Ryan said. Joppo wondered if never existing would have been better.

The wreckage increased along the sides of the broken road as they hovered over the deep cracks in it. The signs of the Sand Raiders quickly became visible. Shattered skeletons tied to posts, half bone, half jagged metal to replace the bones that were missing, all of them painted red. Ryan wasn't sure where they got the paint, it that's what it was.

"They mostly come out at night so we should be safe. The closer we get to Hadoth the less we'll see that nonsense," Joppo said and Ryan shook his head. "Mostly?" he asked, his eyes jumping around to every shadow now, instantly nervous about being attacked at any time. And to his realization and horror, the shadows and places to hide around here were endless.

"Look on the bright side, if we get caught we can give them the screw up back there to eat and they might us go," Joppo said and Ryan sighed. "You do understand that it is impossible for a monster like that to sneak up on anyone, even if they are sleeping," Ryan replied and continued. "I swear, the silver people are up to something and—" Joppo cut him off.

"Relax, I know it's impossible but you know how mobs get. I won't give anyone up to the sand people to eat if they show up, we'll all die together, screaming I'm sure," Joppo replied to him with a smile, but wasn't sure why. He wasn't kidding about any of that.

Ryan wished Joppo would stop saying stuff like that. Then the sound of a blaster fire rang out in the distance and they stopped their bikes. "Sounds like it was close," Ryan said and looked around. There was no telling where it might have come from, however.

"Come on, there isn't anything we can do. We have our own problems, you know how it is," Joppo said with a hint of sadness to his voice. He was well aware that saving everyone was out of the question.

Ryan sighed and did his best to ignore it, without another word he pushed his bike forward down the broken path. Joppo followed him. "You know, many years ago when I was on this very path. Irak and I heard a blaster sound off in the distance, just like that," Joppo said and continued. "We went to investigate like I know you want to," Joppo continued.

"Well we found the source of the blaster, it was a teenage girl and she was surrounded by maniacs," Joppo said and took a breath. "I'd like to tell you we ran to the rescue, but we didn't. There were twenty of them and we quickly backed away. If we tried anything, we would have died too," Joppo said with more than a hint of regret in his voice. There was no reason to tell how that story ended.

"I guess we just have to look out for us," Ryan said bitterly as they took another turn. There was a sign there on the side of the road that was full of small holes and blaster marks. But it was still easily read. 'Hadoth forty-five miles down the path. Travel at your own risk, do not stray from the path' Ryan looked at it.

Adventure and danger lay off the path. Everyone knew that the city was filled with Sand raiders and other equally dangerous things that had evolved out there. "Come on, let's go," Joppo said as they passed the sign.

Chapter Seven

Nyogyth paced back and forth on her quarters. Fuming about being seen and interrupted by Lam when a beep came from her speaker at the door. She stopped. "Come in," she said and prepared herself for the worst. Her silver doors slid open silently and another woman walked in. She was wearing red and black jump suit. Taller than Nygoth with long silver hair that reflected the light. Her blue eyes pierced through Nyogyth at once, as they always had.

Nyogyth saluted her commanding officer. "At ease, and there isn't a need to be so official, but I appreciate the gesture," she said and Nyogyth relaxed, but not much. "Lam says you've been conducting experiments on the alien lifeforms?" she asked. "Yes sir," Nyogyth replied immediately. There was no point in lying about anything now that she had been discovered.

Commander Meria studied her and crossed her arms. She thought about scolding the science officer but decided against it. "Well, I want a full report. Right now," Meria ordered and Nyogyth didn't know what to say.

"Sir, I just want to go home. Those aliens infested our planet since long before any of us were born. I've just been experimenting with Delta waves. It was a side hobby, a theory of mine. I've only been working on a controller for a few years now," she replied and continued. "And the Delta waves work. I can control three of the four types of beasts but just one at a time. I think that we can use them to get our planet back," Nyogyth said and almost smiled, but held it back.

"Attacking defenseless villages in the wasteland is how you test this out?" Meria asked her and Nyogyth didn't look away. "The dirt people are worthless to us. They are so devolved and used to the planet they'd rather die than change their ways. Don't tell me you care about the trash on the planet," Nyogyth said and Meria tilted her head a little.

"No, not really. You're right about all of that but we can subjugate them. Even maggots are useful in the right situations," she replied and Nyogyth was annoyed, she didn't care if she killed them all, none of them deserved to live if they wouldn't fight to reclaim their planet.

"I guess, I sent Lam down to hopefully take care of the situation a few hours ago. But in theory, how much time would you need to control more than one at a time?" Meria asked and she thought about it.

"An amplifier, and about four days to set up," she replied and Meria thought about it. "The Knights won't approve of this. I don't think we can pull it off," she decided and Nyogyth narrowed her eyes.

"Knights, are you kidding me? When was the last time we've heard from any of them? Five years ago? More maybe? Why do we care what they think? For all we know they are all dead by now," Nyogyth said and Meria nodded at this.

"Yeah, I don't know if they are alive or not. We all agreed not to interfere with the world and keep the program going as long as needed," Meria said and didn't feel comfortable breaking the treaty they have held for over a century.

"The Nuclear Knight Program has done its job. They defeated and sealed the Prime Kaiju on the planet, the lesser beasts are aimless now without their leaders. What are we waiting for? The Nanite systems of the stations won't fail but eventually we will. We need to go back home. We have the power to take our planet back, the means to do it. What's holding us back?" Nyogyth asked, pleaded with her.

Meria walked and looked out the port side window. The planet lay far below them. She could see storms raging on the surface, black patches of scarred earth from battles long past. The ocean, once blue, was now a light shade of green. The Earth had been changed so drastically that she wasn't even sure they could live on the surface anymore. The people born there were altered, on the Seran Station, they were considerably weaker. Maybe weaker wasn't the right word, she thought. No, the right word was pure. Uncorrupted. It was then Meria made her choice.

"Alright. We're going home," Meria said and smiled. She'd always wanted to return the human race to its former glory. She was sure the rest of the humans down below were tired of living in the dust and ruins of an alien kaiju apocalypse that no one living today was alive to even see.

Nyogyth smiled, beamed her approval of the choice. "I can get started right away, I think from here we can control three or four beasts at a time with what we have," she said and Meria nodded. "Make it so. Hadoth is one of the biggest cities left on the planet and they are doing their stupid superstitious festival there. We can give the message to their leaders that the world as they know it is over in four days," Meria said and nodded.

"What if they resist?" Nyogyth asked. "Then we destroy everything they have until they see just how stupid they are and stop resisting, or die," Meria said with a shrug. "Good enough for me. Hey. You should make Lam give the message to the waste people. He seems to care for them. I think he'd appreciate being the one to deliver hope to the masses," Nyogyth said and Meria nodded.

"Agreed. Just let me know when you're ready," she said, took one last look at the ruined Earth below before turning and walking out of the room.

Nyogyth smiled as she looked down at the planet. "Home, finally," she said and put her hand on the window. It wouldn't be long before the human race could reclaim the planet they had lost so long ago.

Chapter Eight

The sun was beginning to dip low into the western sky, covering everything with deep red and orange light. Matt woke up and looked around at the shattered buildings that passed by them. "Guys, I need to go, can we stop for a few minutes?" he asked and was doing his best to get feeling back into his limbs. He hadn't moved much in his sleep. Also, sleeping in a metal box, basically, had taken its toll. Pain wracked his body.

"We need to find a place to hide anyway. It'll be dark soon," Joppo said, but as they drove, he didn't see anything that didn't look like it was a good enough place to stay for the night. "How about over there?" Ryan said and pointed towards a building, all the windows had been broken out but it seemed to be sturdy, however.

"If I was a hungry Sand Raider, that'd be the first place I would look for food. If I was an Inkit, that'd make for a great lair," Ryan said and pointed at that building. "That's a death trap," he finished. Joppo shrugged. "Yeah, but this whole place is a death trap, we don't have a choice," Joppo said and knew the risks, there was no such thing as safe out here. The three of them approached the charred black, ancient building and pulled up next to it.

Matt got out of the trailer and did his best to ignore the stiffness in his muscles. He looked around and didn't see any sign of anything lurking. Then a sad, low howl came through the evening air. It got the attention of the three of them in a hurry.

Joppo visibly shuddered at the mournful cry. “Let’s hurry,” he said and shut off the bike, got off of it to look for something to hide the bike with. Ryan did the same thing as Matt wandered off. Ryan walked to a pile of debris, there was a broken pallet laying on top of a pile of twisted metal. The wood was grey and it was clear that it hadn’t been moved in ages. “Joppo, help me move this,” he said to Ryan. “Use your gloves first. You get hurt out here and there isn’t anything we can do about it,” Joppo reminded him.

Ryan reached into his pockets and pulled out weathered, yellow leather gloves. He gripped on the left side of the pallet and Joppo grabbed on to the opposite side. The two of them lifted the thing and it groaned, cracked and threatened to fall apart, but the old wood held.

They maneuvered it to the back side of their bikes and set it up. It wasn’t great camouflage. “Good enough. Anyone passing by won’t notice them and the sand raiders are idiots,” Ryan said and Joppo just sighed. “I sure hope so, come on, let’s go inside,” Joppo replied.

“Oh, wow. Did you guys see that?” Matt asked as he came back. The others turned around to look. Neither of them saw it, but under the pallet, in the pile, were two small skeletons laying side by side, still holding hands. The other two didn’t notice.

“The city is full of stuff like this. The whole place is a tomb,” Joppo said and turned back towards the building. Ryan could only imagine what kind of nightmare these kids saw and how long they had to see it before dying. “Come on, let’s go,” Ryan said and turned away.

Matt wasn’t used to all the death that happened outside of the walls and surrounded them. He rarely witnessed anything horrible, even being a night watchman.

“Sorry,” he said to the skeletons. Matt had heard so many terrifying stories of disturbed dead coming back to haunt and kill the people who messed with their resting places. Not wanting to dwell on it anymore or be caught out here after dark Matt quickly made his way to the others.

Joppo walked to the side of the building and there was a door that was broken and hanging off its hinges. He pulled the door open slowly with his right hand and had his blaster ready in the other. Anything could have been waiting in the dark for them. Ryan was right behind him after Joppo stepped inside.

The building creaked and groaned as the light breeze passed through the cracks in the walls. Joppo looked up and spun around. Inkit's loved to cling on walls, usually right above the doors where prey would be most likely to enter. To his relief nothing was there.

"This should do for the night, but we need to search the place out to be sure nothing is in here with us," Joppo said quietly. However, it was getting to be dark out and most of the predators would be out stalking by now.

"I'll check the back, Matt, you and Ryan make sure to seal the door off and get the infra station set up. It's going to be cold tonight," Joppo said as he put his pack down on the ground and the two of them nodded. Joppo walked off on his own trying to be as quiet as he could.

"You ever spent any time in the city at night?" Matt asked him as Ryan opened the bag. "Yep, once," Ryan replied and pulled out the infra station. It was a small silver cylinder, Ryan pushed a green button on the side and the thing slowly began to open up into a disk.

"I survived then, and I'm sure we'll be fine now," he said as he stepped back from the expanding disk. Ryan didn't want to tell Matt about the silver people. He didn't want to mention that monster was being controlled. He just wanted the night to go by quickly, quietly and get to Hadoth.

"Oh, well. It's my first time. I don't like it," he said and looked out one of the broken windows. "Hey are you insane? Get away from the window. If we're seen it's over," Ryan said and Matt quickly backed away. "Right, sorry," he said and walked back to the infra station. The heat was already starting to radiate from it, but the temperature of the air was already beginning to fall.

"Place hasn't seen anything alive for a while, I think we'll be okay," Joppo said and slowly sat down on the dirty floor, the others relaxed a little and they did the same thing. "It's going to be a long night," Joppo said and sighed. "We could tell stories," Matt suggested and Ryan looked at him. “Do you know any?” he asked and Matt thought about it. “No, not really,” he replied.

Ryan was about to say something when someone screamed outside, it wasn’t panic but bestial and primitive. “Shh,” Joppo said and the three of them waited, didn’t even dare to breathe right now. Footsteps could be heard just beyond the walls. People were passing by their small hideout. None of them were brave enough to look out of a window to see who they were.

Chapter Nine

The three of them waited in the dark, and soon enough, whatever was going on just beyond the wall stopped. The people faded off into the distance and the three of them could breathe a sigh of relief. “Hopefully that’s the only encounter we have tonight,” Ryan said, the others nodded in agreement. Matt smiled, it wasn’t his normal job but he needed to get started. “You know. If I’m going to watch at night. I’m going to have to, you know, watch,” he said and looked towards the window.

“Unless you brought a camera or something?” Matt asked and Joppo looked at one another. “If you think you have to, I guess go for it,” Ryan said nervously. He wasn’t sure this was a good idea but, well, no one lived forever. Plenty of people were killed out here and never seen again. If that was his fate because of one moron’s mistake, well, maybe that was how it all ended.

“Hide yourself with this,” Joppo said as he took his coat off and threw it to him. Matt caught it and put it over his head. Joppo slid his pack to him and pulled out three bottles of water. He threw two of them to the others. Matt caught his but Ryan’s hit him in the face.

“What the hell was that for?” Ryan asked as he caught it before the bottle hit the floor. “First rule of the wasteland, always pay attention to your surroundings,” Joppo said and smiled. Ryan just shook his head and opened his bottle. “Yeah, right,” Ryan replied and took a drink. The water was warm but it would keep him alive until the morning, that was all he could ask for.

"It's been a long day people. I want to leave before the sun comes up," Joppo said and relaxed visibly, leaning against the wall. "Sounds good to me," Ryan replied and relaxed, leaned against the wall. The heat from the infra station was just barely enough to keep the cold away.

"I'll keep watch. Don't worry. I haven't fallen asleep on the job yet," Matt said and took a sip out of his bottle. "Well, I guess it's all about me now," he said and turned his eyes towards the window. He half expected to see someone staring back at him, but there was nothing but the black outside to see.

Hours in the silent dark passed by. Matt constantly looked from left to right every few minutes with his eyes trying to see any kind of danger. If it was out there, he couldn't see it. Matt was thankful that he couldn't see anything, that likely meant that nothing could see him, either. He supposed that was the case anyway. The only sound was the wind blowing through the broken buildings somewhere in the distance. He couldn't help but think of home.

There was no way to know if it was still there. Maybe the monster came back. He imagined the beast coming back for a second pass and finishing the job. He had to hope that wasn't the case and the ordeal was all over. His imagination began to run away with him, showing him images of everyone he knew being crushed under the feet of some beast in the dark over and over again. He couldn't help it.

It was then that something snapped him out of his horrific imagination. The deep boom and slight vibration of something heavy hitting the ground from a distance away, then another deep boom shook the building, too fast to be just one beast. Matt scanned the darkness in front of him to see any clue of what was going on. Nothing but the black was out there.

Another heavy footstep echoed through the ground, then a deep and bright red streak of energy shot through the air. It was behind them. "Joppo, Ryan, wake up!" Matt cried out as the energy faded. "What is it?" Ryan thought he asked as he woke up from a dead sleep. The answer came as the whole building they were in shifted. Whatever sleep remained in Ryan left in an instant and he scrambled to stand up only to stumble against the wall for support.

Joppo did the same thing seconds later. "What do we do?" Matt asked. "Well, we can't stay in here, come on, use your head," Joppo replied and the three of them ran towards the door, broke it open and stepped into the dark. Another red beam cut through the night sky and the three of them looked towards the source.

"Damn it," Joppo said as he could dimly see what was going on in the dark. "Come on, there's a fight going down. Here is where we don't want to be," he said and started to run to his hover bike. "What about our stuff?" Ryan asked and Joppo looked back. "Things can be replaced you can't, come on," he shouted back as a high-pitched roar, a new one, split the air.

"Those damned C class are always screwing with everyone," Ryan said as the frail winged beast shot over head creating an instant windstorm as it did making the three shield their eyes with their arms in a hurry. It was too high up to do any damage but the B class it was tormenting for reasons no one could know was going to follow it. "Come on," Joppo said and pushed the pallet out of the way.

Matt got in the trailer and the two of them got on their bikes. There wasn't any time to back up. "Hold on to something," Ryan said and accelerated forward. Ryan barely had room to make the corner, he took it too tight. Joppo was just ahead of him and made the turn. Ryan made it too but the trailer tilted too far to the side. Matt tried to hang on but he was tossed into a pile of rubble.

"Son of a bitch," Matt said as something stabbed into his left shoulder. He felt the blood began to flow. He grit his teeth and pulled himself forward with effort to free himself from whatever had impaled him.

Matt did his best to stand up just in time to watch as Ryan's hover bike turn out of sight. "Damn it," he said and stumbled forward in the dark. He was sure by the time they noticed he was gone, it would be far too late.

He turned around to see the beast in the distance. Its back exploded with red light as it let loose another deep red ray towards the flying thing darting around in the dark. "Kill that thing," Matt said as he watched the fight. The flying thing twisted around the ray, dodging it with ease. Matt could barely see what the thing looked like. Most of the flying beasts looked pretty similar to one another. Wings, frail body, long neck, tail, nothing special. But they were all pests to man and beast alike.

It screeched and flew back towards the other monster. Matt couldn't see the things very well, but he could hear them. The collision of the two things echoed through the cold night air. The ground was shaking worse now as fighting between the two of them got worse. Then a light appeared behind Matt and he turned around. "Do you plan on dying out here, come on, let's go," Joppo said and pulled the bike around.

Matt stumbled to the hoverbike as fast as he could and hopped on the back, ignoring the pain in his shoulder the best he could in the process. "We're going to Hadoth tonight, hopefully the arrival of the monsters will make the trip easier," Joppo said.

Matt grunted in pain as Joppo started to drive away. He turned the corner and Ryan was waiting for him. "Go, man, what are you waiting around here for?" Joppo yelled at him. He was glad Ryan waited, he was sure he didn't know the way in the dark.

Ryan rolled his eyes and accelerated the same time Joppo sped past him. He was going to reply but didn't bother. Just a few seconds later the flying beast crashed into the building they were staying in. The impact sent dust in all directions.

"Goggles!" Matt yelled and closed his eyes and did his best to cover his wound. Joppo and Ryan both threw theirs on seconds before the cloud of dust covered them. What little could be seen in the night disappeared.

The trio drove through the dust, the noises of the beasts behind them slowly faded, and so did the dust. "I think we're out," Joppo said and took a deep breath of fresh air. Ryan slowed down along with Joppo. "Get in the trailer. I'm sick of you bleeding on my stuff," Joppo said and Matt looked over at the trailer. "Aren't you going to stop?" Matt asked and Ryan shook his head.

"I heard that the sand people can smell blood. I'm sure they are tracking us by now," Ryan replied and he didn't know if that was true or not but he heard rumors. But risking it in the broken city at night like this wasn't an option.

"I'll hold it steady, jump in," Ryan said and pulled ahead of Joppo so that the trailer was right in line with him. Matt looked at the hard, metal surface and hand no idea how he was going to get this done. "Damned sand people anyway," Matt muttered to himself.

"Okay," he said hesitantly, took a breath and pushed himself off the bike. He landed on the metal surface and his whole body burned with pain. "Damn it," he groaned as he fell on his wounded shoulder. The one thing he was trying to avoid doing he managed to do perfectly and rolled on to his back.

"Don't sit up, just take it easy," Ryan said to him. "Don't worry. I don't think I have it in me to sit up right now," Matt replied. He gazed up into the night sky. The cracked moon was bright in the sky with no ruins to block it. He always wondered how it happened, no one was really sure.

Then his eyes shifted to the right and he focused on a star. No, it wasn't a star. This small white dot in sky was moving. "Weird," he said and closed his eyes and tried to think about anything else as the pain spread through him.

Joppo and Ryan sped through the dark down the path and it wasn't long before the rush of adrenaline wore off. Joppo pulled up beside Ryan. "I know you're tired but don't give up on me," he said and Ryan nodded. "I'm not used to this late night adventure stuff but I'll be fine. I hope," he replied, did his best to stifle a yawn in the process. Joppo narrowed his eyes in determination.

Hours past and one pile of rubble looked exactly like the next, the broken pavement road twisted and turned into forever. Their dim lights barely revealed anything ahead of them and the exhaustion was setting in. How many hours had they been driving down this path, Joppo couldn't remember. Time was meaningless at night. Joppo thought he hear the yells of the Sand Raiders over the low hum of his hover bike. Maybe he was just hearing things at this point, he wasn't sure.

The sky began to brighten. At first Ryan thought that he had finally lost his mind, but then realized that the sun was coming up. In the distance metal gates were coming into view. "There it is," Joppo yelled and pointed. They had finally made it to Hadoth, as they approached the gates an intense beam of light came from the top of the gates. It was too bright to see past it so they stopped their bikes and waited, it was their move now.

Chapter Ten

"Who goes there?" a loud voice came from the top of the wall. "Joppo, from Sticktown. We are looking for a replacement for our water system, also we have an injured man," Joppo replied and the light turned to shine on Ryan. He covered his eyes in a hurry. "Damn," he said to himself as the light burned his eyes.

"Alright, open the gates," the voice yelled out, and the spotlight shut off. Ryan rubbed his eyes as his sight returned. The massive, thick metal gates shifted then they swung inwards, opening the way. Joppo saluted to the man on the wall and slowly proceeded forward. "They must know you?" Ryan asked.

"Yeah, come on, hopefully we don't have to stay here too long," Joppo replied and they moved through the gates. Ryan had heard plenty of stories of Hadoth, but he'd never actually been here before, there was never any reason to go before now. Compared to where he lived, the place was a metropolis. There were smells of cooking food, people in every direction, clean people. The streets were paved and the lights along the road were still lit up.

"They have electricity here, to power all these lights? This place is a regular paradise," Ryan said and he meant it. "Oh yeah, it's nice, however they are trapped here. If a beast attacks or anything like that, they have no place to go," Joppo replied. Ryan yawned. "Yeah, but a place like this must have a Knight on standby at least?" Ryan was tired and he was just asking what came to mind right now.

"A knight, they don't stay in one place and no one knows if they are watching or not anymore. Reality is we are all on our own," Joppo said and Ryan felt really depressed by that. Ever since he was a kid, he only heard stories of heroes. "Come on, we need to get Matt here to a medic before he dies on us," Joppo said and drove forward.

Joppo knew the town and Ryan just followed him. It was just a few minutes but they pulled up to a white and tall building. There was someone standing outside wearing a gray uniform speckled with blood, he was tired, and older than Joppo.

"Doc Owens, you're still running this joint?" Joppo asked as they pulled up. The old man turned his head. "No one else is smart enough to do it, so I guess so. How long has it been, a year now?" Owens asked him and only half smiled.

"At least, I wish it was a social call but I have a guy who might be dead in the trailer. I figured I would make sure before we dispose of him," Joppo said and Ryan got nervous, he'd never heard him be so cold and callous before.

"Well, I better take a look," Owens said and walked forward and to the trailer. "Hmm," he said as he looked at the bloody trailer. "This boy is still alive, but he's not in good shape, let's get him inside and put him back together," Owens said, tossed his smoke stick to the ground and stepped on it.

Joppo got off his bike and walked to the back. Ryan almost offered to help but he decided that he would just get in the way. He watched the two of them open the trailer and quickly pulled Matt off the floor. Matt screamed as he was peeled off the metal and his wound was torn open again due to the dried blood. He winced at the scream of pain and did his best not to look. "I'll be right back," Joppo said to Ryan just before the two of them disappeared into the building.

Ryan took this chance to look around. This place wasn't so bad. He had no idea why anyone would want to live where he did after seeing a place like this. There was no way he was going to make the trip back home without some rest. He let out a sigh and put his head on the handlebars of his hoverbike.

"Hey, are you here for the festival?" a lady asked him. Ryan thought he was just hearing things at first, but realized that someone was actually talking to him. He slowly sat up. "Uh, no. It's my first time being here and I don't know anything about it," he replied and looked at her. Despite being in the big city, she looked like him, sort of anyway. Someone who didn't quite belong. "Oh, me too. I got to Hadoth yesterday. I come from Narvoi," she said and smiled.

"Never heard of it, but good deal, I guess," Ryan said. Most of these out of the way wasteland towns rarely interacted. It was no surprise to either of them. "Oh, it's about twenty miles north of here," she said and Ryan was getting annoyed. He was too tired for a conversation and he just wanted her to leave.

"Well, if I see you around later maybe we can meet up at the dance, but take a shower first. And wash your clothes, too," she said with a slight laugh and bounded away, clearly excited about something. "Yeah, sure," he said and shook his head. If there was a festival, there wasn't any kind of a sign of one.

Joppo came back out of the hospital. "Hey, Matt's going to be alright and—" Joppo immediately saw just how wasted Ryan was. "And we need to get you a room," he said and Ryan nodded. "Sure, I like that idea," he said and smiled. "Oh, hey, what do you know about a festival. One of the tourists asked me if I was here for it," he asked and Joppo shook his head.

"Just another reason not to live here. Come on. Get in the trailer. I'll drive you to the Inn," Joppo said, he also knew that Ryan wasn't going to be driving anywhere.

"Okay," Ryan said, not registering in his tired brain what Joppo had said, got off his bike and stumbled back into the trailer. He saw all the dried blood towards the back of the trailer and winced at the smell and sight of it. He climbed in and did his best to stay towards the hatch and closed it after he got inside with great effort. He didn't remember it being that heavy before. Joppo saw that he was inside and started to drive away from the hospital.

Ryan was zoning out as they drove, missing everything along the way. He also wasn't sure how long they drove in this direction but soon enough they were in front of another building. Ryan looked at it and read the sign out loud. "Roll Inn," he said. "Oh, I get it," he said and laughed as he got out of the trailer. "Come on," Joppo said and Ryan followed him inside, thankfully there weren't any steps leading up to the door.

Before the lady at the front desk could say anything Joppo started talking. "Do you have a room open. This guy has been awake for almost a full day and I need him for the trip home." She shrugged. "Yeah. One zop a night, no refunds. Check out is noon the next day or it's another zop," she said, almost mechanically. Joppo reached in his pocket and pulled out a silver coin, tossed it on the desk. She took the coin and from under the desk threw him a key ring with one key on it. "Room nineteen," she said.

Joppo caught it. "Thanks," he said and turned, the two of them walked down the hall. They made it to the room and he unlocked the door. "Okay, I'll be back in a few hours, get some rest," Joppo said and Ryan stepped inside. "Alright, I will," he responded, but wasn't entirely sure if he had said anything at all. Joppo closed the door behind him.

"Wow, this place is nice," Ryan said as soon as he saw the bed. It looked much better than the thing he had at home. He walked forward and fell down into it. Ryan closed his eyes and the world disappeared around him.

Chapter Eleven

Joppo was tired too, but he needed to get the job done. He wanted to be on the road before dark if he could manage to do it. He walked right back out of the inn and made his way back to the bike, hopped on and moved down the road. Memory wasn't as good as it used to be but he was pretty sure that he knew right where to go, at least pretty close anyway.

He took a left turn and moved into the market district. No one was here yet. The sun was just coming up and people were still opening their shops, some weren't open yet. Joppo didn't worry about the rest of them as he traveled to his location. He traveled down until he got to a red shop that, from the outside, was clearly still not open yet. Joppo sighed, shut off the bike and walked to the front door.

Joppo knocked on the door hard. "Hadoth Police, open up, Dave," he said in the deepest voice he could and waited. He heard the clattering of metal on the ground from the other side of the door, then footsteps rushing to the door. The balding man in a red shirt and black pants opened it and the panic in his eyes disappeared at once.

"Oh. It's you," Dave said and rolled his eyes. Joppo couldn't help but smile. Dave just wanted to hit him.

"It's been too long, buddy. How are you doing?" Joppo asked and Dave shook his head. "Same old stuff. People breaking things and I replace and fix them," Dave said and stepped inside his shop. Joppo followed. "Yeah. A beast crushed our water purification system yesterday. That's why I'm here," Joppo said and Dave stopped.

"Three other town leaders were here in the past week looking for the same thing, they said they were attacked from out of nowhere by a B class," Dave said and Joppo shrugged. "Same story here," he said.

"Get out," Dave said and shook his head. "Clearly something is wrong," Dave said and Joppo nodded. "Outlanders are up to something. We had a run in with one on the way out of town who agreed not to kill us if we didn't say anything. I assume they have ways of finding out if we talk or not. So, no, let's just not say anything," Joppo said, he knew what Dave was going to say. He said it anyway.

"This could be something big, you need to tell the council, they need to know. The other six members are in town for the festival. Whatever the outlanders are planning is likely going to be big. If I had to guess, I'd say all of the towns that were hit were test runs for something," Dave said and Joppo shook his head.

"What, the Outlanders are controlling the monsters or something. They can't do that can they?" Joppo asked, Dave just shrugged. "No idea, but you need to tell someone, we could all be in serious trouble, Jop," Dave said and that panic was slowly returning.

"We don't know anything about the Outlanders, all we know is they are weird as hell, we shouldn't assume anything. And don't you go around telling anyone either," Joppo realized that he just said way too much without even thinking. He was way more tired than he thought. "Just, how much is a new system going to cost?" Joppo asked.

"Seven Zops" Dave said, doing his best to stick to business.

"Seven, the last one was only four, what the hell?" Joppo asked and was shocked at the price increase. "Like I said, we're running low and they take a lot to make. We've had to make more and supplies aren't easy to find," Dave replied and Joppo rolled his eyes. "Fine," he said and pulled out his wallet, opened it. Seven Zops was all he had left. He was planning to get a few extra things.

"It's all I have left," Joppo said and started to take the money out. "Okay, just don't tell anyone. Pay me the normal price and I'll make up the difference," Dave said and Joppo stopped, he wasn't about to refuse something like this. "Thanks," he replied.

He was still well aware Dave didn't feel comfortable. "Come on man, don't be like that. What would I tell the council? Weird people from nowhere are doing some mysterious thing that might never amount to anything?" Joppo asked as he shook his head. "It's a waste of time. The outlanders have been a mystery for over a hundred and fifty years and most people don't even know they exist at all. Why cause unneeded panic?" Joppo asked and Dave saw his point.

Without information or proof of any kind of plot, it'd be pointless to raise an alarm. "I guess you're right. But still, all the attacks on the outer villages recently still don't feel right. The beasts haven't been like this since, well, you know," Dave said, trying his best not to think about the darker times of the past. "I'm sure it's nothing, man. Things will be back to normal soon enough," Joppo said and did his best to change the subject.

"Who did they pick for the festival this year?" Joppo asked. Dave walked to the back of the shop and Joppo followed him. Dave didn't answer until they got there. "Some kid from Narvoi, I guess," he replied and Joppo shook his head.

"The two I came with don't know anything about this stupid tradition, I'd like to get out of here before it happens and they get any stupid ideas to get involved," Joppo said, continued. "I still don't believe that there is an A class out there under the ocean, and I really doubt the festival helps," Joppo said and Dave turned and looked at him.

"I know you don't believe and this is why you left, but I am convinced this works and there is one there. Now let's just get your stuff so you can get out of here," Dave said to him and Joppo smiled, dropped the subject. "Yeah, that sounds good to me," he replied and Dave walked farther into the back. Joppo waited while he heard some things rattling around in the back.

It wasn't long before Dave came back with a cart in his left hand hauling the pieces to rebuild the water system that he needed. "You're damned lucky, it was the last one we had left," Dave said and pulled the cart towards him. "Thanks, I have a trailer out front and—" Joppo was cut off by the sound of something neither one of them had wanted to hear.

The city sirens were going, and their droning sound echoed through the thick walls. The two of them looked at one another and there was only one thing this could mean. "Come on, we can get a good look from the roof to see what's going on," Dave said and Joppo's eyes widened. "Why in the hell do you want to go to the roof of a building?" he asked in disbelief. "I don't know, do you want to go look or not?" Dave asked and Joppo smiled. "Let's go," Joppo said and the two of them started to make their way to the roof.

Chapter Twelve

Dave and Joppo got to the roof and had a clear view over the city, straight past the walls. Beyond the walls they saw what they couldn't believe. There were three B class beasts standing there just outside of the city. The first one was about three hundred feet tall, it was pitch black. Its arms ended in long blades. It stood on two legs and looked much like a typical beast did, an oversized dinosaur, mutated into something that defied logical sense.

The second one was bright green and walked on all fours, it reminded them of a dog and its long hair hung straight down. Its tail ended in a club, it stood next to the black one up to its waist. The one on the far end was the one Joppo encountered last night. It was dark red and had smooth skin and was just as tall as the black one.

"Well, this sucks, I've never seen them team up before," Joppo said and neither of them had. They usually hated one another, beasts were legendary for how territorial they were. "You don't think this has something to do with the A class does it, is it waking up?" Dave asked. "No, look at their eyes. They aren't open, it's like they are sleepwalking, no, being controlled," Joppo said over the blaring alarms.

Then, the alarms died, and the two looked around. All of the remaining lights in the city went out at the same time and the only thing that could be heard were the random shouts of terrified people in the distance. "Yeah, maybe you were right. I should have told the council," Joppo said as he watched the monsters standing beyond the wall, waiting for something. "I think everyone knows now, Jop, it's a tad late for that," Dave replied to him.

"So, do we evacuate or what?" Dave asked, he didn't know exactly what to do. "I don't know," Dave replied.

A silver beam shot out of the sky and widened up into a holographic screen. Joppo knew who it was, it was the same guy that they met on the way out of Sticktown.

"Hello fair people of Hadoth, my name is Lam. You know us as the Outlanders, Uplanders. Silver people and so on. We've decided to make our move, and with your help we will rebuild human civilization to its former glory. As you can see, we've found ways to subdue the beasts. All of them," Lam said and looked down to the three titans below him.

"In order to rebuild society, we need you to give us control of all of your hub cities and allow us to take over. We will bring laws, peace and security to the world. In return you will enjoy all the advantages our great civilization used to have before the fall. You have four days to make your choice. It is in your best interest for your leaders to comply with us. Have a good day," Lam said and the screen disappeared.

The three beasts slowly turned around and lumbered away from the city. "At least they kept their promises," Joppo said as he watched them walk away with their thunderous footsteps that echoed like thunder as they did.

"Come on, we need to get to the council. You're a town leader. You'll have a little bit of say on what goes on in the emergency meeting at least," Dave said and Joppo just shrugged. "Sure, I guess. I'm not sure how a small town nobody is going to convince the hub leaders to not roll over for the outlanders and give up everything we have because they can kill us all with giant monsters. Yeah, I'll convince them all to resist," Joppo said sarcastically as all the lights came back on.

"It's worth a shot, you have plenty of time to think of something compelling to say on the way there," Dave said and walked back to the door leading back down. "Yeah, compelling. Right," Joppo said and followed him.

The two of them made it back down into the shop. Joppo grabbed the cart with his water purification unit in it and drug it behind him as they walked out. Outside there were people talking with one another on the streets. It was easy to see and feel the panic that was growing at a rapid pace through the city.

"Help me get this thing into the trailer," Dave said, distracting from his own thoughts. "Right, yeah," he said and Joppo walked back and hopped in the trailer, unlatched the gate. It hit the ground and Dave pushed the mini wagon as Joppo pulled it inside. Dave noticed all the blood but didn't mention it, it wasn't his business to worry about it.

"Thanks," Joppo said and Dave nodded. "You need to get to the council building, your part of the outer members so you might make a difference," Dave said and Joppo didn't know what he was even going to say about anything.

There were only two choices really and he knew that the big wigs were going to take the obvious choice here. "I'll put my thoughts on the table, it's about all I can do," Joppo said and shrugged. "I'm staying here. Someone has to watch the shop," Dave said and closed the trailer, locking it.

"Yeah, I understand," Joppo said and hopped out of the trailer. "Good luck," Dave said but couldn't quite bring himself to smile about anything. Everything he knew was about to be taken over, changed. Or possibly crushed under the foot of an army of beasts. Joppo nodded to him, walked to and got on his bike.

Joppo pulled away from the shop and turned a corner. Everyone's face was the same, he could see the fear in their eyes. Then it occurred to him that the Outlanders might have done something similar to all the towns, even the smaller ones. Or worse decided that they weren't important enough to save and just destroy them. After all they turned his village into a literal weapons testing ground, he suspected their empathy to the waste landers was minimal at best. He did his best not to think about things like that right now.

He took his bike off the side road and made it to the main path. Thankfully the riots didn't start yet, sometimes people in a sudden dangerous situation tended to lose their mind. Right now, everything was still calm. The building that held the council wasn't hard to find. It was the biggest building in town and in the center. In the old days it used to be some kind of sports stadium.

Joppo pulled up to the council and parked beside someone's fancy pink land speeder. He had to admit he was a little jealous that he was stuck with this pile of junk and they got a nice thing like this. He shut off his bike and started to walk toward the main gates.

"Halt," a guard said who was standing next to the door. The man was wearing what passed for armor in the wasteland and his blaster was pointed at him. "Joppo, leader of Sticktown. Member of the outer rim council," Joppo said to him and the guard eyed him through his clear face visor. "Come on man," he said and lifted up his vest to reveal the old gun under his jacket.

"Only council members get one, you must be new. Also, you know that if you deny any council member entry to the hall you can get shot by said member, right?" Joppo said to him. The guard knew that was true. "Yes, welcome back," he said stepped to the side. "Thank you," Joppo said and walked forward, stepping through the gate.

The second he stepped through he could hear the voices all talking at once, screaming about what to do in a frenzy. "I hate the council," Joppo said to himself and as expected. All of the big wigs were here, but no one from the wasteland beside himself. That was to be expected. He wouldn't have been here either if it weren't for the attack.

The hammer of order, as they called it, still lay on the pedestal in the center of the room. Either the meeting hadn't started or general chaos had just taken over before he got here. He didn't know or care, it was coming to an end now.

Joppo walked to the middle of the room, picked up the hammer and slammed it down on the dented red surface of metal that it lay on. The distinct and sharp metal sound made everyone take notice.

"Hi, everyone. Glad to see you're all getting along," Joppo said to them as they looked at him. "You have a voice here, waste lander, but this doesn't really concern you. Besides, you're out numbered," Sirin said to him in an annoyed tone. She was annoyed at the sudden interruption. She had a white t-shirt on and tan jeans. It was clear that in the state she was in, this was the one place she wasn't ready to be just yet.

"Nice to see you again, too. Let's talk about this like rational people, not idiot sand people who'd eat one another," Joppo said and the others separated, at least for now rational sense had returned. "And what would you have us do? Challenge the strangers that can control monsters and destroy everything we have?" Inyath asked, his brown eyes wide with panic. He too was in a state of causal dress. A sleeveless and thin shirt hung loosely over his frail body and black shorts.

The other members mumbled in agreement. "So, what was all the craziness about when I came in here all about. You all seem pretty eager to roll over and die already," Joppo said and was confused.

"It was my fault. I offered a potential solution to the mess that could work," Mithlon said and crossed his arms. "I suggested that we ask the Nuclear Knights for help," he said and the others visibly recoiled at this idea. Joppo understood everything now. Mithlon was the only one here who was wearing a black suit. Joppo was sure he'd never seen the man in anything less than at his best.

"Everyone in this room knows that the knights haven't been seen in five years, maybe more. They are a lost cause where ever they are. Mithy my man, that's just a fairy tale. I was hoping one of you had an actual plan," Joppo said and his hope drained out of him, he couldn't believe that this was the only plan they had.

"See what I mean, Mithlon here has lost his mind, I say we just give up and let the Outlanders take over," Gusline said, he was more than ready to do this. "I am tired of living in a wasteland and I get tired of defending Homdor from sand people every other night. If we can break the cycle, I say we do it," Gusline said to them. The was like the others, only half dressed in casual clothes. He too came here as soon as he could.

"Yeah but their display of force scares me. Who's to say we give up and they don't kill us all anyway and this four-day period is just extra time to prepare enough monsters to wipe us all out?" Sirin asked and that was a fair point. Not that it made much of a difference, four days or one, they had no real defense against the monsters beyond the deterrence cannons.

"There is no way to know. But if we fight back, us and everyone we claim to protect is dead. I still say our best chance to keep on living and let this way of life go," Gusline said and the others were looking at him. The seven members didn't have much more to say. The choice seemed to be an easy one to make.

"Guys. Okay. I know you think the Knights are gone, but I know where one lives. All we need to do is send an envoy out to go find him and he will surely be willing to come back to help," Mithlon said and the others looked at him in surprise.

Joppo was just as shocked as anyone of them there. "What, how do you know where one lives, how do we know this isn't some trick to stall the vote?" Elrad finally asked, he had just listened up until now.

"Guys. Trust me. We have four days, that should be time enough to find them all so we can make a better plan," Mithlon said and smiled. "Okay, spill it. Tell us what you know," Joppo said and the man smiled. "Alright. Who has a volunteer for this secret mission, first of all. The less you all know the better but I promise that I will deliver results," Mithlon said and the seven looked at one another. It was clear that right now they didn't have anyone they could really trust.

"Well. I know a guy we can trust," Joppo said and smiled. "Mithlon, you come with me. The rest of you, don't do anything stupid," Joppo said to them, turned around and walked out. Mithlon shrugged and quickly followed him out of the building.

"We're all going to die," Elrad said as the two of them left. "Yeah. I think so," Sirin agreed with him.

Chapter Thirteen

Joppo lead the way on his hover bike while Mithlon followed him in his pink land speeder. Joppo knew that the machine behind him was much faster than his own but hauling a piece of equipment he needed to take it slower. He didn't care if Mithlon was annoyed at the slow pace. Lucky for the both of them the inn wasn't very far away. Nothing was far away from the center of town, however.

Five minutes of getting through the congested streets and a few turns later, the two of them pulled up to the inn, next to the other bike. "You left your guy in this rat hole?" Mithlon asked and looked around. "Yeah, but compared to what he's used to this might as well be paradise. He's only been sleeping for a little bit. He might be a little loopy," Joppo replied and Mithlon shrugged. "Alright," he replied and Joppo walked forward and into the Inn.

The two of them made their way to the room and Joppo opened it. Ryan was there on the bed, passed out. "This guy?" Mithlon asked as he pulled out a chair and sat down.

"Ryan, wake up," Joppo said but Ryan didn't move. Joppo pulled on the left cuff of Ryan's jeans. "What, where?" Ryan asked in a daze, he couldn't concentrate and wasn't sure If this was still a dream or not. "I need you to wake up man, something's happened," Joppo replied and Ryan turned over with a deep yawn and forced himself to sit up. He didn't notice the new person in the room yet.

"What, it must be important to wake me up. Are we going home?" Ryan asked, rubbed his eyes. "I am, but you're not," Joppo said and looked at him. It was now Ryan noticed someone else in the room. "You're not Matt," he said in a deadpan, tired voice.

"Oh, he's quick," Mithlon replied and Joppo shook his head. "Remember those outlanders. It turns out they really were up to something. They gave us all four days to give up everything, or they are going to kill us all," Joppo said and Ryan groaned.

"Then why did you wake me up now, we still have four whole days," he complained, not really grasping the situation. "Kid, I'm Mithlon, leader of Stiaburg. I need your help with a secret mission. Joppo says we can trust you and the more time we waste, well, you get it," he said and Ryan was quickly waking up. "Okay, sure. What is it?" he asked.

Mithlon smiled. "I need you to gather the Knights, they are basically our only chance," he said and Ryan woke all the way up at hearing that. "Knights? I don't think they are still around. I've never actually seen one," he replied and he knew what everyone else did. This was just a story to make people feel better at night, it had to be more fiction than truth. Every time heard the stories, they were always a little different.

"Oh, believe me, they are out there. But we need to find them, bring them back out of whatever rock they crawled under," Mithlon said and Joppo didn't say anything yet. Ryan looked at him but all he could do was just shrug, it was clear Joppo was leaving this up to him. "Guys, listen. I'm wiped out, can't I have a few more hours of sleep before you lay this on me. Please?" Ryan asked and could barely keep his eyes open.

"Yeah, sure. But I need to get back to Sticktown with the purifier. Their rations won't last long and you know how people get, they never stick to their rations," he said and Ryan nodded "Okay," he said, still not entirely sure what was going on.

"Come on, Mithlon, let's get out of here," Joppo said and stood up. "Fine. The kid has three more hours of rest then I'm waking him up," Mithlon said and the two of them left the room. Ryan groaned, his head hit the pillow and he quickly drifted off back into sleep.

Joppo closed the door and looked at Mithlon. "I don't think he's up to it," he said and Mithlon nodded. "Me either, but I guess we'll find out. We don't know who is a spy for the Outlanders around here. Don't talk to anyone on your way out of town. If anyone asks just say he stayed for the festival," Mithlon said and Joppo rolled his eyes.

"I'm not an idiot, just make sure he gets everything he needs for the trip," Joppo said and Mithlon smiled. "Good luck," Joppo said, turned and walked away. Mithlon followed him. He would use this time to gather up supplies and get ready for the trip. Then he knew that what he had to do next wouldn't be so easily done.

Joppo looked at the other hoverbike and sighed. "Oh, hell with it, they'll give him something better," he said to himself, he didn't know that for sure but he didn't want to keep Matt in the trailer. He walked to the empty bike and switched on the homing signal. Now the thing would follow him back to the hospital. Joppo just hoped that no one got in the way. He got on his bike and pulled himself around to make his way back to the hospital.

By now, without an announcement from the council about the situation that everyone knew about, the city streets were filling up. Joppo was behind a hovercraft that green smoke was coming out of its engine. He did his best not to breathe in the acidic smelling fumes and was thankful that it turned out of his way after a few minutes.

The hospital was busier than when he got there. Joppo shuddered at the thought of contracting the Lorian Flu. He took a deep breath and pulled the two bikes to an empty space and shut the bikes off at the same time then he walked inside.

Owens was at the front desk flipping through some papers. There were a few others in the waiting room but they didn't look sick to Joppo. "So, how's Matt doing?" he asked when he got to the desk. "Lost a fair amount of blood but he'll live. He's resting in exam room B. Just down the hall," Owens said, but didn't look up.

"Did by any chance the council make a choice?" Owens asked and Joppo sighed. "Yes," he replied and shrugged. "I don't want to tell you any more than that. Reasons," Joppo said and Owens nodded. "Yeah.

Most of these people are in here because they are scared that the space people are going to kill everything. Me, I can't wait. I think if even half the stories are true they will come down and save us all," Owens said.

Joppo shook his head. "Optimism is great, but I don't trust them. I'd keep your pack ready," Joppo said and that reminded him. He didn't have one anymore. Now that all the excitement was over his brain was catching up to what he really needed to get back home. "Yeah, you bet. I'm always ready to bug out if needed," Owens replied and Joppo nodded. He then started to make his way to Matt's room.

Matt was laying in his room, looking out the small window. All he could see was a small patch of the sky through the glass. "How are you doing?" Joppo asked him. "It hurts, but I suppose I'll live," he replied, turned to look at him. "Yeah, you look like it. So, Ryan's staying here for the festival. I told him it was stupid but he wouldn't change his mind," Joppo said, he thought he was pretty convincing over all.

"Damn it, here isn't the place he's going to want to be," Matt said and did his best to sit up. Joppo didn't stop him. "I know, but were going back home. I was able to get the part we need so we're good to go," Joppo said, picked up Matt's shirt that was hanging on a chair and tossed it to him. "Good, this big city life is making me feel uncomfortable anyway," Matt replied, caught the shirt and slowly began to put in on.

He was surprised in how much this hurt. Joppo grabbed the opposite side of the shirt to help him put it on. After that the rest was easy and soon Matt was ready to go. "Ryan let his bike go, so you don't need to ride in the trailer on the way back. We're not going through the city this time around," Joppo said and continued.

"We're also going to get a couple of packs before we go, too," Joppo said and Matt smiled. "Sounds good to me. Hopefully the Outlanders don't kill us and come down to help out instead," Matt finished, he too, was optimistic about the idea of help coming to get them out of this mess. Saviors from beyond the stars, the idea made him smile.

Joppo wasn't so sure it was going to all work out that way. "Yeah. I'm sure better times are ahead," he said but couldn't bring himself to smile. "Anyway, come on, let's get out of here," Joppo said. Matt slowly got up and grit his teeth at the same time to fight back the pain. "I'll meet you outside by the bikes," Joppo said and continued. "Take your time," he finished, turned and left the room.

Chapter Fourteen

Ryan woke up with a start. It was half a dream, half reality. Did they really come into his room and say all of that? As he pushed himself up, feeling better, he looked around and didn't see any evidence anyone was here. "Whatever," he said to himself and got up. He wasn't used to sleeping in such a soft bed and wasn't as refreshed as the thought he would be. Sore in fact, but it wasn't anything terrible or anything that would last.

After getting out of the bathroom, Ryan decided that since Joppo wasn't back yet he was going to go explore the town. There would be no telling if he would ever be back, or in this world, how long the place would remain like it was right now.

He left his room, having nothing to take with him and walked down the hall of the inn just as he remembered in how to get out of the place. It wasn't that complicated. As he walked past the front desk he set the key on it and intended to just slip out unnoticed.

"Sir, hey wait," a woman shouted after him and Ryan winced a little before he turned around. "Yeah?" he asked and turned around nervously. "Room nineteen, right?" she asked and took the key off the desk. Ryan nodded. "Good, I thought so, the keys were obvious," she said and continued. "Mithlon left a message," she said and put a piece of paper on the desk, slid it to him. Ryan walked back to the desk and picked it up.

'Meet me at the Night claw café when you wake up. I'll be waiting'. Ryan read on the paper, mumbling the words. He had no idea where this place was. "Um, where's the Night claw café?" Ryan asked her.

"Oh, you can't miss it. Go out the front door and take a right. It's just around the corner," she said with that same smile, it was beginning to creep him out because no one smiled this much where he was from. "Thanks," he said, turned and walked out at a quick pace.

The mood in the city felt different. The people, who were once happy, now seemed sad, worried. None of this made sense but he didn't bother to ask anyone what was going on. All he knew right now is that his dream wasn't a dream and he had the foreboding feeling that everything in his life was about to go wrong.

He followed the woman's directions and sure enough, around the corner, and way they didn't come in. Or maybe he just didn't notice it. The Night claw was busy, there were people sitting outside at tables, talking about something. People leaving and walking in. It seemed happy enough from here. It was one of the most crowed places he'd ever seen. "Okay, here we go," Ryan said to himself.

The first thing he noticed was that everyone had noticed him. His clothes were dirty, worn and old. Everyone here was dressed in stuff that reminded him of pictures of ancient magazines that had survived from the before time. Someone was clearly making these new clothes. He could feel their eyes on him. He did his best to ignore them all as he stepped inside.

Seconds later someone came to meet him, someone in a black suit. "Excuse me, the Night Claw has a dress code. I'm afraid I'm going to have to ask you to leave," the man said to him in a condescending tone. Ryan ignored the tone.

"I'm here to meet someone by the name of Mithlon. Is he here?" he asked and the man in the suit tilted his head. "Excuse me, um, yeah, he's in the back. Follow me," his tone changed at once. Ryan didn't know who Mithlon was, not really beyond a vague half memory.

The two of them walked through the café, took a left turn towards the back of the place and there at a table was another man dressed in black, waiting patiently sipping a cup of dark steaming liquid. "Sir, your plus one has arrived," the host said. Mithlon looked up and smiled.

"Ryan, I assume, please sit down. I hope you didn't have too much trouble at the front gate?" Mithlon asked and Ryan thought about it, but let it go. "Nope, none," he replied and he thought he heard the host breathe a sigh of quiet relief.

Ryan moved to the chair across the table, pulled it out, sat down. "Yeah, I know. Lots of questions but let me get to the point," Mithlon said and smiled. Ryan just nodded and hoped he would start explaining things. He'd listen to this guy ad what he had to say.

"Ryan, I need you to find someone who lives in Narvoi, but it's important that you tell no one, are you up to it?" Mithlon asked him and the name sounded familiar, but he had no idea where that place was but it wasn't the first time he heard the name. "What's in it for me?" Ryan asked. No one did anything for free in the wasteland, he was no exception.

"Ten thousand Zops and I'll let you use my land speeder. When the job is done you keep the speeder," Mithlon replied and Ryan was shocked. "This someone must be important. And the offer sounds really great. But I don't know where Narvoi is and how do I know this someone won't just shoot me once I show up?" Ryan asked and Mithlon smiled, it didn't make Ryan feel better about this.

"You don't, but I know someone who can get you there. However, once I get that someone you're going to need to leave town fast," he said and Ryan was suspicious that this guy was some kind of a crime overlord or something right now. He was telling him as much as he wasn't.

"Two conditions, one you deliver this message to the intended, and you do not read it. Believe me. I'll know if you read it. Two, you tell no one. I know that is me repeating myself but, you know how it is out there sometimes," Mithlon said and lowered his voice.

Ryan thought about it. He could be a water gatherer and go back home. Or do this. This felt like the right choice. "Okay, I'll do it. I'm not sure why you can't just deliver the message yourself but I don't care. You get me my navigator and I'll deliver your mail," Ryan said and Mithlon smiled. "Wait here, order whatever you want to eat. I'll be back," he said, got up and walked away from the table.

Mithlon walked away and met the host who was still shaken by his earlier encounter. "Treat my friend the same way you'd treat me. I'll be back," he said and the host just nodded and walked towards the back. Mithlon left the Night claw and knew what he had to do next.

Chapter Fifteen

The council member immediately walked to his land speeder, got in and pulled away from the club. The sun was already past the midday point, their time was wasting away and everyone seemed to be perfectly okay with it. City people were always like that, however, at least it felt that way. He moved through the city, and was getting frustrated at the other cars on the road that were just getting in his way. On the road he wasn't any more special than anyone else.

Even if it felt like it took forever, he eventually made it to the festival grounds and got out. The sound of the waves crashing into the beach, a light breeze was blowing in from the sea. The stage was a good distance away from here. He looked the thing and it reminded him more of the gallows than anything else.

People were moving back and forth doing their work, setting things up. Mithlon steeled himself and moved forward.

"Hey, where's Francine?" he asked the first worker he got close to. "She's back there, behind the stage last I saw her. That was twenty minutes ago," the man said, "Thanks," Mithlon replied and made his way towards the stage, the center of the chaos.

The stage was draped with the traditional black and white cloth, unlit torches lined the front. As usual the whole thing was just waiting for a bad gust of wind to come by and set the whole thing on fire. He ignored the rest of his surroundings and started to make his way to the back.

"Francine, are you back here. We need to talk," Mithlon said as he walked through the door. "I'm back here, Mith, what do you need because you're about six hours too early," she replied from the back. He moved back there, she wasn't dressed in the ceremony outfit.

"I'm going to have to ruin the festival," he said and she stopped what she was doing, turned and looked right at him. "What are you talking about?" she asked and he half smiled.

"The girl, she knows the way back to Narvoi and I need her for a secret mission," Mithlon replied and crossed his arms. "I'm sure a hundred other people know the way there, get one of them," she replied.

"A hundred other people aren't going to be sacrificed for some stupid myth the council made up fifty years ago. This madness needs to stop and the outlanders are going to invade. Now is the time to put it to an end," he said and she looked away.

"This is the only thing that keeps our society together. We can't just stop. We need to be normal as long as we can," Francine replied and Mithlon shook his head. "No," he said. "I don't care. Bring me to her, now," he said and she stared at him. All kinds of things running through her mind right now.

"Okay, I'll explain the whole situation to her. If I do and she still wants to go through with it, then fine. I'll find someone else. But I don't know who else is from Narvoi so I have to try this first," he said and Francine made her choice.

"Fine," she replied and couldn't believe what she was about to do. She turned around and started to walk away, he followed. The two of them walked through the backstage and moved into a side dressing room. Francine knocked on the door. "Can I come in?" she asked. "Sure, come on in" a voice from the other side said and Francine opened the door.

Mithlon walked in after Francine did. "Hello," she said as she saw who it was in the mirror. A woman who was twenty one years old, all the sacrifices were about this age. She had short black hair and grey eyes. "Hi, okay, uh. I'm just going to get straight to the point," Mithlon said and wasn't quite sure how he was going to say it so he decided on the direct approach.

"Okay, the whole thing is a sham, there is no Class A beast in the ocean and you dying won't keep it sleeping for another year. We just made the whole thing up to keep people calm and something to believe in so we can maintain some semblance of society," he said all in one breath, it was the only way he knew how to do it.

She slowly set her comb down and acted as if she was in shock. "That's not true, is it?" she said and turned to look at Francine. "It is. Not many know that. You were going to die like so many others believing that you were saving the rest of society for another twelve months," she said and the girl was beginning to panic.

"Listen. Before you freak out completely. I know you're from Narvoi. I need you to be a navigator for a secret mission that really could save society. I have someone else waiting and we need to get out of here as soon as you can," Mithlon said to her.

"Die for nothing," she said and was numb to it all. Everything she knew was a lie and handling it wasn't easy. "What's her name?" he asked Francine. "It's Alexis," she said almost absentmindedly before Francine could answer. The weight of hundreds of meaningless sacrifices, no murders was weighing down on her and the slow realization that she was going to join them.

"You people are no better than the Sand Raiders are," she said and stood up. "I'm leaving, I'm telling everyone right now and everyone on the council is going to be executed before the sun sets," Alexis yelled without thinking and Mithlon quickly slammed the door shut.

"No, don't do that. Listen to me. I know how bad this is. I've never accepted it either but you need to keep people together. Outside the walls we're all dead in three months, tops. This was a no choice situation," Mithlon said and continued. "If you really want to make a difference, you need to help me. We don't have anything to lose after the next four days. Those outlanders will kill all of us. I believe they can do it. You can hate us later but right now, we have one chance to shut it down. Are you with me?" Mithlon pleaded with her common sense and desperation.

"What's the mission?" she asked, her rage still boiling inside of her. Mithlon glanced at Francine. "Hey, I kept a secret for the past twenty years that keeps me awake every night, one more won't change anything," she said and looked away.

"You're going to find the Nuclear Knights, or one of them anyway. They are the only ones who can help," he said and she almost broke out laughing. "From one stupid story to another. Everyone knows they don't exist and never did," Alexis replied and Mithlon shook his head.

"Trust me I am tired of hearing that, one lives where you're going. It's all we need, with any luck, to get all of this started. Please, we are wasting time. Name your price, nothing is out of reach for this," Mithlon said, he was ready to pay for this to get done. She thought about it. "Fine. I'll go home. As for payment, let me think about it," she replied but all she could come up with payment was public execution for the council. Alexis did her best to hide her sudden rage that was making her blood boil. She still didn't truly believe Mithlon, however.

Mithlon smiled. "Good, come on," he said and turned, opened the door and walked out of the room. "Get your old clothes on and we'll get you out the back. I'll tell the crowd something tonight. Don't worry. You're not the first one who's gotten out of this mess, thanks for not saying anything. In four days from now all of this is over anyway," Francine said and left, shutting the door behind her.

"Thanks," Mithlon said to her. "Yeah, you owe me," Francine replied. "Do me one more favor. Get out of the city before the outlanders show up. I highly doubt they are going to let us keep any of this as we know it," Mithlon said and she looked at the ground.

"You think it will be that bad?" she asked him. "Worse most likely, but right now you need to look after yourself. Get to a smaller village, a cabin out of the way. Just don't be here," Mithlon said to her. He didn't know how bad it was going to be, not really, but it was pointless to assume everything was going to be just fine. "Alright, I'll leave tonight," she said as the door opened.

Alexis was there in the clothes she came in. “I’m ready,” she said in a low voice. “Good,” Mithlon said and Francine motioned for them to follow her. “So, we are just going to walk out of here. No one is going to notice me bailing on your murder tradition?” Alexis asked and Francine reached over, grabbed a sheet and threw it over head. “Hey!” Alexis cried out instantly. “Play dead,” Francine said. “Mithlon is going to carry you out, no one will even ask,” she said. “Wait, what?” Mithlon asked in surprise.

“I don’t know this seems like a dumb plan,” Alexis said and Mithlon was nodding in agreement, this was a bad plan, he didn’t know if he could carry her that far. She wasn’t exactly small and Mithlon wasn’t used to physical labor like this. “It’s the only plan we have so unless you want to be chased by an angry mob I suggest we get to it,” Francine said and Mithlon sighed. “Fine, open the door, let’s get this over with,” Mithlon said. “Lift your arms,” he said and Alexis did.

The second she did he scooped her up in his arms and immediately began to feel the strain on his back. “Just breathe,” he said to himself and began to stumble towards the door. The three of them made it outside. “Come on, it’s not too far,” Francine said and started to walk ahead of them. “Right behind you,” Mithlon said between breaths, counting every step as he approached the land speeder that felt like it was miles away at this point.

He just counted every step, one after the next, doing his best not to fall over. His speeder felt like it was a hundred miles away right now. Concentrating and his face bright red eventually he made it to the car, Francine was right ahead of him. “Okay. I’m going to put you in the back seat. Stay down until I say,” he said, out of breath. He wasn’t sure how he was going to accomplish it. Francine quickly opened the door and he put her down as carefully as he could. Alexis helped and pulled herself up.

Alexis did her best to inch her way into the back seat without being too noticeable. “Thanks,” he said. “Yeah, just get out of here,” Francine replied and stepped back. Smiled, turned around and walked away.

Mithlon made sure she was all the way inside, shut the door, waved then made his way to the driver's side to get in.

Wasting no time, he started the speeder and drove away from the festival, back to the Night Claw to meet back up with Ryan.

Chapter Sixteen

Ryan was waiting outside of the Night claw when the red land speeder came around the corner with two people in it. "I was beginning to think that you'd never come back," he said under his breath, apparently everything went just fine in finding who he needed to. Mithlon pulled up to the front of the Night Claw. Ryan stood up as they arrived.

"Stay here, this won't take long," Mithlon said to her and got out of the speeder. "Ryan, thanks for sticking around. This is Alexis. She knows the way, you two need to leave right now," he said to him and Ryan shook his head. This was all moving too fast and part of him really wished he just stayed home to help rebuild the damage in Sticktown. Ryan looked at her and a flash of memory came over him.

"I saw her before," he said and remembered it was the girl from earlier, here for the festival. "It was only for a few seconds," he finished and Mithlon smiled. "Good, listen. She has the other half of the information. Once you get to Narvoi she'll open her half to reveal the identity of who you're looking for," Mithlon said.

Ryan didn't like this plan. "And if something goes wrong on the way, how will I know who to look for? What's the point of all the secrecy?" Ryan asked. "Point is I'm paranoid and I don't trust anyone. The less you know right now the better, take my car and get out of town," he said and Ryan looked at the sky.

"It will be night soon. You shouldn't travel at night out there. Can't we wait until morning?" Ryan asked and Mithlon's eyes went wide.

“No, you can’t be here. Actually, its dangerous right now. Please, go. I have everything you need ready in the back of the speeder. There is no time to explain,” Mithlon replied and Ryan didn’t feel good about it.

“Okay, I guess,” he said with a deep breath. “Oh hell,” Mithlon said and looked at Alexis. “She can’t be seen leaving the city, you’ll never get beyond the gates. I’m sure you’ll think of something, anyway. Good luck and don’t get eaten or crushed,” Mithlon said and without another word turned and walked back inside of the Café. “Thanks,” Ryan said and walked to the car, got inside.

The two of them looked at one another, she didn’t look much different than any other wasteland woman he’d ever seen. She thought he looked like he wouldn’t last very long in a fight. “Hi,” Alexis said to him. “Hey,” Ryan replied. Not really knowing what else to say.

“Okay, we need to get out of here. Mister man there says you can’t be seen leaving the city. So, what do you want to do?” he asked her and she looked out the window.

“I’ll just hide under the blanket in the backseat, you get us out of here,” she said and started to climb over the seat with no warning. She slid over the seat and her foot slammed into the side of his head. “Oh, come on,” he said as he turned away, it really didn’t hurt.

“Sorry, it’s not exactly roomy back here,” she said as her leg was pulled inside. “Too bad this stupid thing doesn’t have a top, hiding you from the wall guards would be easier,” Ryan said and sighed. “As soon as we get away from this crowd you can get into hiding,” he said, trying to be helpful.

“I’m not an idiot, I’m not going to be that obvious out here where everyone can see, now let’s get out of here,” she replied, annoyed with him already. Ryan pulled away from the café and turned the corner.

“I didn’t say you were. I’ve just never done anything like this before. I don’t know why we’re making the rush to Narvoi but it must be important,” he said and she looked at him. “How can you not know?” she asked. “The outlanders are going to come and take over everything with an army of giants. Didn’t you see the big face in the sky earlier?” she asked him.

Ryan had no idea about any of this. "No, I was sleeping. It was a rough night," Ryan replied. "Yeah, they are afraid it will be the end of the world," Alexis said and Ryan was confused. "That's funny. I was sure the world already ended a long time ago and we're just dying slowly," he replied and she shook her head. "Well, you're just a ray of sunshine, this is going to be a fun trip," she said and Ryan just rolled his eyes and kept driving.

Soon enough he made it to a side street that was empty. She looked around and got under the blanket in a hurry. "Okay it's really hot under here so please make it quick," she said with a muffled voice. "Don't worry, we'll be out of town in a few minutes," he replied and took another corner. He was doing his best to remember where the gates were and assumed there was more than one.

"What direction do we need to head once we leave?" he asked. "North," she replied. "Got it," he said and looked at the lowering sun in the sky. He wasn't that good with directions really, there was never a need to be good with them back home. All he had to do there was simply follow the road to the river and back.

He pulled in the direction he was pretty sure was North and drove down the street. "Uncover your head until we get there. It could be a bit. I think I'm lost in this stupid place," he said. "Don't you know anything, look for the yellow markers. Follow them and they lead to a gate, it's how they evacuate the city in case of attack and people get confused in the chaos," she replied and he nodded.

Sure, enough there on the side was a yellow diamond on top of a rusty, metal pole. "Thanks," he replied and followed the yellow diamonds. In minutes he found himself coming up to another large, metal gate.

"What's your business?" the guard yelled down. Ryan thought it was really strange that they wanted to know what he was doing leaving town. "I'm on business, but I can't talk about it," he replied and the guards looked at one another.

"Alright, whatever. It's going to be dark soon so you travel at your own risk," the second guard said as the first one opened the gate.

"Thanks," Ryan replied and as soon as the gate was open wide enough, he pulled through it.

"Wait," he said, knowing they were watching him go. He didn't know why but there was something unsettling about that whole experience. He felt relieved the second they took a curve out of sight of the wall. "I think it's okay now," he said and immediately she threw the blanket off and sat up. "Thank Zog," she said. "It was too hot under there," she finished and used the blanket to wipe the sweat off.

Ryan pulled over. 'Oh, I don't even have to ask. You're so thoughtful," she said and got out to get in the front. "Nope. Tell me we're at least going in the right direction to get there?" he said and prepared for the worse. "You're not a complete lost cause, you did good. Alright now we go straight," she said and he looked at her. "That's it? Just go that way?" he asked, thinking it was going to be more complicated.

"Yep, that's it," she said and he shrugged. "Okay, if you say so," he said and pulled forward. Ten minutes of silence and driving when the road curved and there beside them was the vast ocean. "Oh wow, I've never seen it," he said, he was used to the river and as vast it was. This was endless. "Yeah, it's pretty neat. Pay attention to the road," she said to him and he shook his head, put his eyes forward again.

"We should make it to Narvoi in a few hours if we hurry and don't get into any trouble," she said, keeping her eyes on the green sea. "If it was so damned close why didn't Mithlon just go himself? This seems like something that's easy," Ryan complained. All he really wanted to do was sleep in his own bed tonight.

"I don't know," she replied, barely listening to him. She had far too much on her mind right now. Then in the distance, the surface of the water broke and a two-hundred-foot-long, slender neck broke the surface. All she could see was the shadow of the beast.

"Those are my favorite kinds," she said. "Sure, they'll kill you if you go out on the water but from here, I could stare at them all day long," she said with a half smile. Ryan turned to look, he hadn't seen one like that before. "Yeah, looks just as dangerous as all the other ones," he replied.

"Eyes to the road, if we get wrecked out here and we'll be victim to all kinds of horrible sea things that aren't nearly as pretty," Alexis said and visibly shuddered at the thought of the things that dwelt just below the surface. Ryan turned back to the road and sighed. "You should have driven," he said. "Hey, I don't know how to run one of these things. They invited me to the, well, festival," she said and trailed off.

"I don't know anything about that thing, what is it all about?" he asked curious. "Well, every six months to a year they kill someone to keep the A class demon that lives in the sea. I was to be their latest sacrifice. Turns out it's all crap, just a stupid story they used to keep people in line," she replied and Ryan felt as if the whole world was different now, even the parts he didn't know about.

"So, you're like what's it, a princess or something," Ryan wasn't sure of the word but he thought princess was the right one. "No, I'm an idiot who thought she was special and saving the world," she replied. "Oh, right. Well, you can be a princess to me," Ryan said and wasn't sure what to say, everything was weird, awkward.

"Just drive and get me home," she said to him and didn't want to think about it anymore. She watched the beast, heard its lonely roar from the distance as the thing disappeared under the ocean with barely ripple. She wished that she could disappear right now, too.

Chapter Seventeen

Narvoi came into view and It reminded Ryan of home. But instead of walls it had a metal fence around the outside that looked like it was made out of wire. The sun was almost gone and the bright white lights clicked on. Ryan squinted and wasn't sure if it was just the timing or just because they were coming down the road.

"Pull up to the gate, I'll do the talking," Alexis said as he came to a stop. She got out. "Hey, it's me, let us in," she said.

"What are you doing here. You're supposed to be, well, you know," the voice came back. "It's complicated but plans changed," she said and there was silence. "Come on Lenny, you know me. Just let us in. You know it's not safe out here at night," she pleaded again. Ryan thought heard the sound of something approaching, something that sounded like clicking just outside of the light. The last of the sunlight was quickly disappearing and all of the sudden he didn't feel secure, or alone anymore.

The sound of a gate being slid open replace the weird sound in the dark and Alexis got back in. "Let's go," she said and Ryan wasted no time in pulling through the gate.

"Where to?" he asked and she pointed. "My old house is the third one from the left just up ahead. I'm sure they didn't clear it out yet," she replied and Ryan drove ahead. She reached in her shirt and pulled out a gray sheet of paper. "Well, this is it," she said and opened it. "What is it?" Ryan asked. "It's the identity of the knight who lives here. You know, the thing that doesn't exist," she said, and honestly didn't care. She was happy to be anywhere else and alive.

She read it and tilted her head. "That, this must be some kind of mistake," she said and Ryan looked at her, he didn't quite know what was going on. "You might as well skip going to my place, we need to take a left up here," she said in a stunned tone. "Okay, you sound like your whole world was just broken, what is it?" Ryan asked her and she lowered the paper.

"The name, it's Jay Bauman. Or Mr. Bauman. The town's only teacher for the past six years or more," she said, continued. "That can't be right," she said again mostly to herself. Ryan slowed down, all he heard was left but since he wasn't the greatest with directions, especially in a strange place like this he wasn't sure where to go. "Turn up here," she said and pointed.

Ryan followed the directions and soon came to what was clearly an old-world building that had been repaired over the years with makeshift, inferior methods. It was a two story, brownstone building with boarded up windows and old wooden planks on the side in an effort to seal the cracks inflicted by the erosion of time and monster attacks.

In the grass clearing in front of it was an old sign with a hand carved, yet well done word in a board that said 'School'. Ryan figured this must be the place and pulled to the side of the road.

"The teachers always live at the school, it's their payment for doing the work," Alexis said as they stopped. "Makes sense, so, do we just go to the front door?" Ryan asked and she shrugged. "I don't know. I've never been here after dark before, no reason to ever be here if you didn't need to be," she replied and opened the door. "But we might as well get this over with, come on," she said and Ryan followed.

The sun was completely gone now and the dim electric lights did nothing to reveal much else. The sound of the ocean was the only thing either of them could hear out here. Ryan hated being this close to the sea. "Come on," she said and walked forward. Ryan pulled the secret message Mithlon had given him out of his pocket carefully and followed her.

In the dark the distance to the front door felt as if it took forever, if didn't help that he was extremely nervous even if all he had to do was hand over a message.

Alexis knocked on the door, hard and fast. She knew that the school was big and hearing her at the door afterhours might not be so easy. The two of them waited, but after a couple of minutes with no answer it occurred to them that maybe he wasn't home. "What do you think, do we come back tomorrow?" Ryan asked and Alexis shrugged. "Time really isn't on our side and it's a long time until sunrise," Alexis replied and Ryan didn't know where else to look.

She was about to suggest they check the town's only bar when the door in front of them clicked and opened. The sudden brighter light made Ryan look away. "Alexis, are you supposed to be, I mean, why are you here?" Jay asked seconds after opening the door and seeing who it was.

"Yeah. I, well, things changed I guess," she said and looked away. Jay looked at her, then up at Ryan. "Well, what's your story?" he asked him. Ryan was surprised. Jay was short, older than he was and skinny, too. This couldn't be the right guy. "My story? I am just a driver and I have a message," he said and held out the paper.

Jay's eyes scanned the paper suspiciously and his aura seemed to darken just for a second as he took it. Jay opened the message and a small electric spark appeared the second he did. He didn't seem to notice and quickly read the message.

"Come inside, both of you," Jay said and stepped back. Alexis walked inside first and Ryan followed him. Jay shut the door behind them and locked it. "Second room on the left, we can talk there," Jay said and Alexis lead the way. "The main classroom," she said and this whole place brought back memories, not all of them so good.

The three of them walked forward. Ryan had never seen such a big room for kids before. When he was growing up he was sure the place he called school was no bigger than this one room. It was clear the place was old, there were maps on walls of places he didn't recognize.

Places on the other side of the ocean. Dots of land in the sea with weird names. A white board, desks that were made of wood and metal. So many things he'd never seen before. He was almost lost in it all when Jay's voice broke him out of it.

"I knew telling Mithlon who I was would bite me later," he said and sat down into his chair behind the big desk.

"Then you know what's going on out there?" Ryan asked and Jay nodded. "Yeah. I know," he said. "But I don't know what you want me to do about it," he said and leaned back into his chair. "Aren't you a knight, like, the real deal, you can't be. You seem way too nice. I've always imagined the Knights being mean, gruff and no-nonsense kind of people. You, you're Mr. Bauman. Teacher of the year type," she said all at once. She supposed it was pretty easy to be teacher of the year if you were the only one.

Jay stared off into space. "Yeah. I am. But I was never like what you described. Once we were finished I mean, we won, we decided the world would be fine the way it is. Life has been good for five long and happy years," Jay said, almost mechanically. There was obviously a lot of history but just before he started talking he shook his head, reached under the desk and pulled out a black bottle.

"Either of you two drink? I could use one," he asked them. "No, thanks," Ryan said and Alexis shook her head no. "Fine," Jay said and smiled again as he opened his bottle and opened the bottle.

"My main problem is that, just maybe the outlanders as you call them, can actually make things better around here? Wouldn't it be nice to turn on a faucet and get water instead of going to some river risking your life? Wouldn't it be fun if you didn't need to worry about being crushed by a beast? Eaten by an Inkit or a wide variety of other mutated things out there?" he asked them then took a swig of the bottle that had no label.

"That would all be great, but they, well they talk like invaders. Didn't you see that big head in the sky. Four days to surrender or else we all die. Who does that? Our life might be primitive compared to where ever they live, but it's still ours," Alexis said and Jay nodded, looked at Ryan. "How about you, kid?" he asked.

Ryan thought about it. He slept through the whole announcement and people in the city didn't seem too concerned. "I think that if you're going to help someone, you don't threaten to kill them all if they don't take your brand of help. That's just my idea of things," Ryan said and Jay nodded, took another swig of his bottle.

"Seran station has always been a little bit insane, but this is crossing the line, even for them," Jay said and the other two had no idea what he was talking about. Jay nodded to himself, deep in thought. "The message you gave was a final plea for help. Mithlon believes they are going to kill all the waste landers anyway no matter what they decide to do," Jay said again.

"Do they really have the power to control the monsters? The big head appeared in the sky but that was it, no monsters or anything," Jay said and Alexis nodded. "They brought some B-class monsters just to prove a point to Hadoth and everyone in it," Alexis said. Ryan decided to come clean.

"I saw who was controlling the monster that attacked my village. It was a woman wearing silver, she had purple eyes. Her weapon of choice was a three hundred foot B class monster. After the attack, I don't know how, she was waiting for me at my house. I shot her with my blaster but it didn't do anything," Ryan said and Jay nodded at his story. "She threatened to kill me, and my friends. What kind of helper does that, it seems pretty obvious to me these people are crazy," Ryan finished.

"I imagine the plan is to gather up the others and face down an army of monsters in the final fight for the freedom of the world," Jay said and rolled his eyes.

"I guess that's the plan," Alexis agreed.

"Four days isn't a lot of time, I mean, do you know where the others even are?" Ryan asked him and Jay just shrugged. "Nope, no clue. After we separated we kind of lost touch," Jay replied and the other two immediately appeared to lose hope.

"I said I didn't know where they were, I didn't that I couldn't find them. However, they may not be so eager to get back to work. I guess we can ask," Jay said to them and glanced at the ticking clock that was on the wall behind them.

"Since the world isn't going to be the same after this anyway, no matter how it goes, I suppose you can go with, wait here," Jay said, stood up and walked out of the room before they had a chance to even ask him what he was talking about.

"Go where?" Ryan asked and wondered where it was they were possibly going in the dark, everyone knew it was stupid to travel after dark. Alexis just shrugged.

Only a few moments later Jay came walking back into the room and he had a silver bracelet on his left arm. Alexis had never seen that before, even though she saw him nearly every day for three years. She'd ask about it later, now wasn't the time.

"Stand up and get close," Jay said and pushed one of the green buttons on the top. The two got up and closer to him. "What about the school?" Alexis asked him. Jay smiled. "I left a note on the door," he replied, pressed the second button and the three of them disappeared in a flash of white light.

Chapter Eighteen

The three of them appeared in a vastly different place. Alexis and Ryan staggered and almost collapsed on to the white metal wall to their sides. Jay shook his head, getting rid of the dizziness in a hurry. "Welcome to Station number five," he said, "better known as Oriab," Jay said and the wall in front of them slid open.

"What are you talking about, what does Oriab even mean?" Ryan asked as he regained his balance. "I never bothered to ask, I just accepted it," Jay said and stepped out of the chamber they were in.

"Master Jay, you've returned?" a robotic voice said as a black floating orb approached him. "Yeah, I said I wouldn't ever be back but here I am, cool right?" Jay replied and the orb floated to the others. "Guests or prisoners?" it asked. "Guests, Thon. Don't shoot them," Jay replied and walked forward.

Ryan and Alexis were stunned by everything around them. They had never seen anything like this. Everything was clean, smooth and metallic, it was also massive. "Where are we?" Alexis asked. "About three hundred miles above the earth, give or take a couple. Follow me," Jay said and started to walk. His footsteps echoed in the metal room they were in.

"Thon, don't wait for me, I need the command center fired up, go," Jay said and the floating black orb immediately shot ahead of them.

"Alright you two, listen. Oriab is huge, confusing and easy to get lost in. I'm going to need you two to stay close to me for a little while," Jay said as they walked. "I have so many questions," Alexis said mostly to herself. "Answers later, follow me now," Jay replied and walked through the metal corridor.

The trip wasn't very long before a large, round door slid open to reveal a room that looked like it was supposed to have lots of people working inside of it. Many stations with chairs sat empty gave the two of them the feeling that this place could be haunted or something. Ryan didn't know what happened but he was sure it couldn't have been good. Jay ignored all of it and walked to the big screen with a console.

He pushed a few buttons and the screen turned on, it was a flat map of the whole planet. "Now we are in business," he said to himself as the two of them watched him work. Then three other red dots appeared on the map, not one of them was close to the other. "I never knew the world was so big," Ryan said. Alexis just shook her head. "That's what you get when you don't go to school, however, it doesn't look anything like the old maps where I went to school," Alexis replied.

"Wait, I thought there were more than four of you," Ryan said, trying to remember the stories. "No, just four," Jay replied and pushed a few more buttons. "But the stories go back, all the way to the beginning. Over one hundred years, are you immortal or something?" Ryan asked again.

"Or something," Jay replied and turned. "Alright. I have a lock on them all. Alexis will talk to Grace and I will talk to Mike. Ryan, I'm counting on you to talk to Jack," Jay said and turned around to face them both.

"One of us, they are your people, how could we convince anyone?" Alexis asked and Jay just shrugged. "I don't know, you'll think of something but if we all work together we can get a lot more done at the same time," Jay said and the others didn't know what to say.

Alexis and Ryan looked at one another. "Well, I guess we won't be bored. I didn't think we'd have this big of role in things," Alexis said and smiled. Ryan wasn't sure he wanted to do any more than this and he almost rolled his eyes at the situation, but stopped himself. He wondered if he would ever see his home again or not at this rate.

"Good, we'll need to get you cleaned up, first," Jay said and walked away. "Follow me," he finished and Alexis walked after him. "Other kid, you stay here. Thon will be with you shortly," Jay said and Ryan stopped in mid step and wondered what made her so special.

Ryan found himself alone and creeped out in this steel, empty room. "Hello. I am Thon. I keep this place in order while the Knight is away," Thon said to him and Ryan jumped and fell forward as the voice scared him.

"Don't sneak up on me, please," Ryan said as he put his left hand over his heart. "Oh, sorry about that. You and I must start the procedure to reactivate Valzin, please follow me to your guest quarters," Thon said in the same robotic voice. "Yeah, sure. What's a Valzin?" Ryan asked as the black orb floated out of the room and he followed.

Alexis and Jay left the command center. "I know, lots of questions, lots of everything. For a few minutes, just drink it all in. Oriab station is a relic from a dead age. Most of this place is unknown even to me. When I got on board I was taught how to use the command center, the basic functions of this place and of course Valzin," he said as they walked down a metal hall.

"I was just like you, amazed at all the grand emptiness, the sterile walls and the crushing loneliness. You think the wasteland is bad. Just spend a few months out here with nothing but a machine to talk to," he said and visibly shuddered at the memory.

"It sounds like fun," she replied sarcastically. "Trust me, at nice as this place is, you'll be begging to see anything else in a few days," he said and turned a corner, pressed a red button on the side of a door. The door slid open and revealed a massive room filled with six layers going up with fifteen grey doors lined up all the way to the far end on both sides of the room.

"Living Quarters, they are all empty. Take your pick but don't bother looking because they are all the same. I'd suggest one close to this door here in case of emergencies," Jay said, slammed his hand against a similar red button and the door slid open. She half smiled and looked inside.

The place was a better room than she'd ever seen in her life. It was warm, well lit. It was one just like she had seen in an ancient paper book. Not quite as fancy as the picture, but reality was much better. "Bathroom is over there to the left. You can get new clothes from the machine on the right. It's night in most of the wasteland. Since we can teleport to where we need to go you can get some sleep. We have time," Jay said and looked around the room. "I'll wake you up when it's time. It won't be long," he said, stepped back. The steel door slid close without a sound a second later.

The room had a port side window on it. Alexis walked to the window and gazed down on the Earth below. The shape of the land, the clouds and the green water made the world she'd grew up on and right now she didn't recognize any of it from this distance. But the whole planet looked as if.

Also, she wondered why there was a window in the room anyway. It was nice and everything but still, it felt dangerous. She walked away from the window and looked around. The first thing she wanted to do was take a shower.

Ryan walked down a hall, following the black orb. "Where are we going?" Ryan asked. He felt as if he had been walking forever and going nowhere. "We are going to see Valzin, you already know this," the machine replied in the same monotone voice. "Sure, but where is it. I didn't think it'd be that far away," Ryan replied to a black orb awkwardly.

Thon suddenly stopped, floated to a pedestal on the wall and lowered itself. "Get in this elevator. I will take us the rest of the way," it said to him and Ryan watched as the door slid open. "Okay," he said and stepped inside. The door closed and the second it did, the thing jolted to life, Ryan grabbed on to the railing on the side. He'd never been in one of these before. As the thing began to move a little more it felt much like a hoverbike so he got used to it.

"When we get to the main level I'll tell you where to go," Thon said, his voice coming from the walls. Ryan jumped, not expecting it. "Sure, I just hope that in five years that this thing isn't useless," Ryan said mostly to himself.

"Unlikely," Thon replied to him and the door slid open to a black chamber. Ryan couldn't see anything past the door way and this made him feel nervous. Everyone knew that it was bad luck, and stupid to walk into a dark room without any light. It usually meant death wasn't far behind. He hesitated from taking another step.

"Thon, I don't like the dark. Could you turn on a light?" Ryan asked in a low voice. For a second there was no response. Then loud, deep click came out of the black and the distinctive hum of electric power, then the room began to lighten up slowly. Ryan walked into the chamber just as slow. There was a shape in the dark behind a glass wall in front of him. A giant lurked beyond and Ryan wasn't sure what to make of it.

"Oh," he said to himself when he realized that he was standing face to face with a thing of legends. The Valzin knight. He'd never seen it before, but it matched the old stories. And it terrified him. The face of the thing had deep red eyes with yellow pupils. Its mouth looked like it was smiling, filled with razor sharp teeth. The black armor reflected the growing white light. "This, why is it so damned scary?" Ryan asked and backed off. The old stories were close but they didn't do it any kind of justice.

"Valzin is scary because weapons are scary, the knights are not peacekeepers. The knights are, were, intended to be the ultimate weapons created by mankind. The idea was that if every superpower had a knight. No one would be foolish enough to use them against one another in war," Thon replied and continued. "Thankfully, only two years after the Nuclear Knight program came to completion the world changed forever and the Knights obtained a new purpose," Thon said and even if his voice was mechanical Ryan thought he heard a sense of relief in it.

"The knights had a new purpose, until they didn't anymore," Thon said. Ryan didn't have a clue of what that meant but he could feel the horrific visage of this knight staring into and through him. He had to look away from the face that made him feel tiny. "Okay, what do we do?" Ryan asked and a line of green lights lit up on the floor. "Follow them," Thon replied to him so Ryan did.

Jay was waiting for him at a console. "I need you to turn that red key at the same time as I do. This is a lot easier with two people and usually the pilots work together to restart the system. Now I have you," Jay said to him and put his left hand on the red key that he was close to. "Sure," Ryan said and looked at it. "Which way do I turn it?" Ryan asked. "Towards me, but if you don't do it exactly at the same time the whole station will explode. It's a failsafe," Jay said to him and Ryan took his hand off the key at once.

"What?" he asked, scared all of the sudden of the idea that he could die with one mistake. "Kid, I'm just messing with you. Take it easy. If we mess up all you have to do is try again. No explosion," Jay said and Ryan narrowed his eyes. "I'm twenty-five years old. I'm not a kid," Ryan said, the continued. "And don't mess with me like that," he finished. Jay rolled his eyes. "Fine, be that way, no fun and boring," Jay replied and motioned towards the key.

Ryan put his hand on it. "On three, turn it towards me," Jay said and Ryan nodded. "One, two, three," Jay said and they both turned the key at the same time. Jay smiled as the console came to life with a click.

"Good deal, that's all I really needed you for. It's the middle of the night down on Earth and we have some time. I decided to gather the rest of them tomorrow. Thon will lead you to the residential areas. Do try to get some sleep," Jay said to him but he wasn't sure if any of them were going to get any sleep tonight.

Ryan shook his head. "That was all, seems kind of simple," Ryan said and did his best not to turn his head or see the horrible face out of the corner of his eyes. "Yep, that's it. I'll do the rest, it's a one person job from here," Jay said and Ryan just shrugged. "Alright," he said and turned around.

"I'll lead you with the green lights, follow me," Thon said to him and just like before the green lights lead him back to the elevator. "See you in a few hours. It won't be easy but do try to get some sleep," Jay as Ryan turned around. "I'll do my best," he replied and walked off.

"Well, Valzin, how've you been. I hope you slept well. I guess we have one last job to do. You know how it is, right. Good, bad and all that other crap. Maybe we'll get lucky and we can talk some sense into Seran station. I'll contact them in the morning before they get up to see what I can do," he said to the machine. Then he wondered if he was going crazy because he was talking to it. He'd just keep this to himself.

Chapter Nineteen

Jay sighed as he finished putting in the commands to start recharging Valzin. "It's like I just turned it off yesterday," Jay said as he stepped away from the console. "Not yesterday. Five years, six months and twenty-eight days ago," Thon corrected him and Jay shook his head. "I didn't ask for a count," he replied. "Is the communication room still in working order?" Jay asked. "Everything is in working order. Do you think I'd let this place fall apart?" Thon asked him in response.

"No, sorry I asked. I have a feeling that all of this can be avoided. I'm going to try and talk to Saran station and see if I can get them to not kill everyone down there," he said and there was no response. "Well, what do you think, can I get them to see a better way or not?" he asked.

"Honestly, no, but good luck," Thon replied and Jay was tired of talking to him, he never did like talking to machines but he'd never admit that out loud. He left the bay area and started to make his way to the command center. He could contact the station from there just as well, too.

The trip there didn't take very long at all. The longer he was back in this empty and metal box in space the more came back to him just how quiet it actually was. Jay sat down in a chair in the middle of the room and pushed a few buttons on the arm rest. "Oriab station calling Seran, come in," he said and waited.

There wasn't a reply. "I know you can hear me over there. Everything on this end is working just fine so do yourself a favor and pick up.

No, I don't care what time it is," Jay added. He was sure that someone would at least pick up on the other end. Then the large screen turned on. Meria's tired face filled the screen.

"Jay Bauman, what a surprise. I didn't expect to hear from you, oh, ever again," she said. She was dressed in what looked to be nothing more than a white nightgown. "Nice to see you, too. Listen. I hate to be a bother but where's Commander Mina?" he asked her and Meria sat on her bed. She just smiled. "Mina retired, by that I mean she died. It was terrible but we managed to carry on," she replied and he looked to the side. "Oh, I see," he replied.

"I am the commander now," she said. Jay almost rolled his eyes. "Great," he replied and continued. "So, about this taking over the world thing, can you, you know, drop it?" Jay asked her. Don't you think it's time we take the planet back? The human race has been living on the fringes for too long. This century alone set us back thousands of years. You and I know that this has to stop," she said to him and took a drink of something that was red.

"I agree, sure. But why all the force. Didn't you ever just consider, oh, I don't know, asking nicely?" Jay asked her, he wasn't going to comment the way she looked. Being distracted right now wasn't going to do him any favors. She knew he had taken notice right away.

"The truth is we don't expect the primitives to just roll over. I don't care if we kill half of them and destroy all of their places to live. They're barely worth calling homes being a bunch of sticks tied together. It won't be a big loss," she said and Jay shook his head.

"No, sorry. You need to reconsider this plan. I know you can control the monsters, but I also know that you have a Knight on your station. I also know you won't risk attacking the station because, well we both know why. I am asking you, nicely, to change your plans," Jay said and Meria took drank the rest of her red liquid from her glass.

"Sorry, Jay. We can't do that. The world needs to be fixed. Don't think we won't fight to take it back. If you want to side with the lowlifes down on the planet, fine. You can't win against an army of beasts. No force on earth can stand against that much power, you'll die if you try. I still like you and your friends. I'm going to do you the courtesy of not killing the other knights in their sleep. Actually, I don't have anyone on this station who'd be able to do that anyway, it'd be a waste of man power," she said and continued.

"I know you're going to gather them up and convince them to fight this, but that's good. Your part of the old ways. You can fight and die in a last blaze of glory fit for the end of one of those old timey movies," she said with a smile. Jay flinched, the woman had a point. It was going to be next to impossible to fight against forces like that, if it was true. Lies were also a thing so he wasn't convinced an army of monsters was possible just yet.

"Alright, you know. I mean, maybe this facetime session isn't good enough to make a deal. Why don't you come over here and you and I talk more about the details in person," Jay said and smiled. "Good night, Jay Bauman," Meria said with a smile and cut the communication between them.

"Well, it was worth a shot," Jay said and switched the screen over again to the location of the knights and sighed, wondering if it was even right to contact them. They could make their own choices after all. Maybe they would come back on their own. He didn't know how any of this was going to go.

"Thon, wake me up in a few hours or if something happens on the earth that's important," Jay said and leaned back in his chair. He'd spent so much time sleeping in this chair, despite how alien this place always felt to him it was easy to sleep. Jay closed his eyes and quickly drifted off to sleep keeping all the stressful things out of his head the best he could.

Alexis got out of the shower, the steam rolled out of the room and fogged everything up. It was the first warm shower she'd ever had. The towel was wrapped around her body and she quickly moved to the bed. As she did a green light ran over form.

"Materializing sleepwear," a voice said to her, it wasn't Thon. Then on the bed, a thin silver outfit appeared. "Nice," she said and quickly picked it up, it felt weird in her hands, too smooth almost. She quickly threw the towel off and cringed at the cold air. The night clothes came on in seconds and somehow fit perfectly. She wasn't going to ask how the machine knew how to make the right size.

Alexis threw the covers back and in her mind, she expected to see something horrible. A blood stain or worse. The sheets were white and cleaner than anything back home. She sighed and slipped into bed. Sleeping in strange places was easy for her, but this more than strange. Alexis stared into the white ceiling and her mind started to wander, questions began to form.

"Who slept in here before I did?" she asked randomly. "This room belongs to Paul Lancaster, while he is away it is set to guest mode," the voice responded to her coldly. She tried her best not to jump. She turned her head and noticed that there was a handle on the wall. She reached out and pulled on the handle, a small panel fell out. Inside was a red, leather bound book. Alexis reached in and pulled the book out. It was tied closed.

The ancient string felt like it was going to fall apart as she pulled it and undid the poorly made knot holding the book closed. Opening it up, she began to read. The handwriting was sloppy, or, maybe it was just how they wrote back then, she didn't know.

Alexis read the story of fifteen-year-old Paul Lancaster. His life was pretty boring. He wrote about how he didn't like school, wrote about his show. Something about people in bright colored power armor that came on at night at seven on Thursdays. Alexis flipped through the pages, each page as insightful into the past as it was boring. However, once and a while a project was mentioned. Something Paul called the Journey, if had another name it wasn't written down here.

Then she came to the last two pages.

June 15, 2150

The news is going insane. Disasters everywhere, no one is saying what's going on. I'm scared and Dad still isn't back. Mom either. The moonquakes are so much worse. Our quadrant hasn't been affected so much but Jim is going nuts. He wants to get to a space station as soon as we can. The evacuations are beginning, the alert just came over the holotron. I have to pack now. Not much time.

June 21,2150

Mom and Dad didn't make it. Jim and I made it to Oriab station after days of going from sector to sector looking for a ride off the moon. We made it just hours before the disaster literally walked on us. It walked. I don't know what's going on. All I know is that the beasts glow brightly, then they fly to earth. Every country, city on the planet is under attack and all we can do from here is watch. They ignored the space stations, I don't know why. I'm in my room and I can see the things falling to earth, like comets if I had to pick a word.

I think this is the end of the world. I'll write later.

June 23,2150

I was right. The knights can't stop the four really big monsters like the leaders promised. All the smaller ones keep getting back up after they are killed. I guess I'm lucky I'm a space station now. Earth is being ruined and evacuation is no longer possible. Not much else to say. Everyone on the station is being assigned a job, it will be something to take my mind off of the disaster. I get my assignment tomorrow. If I refuse, they'll send me to Earth. This is the punishment for not doing what you're told now. I hope I can do it. I'm scared.

September 4, 2150

Work is hard. Twelve hour days in the energy chamber sucks and it's pointless, the nanomachines will keep this place running forever. They just need to keep us busy I think. Not much time to write anymore. I haven't seen Jim in three days now. I don't think I will write in this much anymore. I need to put kid stuff away. Not like this is a good use of my energy anyways. I don't feel very good, either. I think I caught what's going around the ship. Anyway, no one talks about the state of our home world anymore. I feel the need to record the image of the thing that destroyed the world.

Alexis turned the page and it was kind of an image everyone knew. It was some beast, a bad drawing of one. She never saw it before, however but the design was unmistakable. It looked like all the others, but it was black, had red eyes and according to this was taller than buildings. Alexis didn't know if it was accurate, or it really was that big.

This monster killed my whole world. This was written in black, dark letters as if they were scratched in with fury above the monster.

Alexis turned the pages, but that was the last entry. She closed the book, tied it up like it was and put it back where she found it, closed the container back up. "What year is it now?" Alexis asked and waited for an answer. "It is the year 2300," the computer responded, she didn't bother asking for the day.

"Wow," she said to herself and turned over on her side. Her mind raced with so many questions, but the lights slowly began to dim. Alexis closed her eyes and drifted away to dreams.

Chapter Twenty

Jay was passed out in his chair when all of the sudden a high-powered stream of ice cold water sprayed him in the face. He toppled out of his chair and rolled on to the floor. "What the hell was that for?" he demanded, at the same time did his best to catch his breath.

"Your alarm clock, sir, three hours as requested," Thon replied to him. "Yeah, what's the weather doing down on earth, near the locations?" Jay asked as he pulled himself up off the ground. "Weather is fine in three of the locations. A storm is heading towards Liberville, it will be there in three hours. Beast activity is unchanged, the threat is minimal," Thon said.

"Good, wake the kids up and get them to the mess hall. We'll eat and get to work," Jay said and looked down at his soaked clothes. "And Thon, be nice. Don't use the water, the steam or anything else that's going to make a mess," Jay said as he turned to walk out.

"Fine," Thon replied to him.

Ryan was sleeping on a bed. He had followed the green lights the night before, made it into the room and passed out in the room in the clothes he had on. This was normal for him. Then a noise tore him away from his dreams. It was music that sounded weird. "What is this noise?" he asked in a half mumble.

"It's called classical music. Your presence is required in the mess hall. Before you go, you should clean yourself up," Thon said to him and Ryan rubbed his eyes. "Fine. I'll be there in a few minutes, let him know," Ryan said and stumbled his way into the bathroom, only half awake. "And shut that annoying crap off while you're at it," Ryan said as the bathroom door slid shut behind him. The music shut off.

Alexis woke up to the same classical music and stretched out. "Time to get up already?" she asked and smiled. "Yes," Thon said and she threw her legs over the side and sat up. "I slept great," she said and stood up. "I am glad. Please pick out your clothing and meet Jay in the Mess hall. I will guide you when ready," Thon said to her.

"Thanks," Alexis said and wondered, if she could wear anything she wanted, new clothes was first on her list. She, like everyone else, had been forced to wear old clothes from anywhere the merchants could find them in stockpiles. Most of them were just clothes handed down from older generations.

"Well, nothing too fancy," she said to herself. "How do I operate the clothes menu?" she asked. Then a hologram appeared in the air in front of her. "Pick what you like," Thon replied. Alexis started to flip through the choices, she'd never seen this many options before and the stress of picking something to wear was beginning to stress her out a little. "Don't stress out, it's not a contest. Just pick anything that looks good," Thon said to her.

"Fine, I will. Don't rush me," Alexis replied, then she saw something she liked. "This will do," she said.

Jay was sitting in the mess hall when the other two walked in, following the green lights. He turned to look. Alexis was wearing clean clothes, jeans and a black t-shirt and she even had new shoes on. He smiled, Ryan on the other hand didn't pick anything different to wear. He looked cleaner but otherwise, still wearing the old clothes he was used to.

"I don't know if you've noticed but you could wear anything, why do you choose to wear that stuff, I can smell it from here," Jay said and Ryan shrugged. "I didn't like anything that was on the list," he replied and Jay sighed. "Fine, wear what you want," he said "Thon, we need some shale and pure water," he said.

"Bread, wasteland common food? Why?" Alexis asked, disappointed. She was hoping to try some of the more exotic foods of the place. "You've never eaten this before. If you eat it now, trust me, it will make you sicker than you ever been. You need to adjust gradually to the new food, so just eat what you're used to and save yourself the trouble," he replied to them as two hovering plates came out of the distance and landed on the table with the bread, and glasses of water on it.

"Well, enjoy," Jay said and the two sat down. The shale bread, even if it was the main part of most wasteland meals, looked unlike any either of them had ever seen. "Looks better when it's not actually made with cardboard, eh?" Jay asked them and the two of them were pretty sure that their food wasn't made out of cardboard.

"Yes, thanks," Alexis said and they both sat down at the table. Ryan nodded and the two of them began to eat. "This is good," Ryan said and it was far better than anything he was use too. The bread was warm, soft, opposed to the flaky, hard and usually tasteless stuff he had back at home.

"Alright, so I have to know. What happened to everyone who used to live here?" Alexis asked, the journal still haunting her thoughts.

Jay shrugged. "I suppose they all used Seran station's time machine to escape," he said as he took another bite of his omelet. "What is Seran station?" Alexis asked, but she already had an idea of what it was. "A place, like this," Jay replied. Ryan was surprised there could be any more places like this.

"What is a time machine, some kind of giant clock?" Ryan asked trying to get over the idea of more than one of these places existing. Alexis wasn't too impressed either. Jay shook his head. "No, it's a machine that lets you go back in time, like, yesterday. Or before the disaster. You know. Time travel. All the people on this, and all the stations went back before the disaster to live out their lives," he said casually.

Such a concept didn't even make sense to the two of them. "So, why did the disaster take place. Why is everyone living in a wreck?" Alexis asked and started to get angry, if they could go back in time surely, they could have prevented all of this from happening.

"Right, that's what I thought too. But it turns out that time travel scrambles your brain, basically wiping your memories of the future. You remember who you are and stuff, but other than that, not much else," Jay said and took another bite. "Oh, I guess that makes sense," Ryan said, he wasn't convinced that time travel was actually possible. Alexis remained unconvinced this story was actually true. Jay changed the subject in a hurry.

"Alexis, while I admire your ability to pick new clothes. I think you should make a stop into the winter gear section. Liberville is miserably cold and Grace likes it that way. I think she's a little insane but that's just how it is," Jay said and finished his food at the same time as the other two did.

"I, yeah. Do you have a picture, what does she look like? How will I know who to look for?" Alexis asked and Jay nodded. "No pictures. Before you teleport out I'll give you a locator. All the Knights have a chip implanted so we can find one another at any time, if we need to anyway," Jay said and looked at Ryan. "Jack lives at Nogra. It's a nice place, you'll like it," Jay said and smiled, it was a smile that made Ryan uncomfortable.

"Oh, well, alright. I'll just track down someone I've never met and get him to reveal his secret and come fight for us. This should be great," Ryan said sarcastically. "It will be fine. Here, if you can't convince him to do it, let him listen to this," he said, reached in his pocket and slid a small orange and white square across the table to him.

"He'll know how to activate it, so don't lose it," he said and Ryan pulled it towards him and put it inside his vest. "You too," he already had another one out for Alexis, she took it and put it in her pocket. "Thanks," she said.

"Alright. I think it's time to get started. The sun should be coming up in all of these places in a few hours. We should start to get ready to go," Jay said and stood up. Alexis and Ryan finished their water and stood up with him. "Alright, let's go," Ryan said and wasn't eager to go, but he wanted to get all of this over with, too.

The three of them left the mess hall and followed Jay out of the room. It wasn't long before they found themselves entering a teleportation room. It's wasn't the same one from when they arrived into this place, it was similar, but smaller.

Jay reached on a table and tossed them both a metal, square box with a black screen on it. "It's really simple. Push the green button. Follow the instructions on the screen. Just about anyone can do it," Jay said. The two of them looked at them and it seemed pretty simple to them.

"Anything else?" Ryan asked. "Yeah, you're not coming back here. When you find and convince them to get back to work they will need your help to activate the Knights, after that we'll take It from here and you can go home if you want," Jay said. Ryan was relieved, he wanted to go home more than anything else. "I can't go home," Alexis said and Jay nodded.

"Oh, right, you were the sacrifice for the ritual and escaped. People are going to be okay once they realize that the big monsters aren't going to rise out of the sea and kill the world," Jay said and continued. "Well, you can stick around the stations for as long as you need to," Jay said and smiled. Ryan thought it was creepy how he called them the big monsters.

Didn't he see the things walking around down there, weren't they big enough for him? Ryan wondered to himself but dared not say it. There were some things he just didn't want to know about.

"Thanks," Alexis said and then a black coat appeared in the air and fell to the ground. "To keep you warm, miss," Thon said and it made her jump a little. She picked it up and it fit, she buttoned it up and found gloves and a green hat in the pockets. She put them on and was already feeling overheated just standing there.

"Who's going first?" Jay asked and Alexis shrugged. "I'll go first," she said and stepped on to the platform. "Good luck," Jay said, pulled a white lever on the wall with a flash of light, she was gone. Ryan stepped on to the platform next. "Don't lose your head," Jay said to him and Ryan's eyes went wide, but before he could ask about it, Jay pulled the lever again and he was done.

"Thon, keep me updated on beast activity and Valzin's status, too," Jay said. "Yes, I will. Good luck," Thon said to him and Jay disappeared in a flash of white light.

Chapter Twenty-One

Alexis appeared in a flash of light and immediately wished that she would have worn something better than shoes as she found herself ankle deep in snow and the cold bit into her face. "What the hell," she muttered to herself and looked around.

There were trees she'd never seen before. The things on the branches were needles, not like she was used to in her home town of Narvoi. They were tall and looked like white cones covered in snow. The wind was light but even so, it felt like fire against her face. She reached behind her shoulder and pulled up the hood over her head. It helped a little bit.

She steeled herself against the biting cold and pulled the tracker out of her pocket, pushed the green button and just like he said and an indicator appeared, it was pretty close. She looked forward and realized there was a path just a few feet away. She pulled herself through the snow, it was tough to do much like walking through mud or something, she thought. She'd seen snow before, but never so much in one place.

Alexis made it to the path, the snow wasn't as deep here. To the right the path curved into a white, endless abyss. She didn't know where that direction went, to the left is where the indicator was pointing. She started to walk in that direction, her feet crunching the fresh snow with each step and that sound was the only sound she could hear. It made her nervous. When things got this quiet, usually something bad was about to happen. The trees along the path made seeing any enemies, if there were any out here, impossible.

Nothing changed in this frozen world. Everything was bone white and it was beginning to hurt her eyes as the sun reflected off the surface. It was terrible in a lot more ways than she imagined it would be. The feeling in her toes and fingers was beginning to go away and Alexis wished that they could have teleported her closer to the town, at least.

Time was meaningless in a place like this but she concentrated on putting one foot in front of the other. The desolate, snowy path felt as if it would never come to an end. Then coming out of the last curve, she saw the gate of a town in front of her. There were stone pillars on each side and lit torches on the outside of them.

This had to be the place, but there wasn't any indication it was, no obvious markers or signs. Alexis, for all she knew, could have been walking into the equivalent of a sea raider camp and was about to be turned into a meal.

It was too cold to not take the chance so she moved forward all the same. The town was deserted, but it was early in the morning and very cold out so this felt normal. She looked and saw buildings lining the road into town, not one was without snow on it. Alexis pulled her locator out of her pocket and the directions indicated to keep going straight. Putting it away she kept walking forward, deeper into the unknown.

She walked forward when suddenly the locator emitted a small beeping sound. She pulled it out and it said indicated to turn left. She looked in that direction and her eyes widened. It was a graveyard. "No," she whispered to herself. The place was small, the fence surrounding it was twisted and covered in ice.

Alexis walked to the gate and saw that someone had opened it. The lock and chain were hanging off to the side. Alexis didn't know what to expect. She pressed through the iron gate and moved into the graveyard.

The person standing over a grave was immediately easy to see, being the only other living person here, they stood like a tall dark statue in the snow. Alexis wasn't sure what to do. Either this was Grace, or she was dead. From here it was hard to tell anything about the person standing in the snow and now she felt like it would have been really awkward to just walk up and ask them, especially here. On the other hand, time was being wasted.

Alexis made her choice and walked forward. It wasn't long before the sound of her footsteps attracted the attention of the one standing at the graveside.

"It's a little early for visitors, don't you think?" Alexis asked, saying the first thing that came to her mind. "No," a voice replied. It was clearly a woman, but, the voice was just as cold as the air around them.

"I'm looking for someone named Grace. I have a message," Alexis said, trying to get right to the point. The woman looked up at the stranger. "A message?" she asked. She was wearing dark sunglasses and a red hood covered her head. She was covered from head to toe in red winter gear.

"Yes, a message. For Grace. Are you her?" Alexis asked again. The stranger shook her head slightly and started to turn and walk away.

"Jay sent me," Alexis said and figured that only Grace would know what she meant, to anyone else it would be meaningless. The woman stopped and turned back. "Damn it," she said and looked at Alexis. "Walk with me," she said, turned and started to walk back towards the gate. Alexis looked at the grave marker. It was nothing but a thick board driven into the ground.

Here Lies Ben Randolph, rest in peace. Age four. Alexis read those words and understood the situation. She made a mental note to be nicer about things in the conversation. She turned away and walked quickly, following Grace, or, who she was pretty sure was Grace, anyway.

Alexis met the woman outside of the gate. The second she stepped outside, the one Alexis came to meet locked the door. "It's not good to talk business on the dead ground. What does Jay want?" she asked.

"The knights are needed. The outlanders are going to kill everyone. Well, I guess that's all," Alexis said all at once.

Grace looked back at the graveyard. "Good, this whole world is a hellhole and everyone in it can burn for all I care," she said, turned and started to walk away. Alexis was actually expecting that response. This was the response that most people would give, there was nothing easy about living like this.

"Grace, wait," she said and walked after her, but she didn't wait or even slow down.

Alexis managed to catch up. "What happened, I get it, you're bitter but we need you," Alexis said to Grace as they walked. "Need, happened? I assume you know who is back there then. You read the marker. This world took everything from me, even after we saved it. There isn't any point to care anymore," she replied.

Alexis really didn't know what to say. "You came all this way. I might as well let you warm up," Grace said and kept walking. "Thanks," Alexis replied. "Why do you live in such a cold place?" Alexis finally asked. "It isn't always cold like this, you just managed to show up when it was," Grace said. "Beasts don't like the mountains so much. We only have one wandering around but he really doesn't bother anyone, just a D class, as you'd call them. I call him Salvador. Used to be a famous ape in the old world," Grace said. It was hard to know if she was smiling at all because her face was covered.

Alexis got an idea as a small house in the became visible in the distance. "Salvador could become a killer, the outlanders weren't kidding. They can control the beasts and use them as weapons. Is that what you want?" Alexis asked, Grace didn't reply and she hoped that started to get through to her.

"This is my place. You can stay here for a little. I know you can teleport out at any time," Grace said as they got to the door. Grace opened the door and stepped inside, Alexis followed and shut the door behind her.

"I know the outlanders can do lots of things. But we can't stop them. The knights are strong, but they were never meant to be warriors like that. Traditionally when a monster attacked, one of us might show up and drive the monster off or kill it for a little while, save the people. The cycle was that way until five years ago," Grace said as she started to take off her winter gear.

At least she was talking now, a little. Alexis took her gloves off, stuffed them in her pockets. "This world has seen its last days. If the Seran people found a way to change the world, I say let them do it," Grace said and hung up her long coat on the hook by the door. "Yeah, but like I said, they don't care about us. I'm convinced they are going to kill us all if we surrender or not. Didn't you see their announcement in the sky? They brought four B class monsters to Hadoth just to prove a point," Alexis said.

Grace shrugged. "Most of us are dead anyway, take a look around. Going to get water is practically a suicide mission. A giant beast can walk through your town at any time. People are eating one another in the wastelands and supplies are so scarce that anything from the before time is highly coveted. The only reason this world hasn't reverted to the stone age is because of the space stations. Humanity has basically given up, just waiting to die but too scared to admit it," Grace said and sighed.

Alexis couldn't argue with any of that. It was all true and a daily part of life. People died or disappeared so often that it was hard to feel much if you weren't related. If you went out into the wasteland alone, people just assumed that it was going to be the last time they would ever see you. "All of that is true," Alexis said quietly.

"However, who gave them the right to do it. Face it, if humanity needs to die, shouldn't it be from people who live on the planet? On their own terms and not some exiled people from space who can control monsters. Come on you really can't be okay with this insanity?" Alexis asked her and Grace looked away.

"Yes, I can. I have nothing to lose. After Ben got radiation sickness and died I pretty much stopped caring. So, should you," Grace said to her. Alexis sighed and started to feel like all of this was pointless, there might not be any way to get her to help out.

"Grace, why do you keep living?" Alexis asked, frustrated with all this despair, as understandable as it was after all. "I don't know. Every day I look at my blaster and wonder if today is the day, but so far, I've been too scared to do it, I guess," she said almost automatically, like a machine.

Alexis reached in her pocket and pulled out the item Jay gave her and put it on the table in front of her. "Jay wanted you to see this if I felt like I couldn't get you to come back," Alexis said and Grace looked at it. "A recording," she said to herself, grabbed the thing and pulled it back. She lifted up the sliver part like a lid a pressed the red button underneath.

The two of them listened to Meria's message, her arrogance made Alexis cringe. Grace kept a straight face until the message was over. "I've always hated her," Grace said and her eyes narrowed. Alexis was surprised. All of this surprised her after all of this despair, something new at last. Even if it was hate.

"If you want to die and are too afraid to do it yourself. Why don't you come with me and do one last mission? It's a suicide mission anyway. All you have to lose is your life, so why not go out in a blaze of glory?" Alexis asked her and Grace set the recording down on the table after shutting it off. Grace shook her head, thoughts running through her head.

"Death by fire, why not. I'm sure Ben won't mind if I join him sooner than later," Grace said but her tone didn't change, the depression hadn't left. Alexis didn't smile. "I'll need your help. I'll assume you've been to Oriab?" she asked him. Alexis nodded. "Good, we're not going there, however," Grace said and stood up. Alexis stood up, too.

Grace walked to the back of the room and moved a small panel on the wall, pulled out a silver armlet. She studied it for a few seconds, then put it on her wrist. "Get close," Grace said and Alexis did so. The second she got close Grace pushed a button and they both disappeared in a white light.

The two of them reappeared in a white chamber that was similar to Oriab's and Alexis was almost sure that they had returned. The door opened and a dark red orb was there to meet them. "Grace, you've returned, welcome back to Dylath station," it said to her in a higher pitched, female voice. "Thank you Thal," Grace said and walked forward.

"What's your name?" Grace asked her, finally. "I'm Alexis," she replied. "Thal, do yourself a favor and don't kill Alexis, she's my guest," Grace said to the red orb.

"As you wish," Thal replied and continued. "The Nanic unit is intact, do you wish me to begin reactivation protocol?" Thal asked her. "Yes, let's go," Grace said and started to walk away. Alexis followed Grace.

Immediately on looking around her surroundings. She could tell this station was very different than Jay's. "What kind of place is this?" Alexis asked. "It's a medical station," Grace said with a hint of sadness in her voice. Alexis had questions, but at the same time believed she had the tragic answers, too.

Chapter Twenty-Two

Don't lose your head. Those words echoed through his brain as he appeared in some kind of a forest. Immediately he looked around and was worried. He hadn't ever been to a place like this before. He was used to more sand, rocks and vast patches of emptiness. Ryan quickly pulled out his locator and pushed the button.

Where ever this Jack guy was, it was directly in front of him. He took one step in that direction when a scream of a beast echoed from the trees. "Oh, come on," he said to himself and started to, against his better judgement, run in that direction. Normally, you ran away from the monster. That is what a smart person usually did.

Ryan didn't need to go very far before he broke through the trees and nearly fell down a hill before grabbing on to a tree. Far in the distance he could see a large insectoid thing attacking a village that was hard to see because it half blended into the trees. Ryan hadn't ever seen one that looked like this before, it was a mix between a beetle and typical reptile monster he had always known.

Its body was mostly bug, however. It was dark brown and had bright yellow eyes. A long black horn on his head. Its arms were not arms, but long black spikes. It walked on two, thick legs through the village. It screeched with the same high-pitched roar he heard earlier.

"What pissed you off I wonder?" Ryan asked as he watched the walking giant hybrid bug thing vented its rage. "Egalon is the devil of the island, Egalon needs no reason to rage against us, it will go soon," a voice said behind him and Ryan turned around in a hurry to see a shirtless teenager standing behind him. He was covered in crude tattoos and held a long, black stick in his right hand. "You name these things? Where I come from we don't care enough about them to do it," Ryan said and the boy's eyes widened.

"You're not from here," he said and before Ryan could move the kid swung his stick and slammed it against his head. Ryan's pain was short lived just before everything went black.

Ryan woke up on the floor. His head was pounding and his vision was blurred. He had no idea where he was. "Welcome back," another voice said to him. "Thanks, where are we, who are you?" Ryan asked as he slowly sat up.

"Name's Rich, and you are unfortunate enough to be in Nogra territory. We'll be kept in here until we are either sacrificed to their devil, or eaten. Who knows, maybe both," Rich said and for their situation didn't seem too worried about it. Rich was a short, balding, and too fat of a man with brown eyes who appeared to be way too happy for being in a cage. It was clear this man had a good life. Ryan didn't want to know how.

"Nogra?" Ryan asked and slid towards the opposite wall. "Island raiders. They live here on the island, capture people who sail too close. You know, typical dirt bag society," Rich said with a sigh. "I'm looking for a man name Jack, I can't be in the right place," he said and his hands went to his blaster and locator, but they were both gone. "Damn it," he said and Rich looked at him.

"Yep, pirates, basically. Primitive crazies who worship their God king," Rich said and sighed. "I'm not gonna stay here long," Rich said as he leaned up against the wall.

Ryan didn't care about this guy, but now he knew he was screwed. "Damn it, I knew I shouldn't have agreed to this stupid job," he said as he moved over to the opposite side and slid up against the wall. There were a lot of things he was growing increasingly angry about. Jay could have warned him about a whole lot more.

"Don't worry, kid. You're scrawny, they likely won't eat you. They'll just throw you in the pit for entertainment," Rich said with a heavy, grim laugh. Ryan didn't like the sound of that, nor did he like any of this. It was about then he heard footsteps coming in their direction.

"Sailor man, come with me," a guard said, he was covered in tattoos and wore clothes that looked more like rags to Ryan than actual clothes. "Invader, you come too," the man said and opened the old jail cell. The both of them stood up. "Don't be stupid, kid. This guard won't hesitate to kill you if you try to fight or run," Rich said as he stepped out of the cell. Ryan didn't plan on it, even if he did, he wouldn't know what to do next. This was a completely alien land to him. He was safer here than outside, at least right now.

Rich and Ryan walked side by side as the guard walked behind them. There was only one way to go. The sunlight streamed in from the end of the tunnel. Ryan felt his heart beat grow faster as the unknown rushed to meet him.

The prisoners stepped into the light and into a floor covered with white sand, surrounded with high walls lined with torches and above them screaming people who appeared to be excited about what was going to happen. "Are you kidding me, what kind of nightmare is this?" Ryan asked as he looked around.

"The Nogra Nightmare, you must be from far away if you've never heard of these people," Rich said under his breath. Ryan was about to respond when suddenly the crowd went quiet. A man walked into the pit, dressed in a dark green cloak, holding a black staff in his left and as he approached. He dropped his hood and revealed that he wasn't like the others. No tattoos, deep red eyes and skin so pale he looked dead.

"Once again you have made your delivery on time. The Nogra people thank you," the man said to Rich. Ryan wondered what kind of delivery would land him in jail. Then the man looked at him. "You, we don't know where you came from. You will be placed in the pit and fight until you die," the man said to him. The crowd cheered at those words.

"I'm looking for a man named Jack. It's important I find him. If I don't everyone here could be killed. I don't have time for this," Ryan said and the man shook his head. Pointed his black staff at Rich who disappeared in a flash of white light.

"Well, you found him," Jack said quietly. "This is my Kingdom. I am god here, the supreme ruler. I am well aware of the situation. So, I will make you a deal. I will give you five minutes of time to give me a good reason, if you can beat our champion," Jack said, turned and walked away.

"Damn it," Ryan said to himself. "I'm not really a fighter, you know. I don't think this should be how we do it," Ryan said to Jack, but he didn't listen and left the arena. After a few seconds he saw Jack sit in some kind of bone covered throne in the upper tier of the arena.

"Nogra, today our champion will have a fun warm up before the main event. This invader, the one responsible for bringing the wrath of Egalon down on us today," Jack yelled out to the crowd, who in turn went wild.

"Oh yeah, blame me for a monster attack, awesome," Ryan replied but no one could hear him over all the screaming. The gates behind him opened with a loud and low rusty squeak. He turned around to see a woman who towered over him, she was dressed in black leather armor. Her hair was bright red, her eyes a green that almost burned. In her left hand was a massive homemade, twisted thing he was sure was meant to be a sword.

In comparison, he might as well have been a toy who had to look up at her. Ryan didn't think any of this was very fair. "Choose your weapon, invader," someone said to him from the side. He turned to look and saw a rack there filled with a variety of weapons. Weapons that all were all the same size he was.

"Damn, who are these people, giants?" he asked himself because none of this made sense to him. He walked to the rack and inspected all of the weapons there. All of them looked dangerous, made out the same black material.

Ryan's eyes landed on something more manageable, he supposed it was a sword for kids in this culture and picked it up. The second he did, he realized that this wasn't metal at all. It was harder than any wood he felt, but it was organic.

He pushed the thought of where it might have come from out of his mind, gripped it tight. He turned to face his enemy, one he didn't know or ask for and prepared to fight.

She kept her eyes on him the whole time and watched as he moved back to the center of the arena. This thing, what was it? There was no way this thin, pathetic figure could have been a person. She'd seen claw men bigger than this thing couldn't have been a challenge. She felt insulted to face someone who looked like they were made of rotten flesh and bone.

It was a strange thing when this puppet of a creature started running at her. At least it wanted to die like a fighter, she supposed that there was some kind of honor in that. Or maybe it just went insane. She didn't care either way.

Ryan knew that the best way to win, was to attack with everything he had. He ran forward and almost started to scream, but decided against that. The towering behemoth in front of him didn't flinch as much as she looked confused at his actions. Ryan held his strange blade in both of his hands as he ran forward. Ryan swung his blade as hard as he could without aiming at any particular piece of the body. He was aiming for anything he could hit.

She took one step back, grabbed him by the back of his neck as he stumbled by and threw him back to where he started with ease. She watched the weak thing hit the sand. Tired of this nonsense she moved in for the kill.

Ryan had never been thrown like that before. Not by a person anyway. With all that black armor, there was no telling if she was a person at all. This champion of Jack's had to be some kind of mutated monster or something. That kind of physical power was insane. Ryan attempted to stand back up but an armor clad foot put him right back down as it landed on his chest. It knocked the wind out of him and he almost blacked out again.

She held him there under her foot, raised the sword over where she thought his heart might be and thrust it straight down. She watched as Ryan disappeared in the white light and her blade thrust through the sand. She looked up at Jack "Spared?" she asked him.

Jack was standing before his throne. "Not by me. The devil Egalon took him," Jack yelled back. "You or your blade weren't worthy of killing such a weak thing anyway. You need a better challenge. Like this," Jack finished and tapped the end of his staff on the ground.

Two gates on the sides of the arena opened up and three tall, dark brown and white crabs that walked like men came from each side. "Finally, a challenge," she said and eagerly walked forward. The mutated sea monsters would be tough, but it was going to be a good day.

"I will return," Jack said to the people beside him. They nodded, but did not question him. He turned and walked away from them all.

Ryan thought he saw his life flash before his eyes. When everything turned white he was sure he was dead. Thankfully being dead didn't hurt as much as he thought it would. The white light faded away and he realized that he was in a dark, fire lit room, on the floor. Ryan groaned and sat up, when he did Ryan could see the walls were covered with various objects he could only call trophies. Skulls, swords, shields, guns and many other items of war, death and Ryan didn't care to look at them anymore. "Who was dumb enough to send you here. Was it Grace, Mike? Tell me," Jack asked as he walked into the room.

"It was Jay, you must know why I'm here," Ryan replied as he stood up. "Jay, I should have known. Listen. I have a good thing here. Why would I want to leave?" he asked him. "Don't be stupid. You must have seen the message. You know what the outlanders plan to do. All of this will come to an end. They won't put up with anything from the old world," Ryan said to him. Jack didn't know what he was talking about, he also didn't like being called stupid in a place where he was the supreme ruler. He considered killing him right here for it, but for now restrained himself.

"What do you mean, what message?" he asked. Ryan realized that maybe he didn't get the message at all and started to pat himself down. He missed it in his panic but the thing Jay had given him was right where he left it, he pulled the thing out of his vest and handed it to Jack. "Your guards missed this," he said and Jack took it. "Stupid useless guards. They only look for weapons I guess," he said and opened it.

Jack watched the message. "Meria, that slimy witch," he said as it finished. He almost threw the thing against the wall but stopped himself. "Start talking," Jack said to him. "In Hodath, the outlanders brought four monsters to the wall and said that in four days if they, and all of us didn't surrender authority to them, they'd just kill us all, basically," Ryan said to him and Jack sat down in a chair against the wall.

"The plan must be a suicide mission to fight the space dwellers against an army of monsters. I wonder why Jay has to be so dramatic," Jack said mostly to himself. "Yes, and no. I don't believe it's a suicide mission. I've heard the stories of the Knights. If you're one, that's amazing," Ryan said, speaking as if he had met an idol for the first time.

"Stories lie sometimes. People talk, people remember things wrong, too. But I was one," Jack replied, but there was no enthusiasm to the words. "Will you come back? If we can beat this crazy lady. We can save the world," Ryan said and Jack shook his head.

"Save the world. There isn't much world left to save. It is infested with giant, immortal monsters and our only saving grace is that the main four are sealed away," Jack said almost with despair in his voice. "Well, can't we just blow up their whole station?" Ryan finally suggested. "It would be easier to do that," he finished.

"Yeah, sure. But no one wants to risk the time machine getting blown up. We'd need to take the station, infiltrate it and take it over by force and there are about three thousand people on that station who wouldn't want to give it up," Jack replied.

"Is that time machine even a real thing. I don't believe it," Ryan said, despite hearing about it twice now. "Yeah, it's real. It's up there and they keep it all to themselves," Jack said. "I guess I can't let my people down, even if they are all cannibals and insane," he said and continued.

"Let's go," he finished. Ryan was thankful that Jack had spared him from death and walked to him.

"I'll need my blaster back," Ryan said and Jack smiled. "You'll get something to replace it," he replied and the two of them disappeared.

Ryan and Jack reappeared in a white chamber like he had seen before. "Welcome to Cerberus station," Jack said as the door opened a dark green orb was waiting for them. "Welcome to—" Jack cut him off. "I already said it Xoth, I'm going to need you to activate the station right away, we have work to do," Jack said as he stepped out.

"You have unauthorized personnel on board, do you wish for me to vaporize it?" Xoth asked in its mechanical voice. "No, I'm going to need him for now. Get to work, time is wasting," Jack said and Ryan followed him, he assumed he was going to help activate another Knight. "Oh, and if you ever call me stupid again, I'll kill you," Jack said and Ryan swallowed in fear. "Sorry, sometimes I get carried away, it won't happen again," Ryan replied and shuddered a little bit.

Chapter Twenty-Three

Jay appeared behind an old wooden building. He looked around and made sure that no one saw him show up. Once he saw that he was alone, he took a deep breath and walked around the building back to a muddy street. The sky was cloudy and the air was cool and people were walking back and forth on the side. Jay watched as a hoverbike slowly went by.

It was beaten and looked like it had been in a couple of fights or wrecks. This was every village in the wasteland in the spring time. A muddy mire mixed with the smell of despair in the air.

Jay ignored the scene and turned and looked down the road and saw what he was looking for. The biggest building on the road and it even had an ancient neon sign above the door. 'Welcome to Joe's' it said in bright green letters and it flashed on and off. Jay didn't need a locator to know where to go next. He looked both ways before crossing the street because you never knew what insanity would come down the road and walked in that direction.

It was only a few seconds of travel but he made his way to the bar. Opening the door, the smell of broweed smoke and cheaply made, and questionable alcohol was instantly overwhelming. People huddled in dark corners and the sound of the local band playing something that resembled music softly to keep the peace. Jay looked around and there at the bar he saw the man he was looking for, right where he expected him.

Jay walked to the bar and sat down. "Hey," Jay said and Mike looked at him. Mike was a big guy who made Jay look tiny in comparison. "What are you doing here?" Mike asked, getting straight to the point and quickly becoming annoyed. "You know what I am doing here. I'm getting the band back together because the morons in Seran station don't want to play nice anymore," Jay said, he didn't seem to care if anyone over heard him or not.

"About that nonsense, you think I care about what they do. We both know they can't control the monsters. No one can," Mike replied gruffly and took a big drink of the beer, or what passed for beer in these parts, in his glass.

'I'm telling you, they can. Someone figured out a way to do it and in what, three days, they are going to unleash a whole army of the monsters on the world. The raiders, the Technocracy, the wastelanders. Everyone is going to be killed. Meria practically told me this herself, but I recorded it," Jay said and someone on the other side of the bar heard what he was talking about.

"Say what now?" a woman said as she set a glass down on the bar. "Don't mind my friend Daisy, he's spent too much time in the sun, crazy and all," Mike replied and Daisy stared at the two of them. Jay just smiled.

"I'm not crazy, but yeah, don't listen to me," Jay replied to her and rolled his eyes. "Jay, it was nice to see you again but I think you'd better leave. None of us are going to go back to work. We've done our work, we're done," Mike replied to him a little quieter. It was then the front doors swung open as if someone just kicked them in.

"What in the world?" Jay asked and turned around. "It's just the local hard case group who took out an Inkit and think they're all invincible now. Don't bother them and they won't bother you," Mike said and finished his beer. Jay watched the group of six people walk in, dressed in leather, all of them had a blaster hanging at their sides. "Hunters?" Jay asked.

"No, they aren't hunters, they just got lucky. Or claim they did. Who cares?" Mike asked and he clearly didn't care about them. "Alright, if you say so," Jay said but just before he could turn around he watched as their leader, or what he thought was their leader anyway, push some older guy out of the way who didn't move fast enough.

"Out of the way," he said as the man hit the ground. Jay narrowed his eyes as he watched this but didn't do anything yet. "Jay, let it go," Mike said, he didn't have to look to know what was going on. "You know I can't," Jay replied as he watched the gang move closer to the bar. Mike started to get up to go somewhere else.

"Don't tell me you've turned into a sidewinder?" Jay asked him and Mike sighed. "No, I just don't want any trouble, I just want to remain in a quiet, peaceful life," Mike replied as he got up and left the bar. Jay shook his head, but there was no way he was giving up his seat for these guys.

"Boy, you're in our place, get out," the man said to him. Jay didn't move. "Oh, I understand. We have ourselves a hero," the man said to his five friends. The rest of the people in the place did their best not to look in that direction. Jay could feel the tension in the air growing and he smiled.

He liked it like this, back in the old days he used to pick fights with people like this all the time. Jay stood up and turned around. He barely came up to the man's shoulder. "My mistake. I'll let you have your spots. They weren't that good anyway," Jay said and stepped to the side.

The gang of men watched him step away. Jay turned his back and expected to be hit in the back of the head, but it didn't happen. The guys took their spot at the bar and Jay walked towards Mike. "Well, look at you. You're all grown up, the others would be proud of your maturity," Mike said to him, honestly impressed.

"I deal with stupid teenagers all day who think they can all take on an Inkit and Crabman on their own at the same time. I've gotten better and dealing with people like that since becoming a teacher," Jay said, Mike raised his eyebrow. "Teacher?" he asked, not believing him.

"Apparently all you need to do is walk in and take the job. I wanted to try something different so, well, there you go. I applied and was hired. Five years running Narvoi teacher of the year," Jay replied and Mike finished his drink.

"Nicely done. I thought about doing something but I decided that I did enough and wandered around from town to town. Doing anything I want, staying low. It's been a pretty good time," Mike replied and looked around. "Just got here three days ago and was thinking about leaving," he said and set his bottle on the table.

"Why don't you come back with me, all you're doing out here is wasting your time and life," Jay said and Mike shook his head. "You don't get it. Every night all I see are those things. It's an endless nightmare. Even if I did go back I don't think I would be much use," Mike replied and Jay sighed at this. "Me too, nightmares every night. We separated but, not really. I'm willing to bet we all have the dreams. You're not alone and I think the only thing that will make them go away is to do what we're supposed to," Jay said to him.

"We did what we were supposed to do. We took down the monsters. Saved the world, or what's left of it. Are we really responsible for defending it from other people?" Mike asked him and Jay narrowed his eyes. "No," Jay answered. "But it's the right thing to do. Look around. This is the world now. Humanity adjusted, maybe we should try to save it. I mean, we might fail. We might all die. Either way I think it's going to be our final act, too," Jay said and shrugged.

Mike knew that Jay was always looking on the dark side of things, but right now he couldn't help but agree with that. Everything about all of this had the grim feeling of finality to it.

Mike took a breath and looked around. He didn't know anyone here. He didn't care about any of them and that was the way it had been for the past five years. Life was as meaningless as yesterday's weather lately.

"Oh, hell. I have nothing to do anyway. If we die, we die I guess. Nothing lost," Mike said and Jay nodded. "Yeah. I guess so," Jay replied, but he didn't smile. He wished that he could go back just a few days before all of this happened, too.

"Let's get out of here," Jay said and got up. Mike did too and the two of them made their way towards the door. The two of them left and walked around the corner of the bar. "See anyone?" Jay asked as he looked around. "Nope, you're good," Mike replied. Jay hit the button and the two disappeared in a flash of white light.

A second they were in the black teleportation chamber. "No power?" Jay asked. "No, it's always this way," Mike replied and the door opened. "Welcome back to Syrgoth Station, Mike," a black orb said, waiting for them. "Hello," Mike said and stepped forward.

"This place always gave me the creeps," Jay said and Mike nodded. "Yeah, it's a nice place, isn't it?" Mike replied and swallowed his fear. "I guess we better go say hello to Azagon," he finished and started walking.

"Knight Azagon is in stasis mode," the shiny black orb said in a mechanical voice. "I know, it's how I left it, go do something productive, robot," Mike said and brushed the thing away. The orb floated away. "Doesn't it have a name?" Jay asked. "Yeah, but it's never told me what it is. But I just call it spot. It seems to work," Mike replied as they walked down the hall of Syrgoth Station towards the holding chamber in order to start the process in reactivating the weapon. "My name is Atador," the machine replied to him. "No, it's Spot, no one knows what an Atador is," Mike replied to it. The computer didn't reply after that.

Jay was sure Mike had lost a few sanity points in the past five years but decided not to say anything about it.

Chapter Twenty-Four

Grace and Alexis sat in the command center of Dylath station. Neither one of them were too eager to say anything to one another. After seeing Nanic for the first time Alexis didn't have much to say and Grace was overcome with memories of the past. "Grace, how did you begin to be a Knight, I mean what got you started?" Alexis asked her. "Bad luck mostly," Grace replied.

She was about to say something when the communication screen popped on. "Grace, it's Jack, you there?" the voice came over the speakers. Alexis jumped at the sudden noise Grace just looked up and nodded.

"You can see me, right?" Grace asked him and the man smiled. "I see you got a tag along too and they dragged you into this nightmare," Jack said and looked to his left. Ryan was there staring at some kind of hologram, trying to figure it out. "I don't know. Does anyone have a plan or are we just going to wait for the crazy people to do something?" Grace asked and Jack shrugged.

"I don't know," Grace said and continued. "The only plan I had was to show up. No one ever said I actually had to do anything," she said with a low voice. "Some knight you're turning out to be," Alexis said after hearing that but Grace ignored her.

"True, but since we're up here again we might as well do something. But who knows. Maybe the deadline will pass and Seran won't do anything. Maybe it's all just talk after all," Jack replied to her. Ryan waved his hand through the hologram and it shut off. "How many times do I have to tell you if you do that you shut it off?" Jack asked responding to Ryan's frustrated sigh.

"We can only hope," Grace said and honestly did hope that it was all talk after all. She was pretty sure that none of them on either side were looking for a fight. Soon another screen opened up in the main one. Jay and Mike in one screen.

"It's good to see everyone again. I was wondering if my messengers would get through to you or not. I am glad to see they accomplished their missions," Jay said into the message. "Mine almost turned into a punching bag for Katy, but otherwise everything turned out okay," Jack said and smiled. "Hey, that sucked," Ryan said from the background.

"Shut up and keep watching the magic hologram," Jack said to Ryan. Alexis couldn't help but laugh a little bit.

"What's the plan?" Grace asked, getting to the point. "Well I was hoping we could talk about that," Jay replied and Mike looked away a little. "I say we just blow up the station and be done with it. That'll just take a couple of minutes and we can all go back to our normal lives," Mike said without thinking about it.

"No can do, Mikey, you know why. Think about it," Jack replied and the others shook their heads at the mere suggestion. "Oh yeah, the power grid thing," Mike said and remembered that all the stations were connected and had to stay where they were to keep the balance. He always thought that was a major design flaw.

"I have a suggestion," Alexis spoke up and there was silence. "Well what is it?" Jack finally asked and she shook her head. "Oh, right. Well. If we can't attack them directly, maybe we can exterminate the army. Kill all the monsters before they can kill the people," Alexis said and the knights became uneasy with that suggestion.

"Two reasons we can't do that. One, they aren't evil, not really. Two, they are immortal. We've killed hundreds of these things and they always regenerate eventually. Sometimes in a day, sometimes longer.

Without the alpha beasts, they are just like people. Just trying to get by on a world they don't belong on," Jay replied and the others nodded.

"People?" Ryan said, shocked at the comparison. "I lost my parents to one of those things. We lost our whole world fell to these things and you compare them to just being people?" Ryan asked them and came to the screen.

"There is a lot of history, things you don't understand. The monsters aren't evil. We can't kill them all, even if we wanted to," Jack replied and the others knew how he and Alexis must have felt about them shooting the idea down.

"Okay, well, then I guess we have two options," Mike said and continued. "We make a stand against whatever army they bring up and fight it until one side is finished. Or we sneak into their space station, find out how they are controlling them and break it," Mike finished.

"I like that second plan, we can just zap on over there and take the place out," Alexis said sarcastically. "Seran station is filled to the brim with people. It's the last populated station. We're not going to just zap over there and expect that no one will see or notice us. I'm sure all of their shields are still up," Grace said, but wasn't sure about any of it.

"Then it's settled. I guess we need to do both plans," Jay said and no one had any idea what he was talking about. "We have two stragglers we can sneak aboard the station while we take on the army on the ground," Jay said and nodded.

"Wait, you mean you want us to go to the station and, well," Ryan couldn't finish it. It was a suicide mission and everyone knew it. "You'll live. Meria might not appreciate you blowing up her science project but if you succeed I don't think she'll outright kill you for it," Jay said, but he didn't sound too sure of himself.

"If that what it takes to save everyone, I guess I'll do it," Alexis said and Ryan shifted uncomfortably at the idea. "Fine, I guess," he said quietly but he really didn't know the first thing about being an infiltrator.

"Good deal. Get them sent over to my station and I'll start putting them through the training protocols. We only have a couple of days left to get ready and—" Mike was interrupted as an alarm began to sound on all four of the stations at the same time.

"Someone shut that crap off," Grace said and winced at the sound. Seconds later at her command it shut off. "Someone's being attacked on the ground. Are we going to do anything about it?" Jay asked them and silence was the only reply. "Guys, who's being attacked? Aren't you going to do something?" Alexis asked, pleaded with them almost.

The screen shut off and it was replaced by a map of the earth. "A C-class monster came out of the ocean and is attacking Nulbar City. They are fighting back with the coast cannons but it's not doing much good," Jay said and a live feed came up replacing the map.

It was a hulking sea beast, covered in dark green scales that was lumbering on two legs. It looked like a shark that grew legs and arms. It was clumsy as the bright white beams of the coastal cannons slammed into its chest and face. It screamed in response but advanced all the same. "Is it under control?" Jack asked as he watched it.

"No, the one that attacked my village looked like it was sleepwalking. This thing looks like it's, lost, confused maybe? I don't know," Ryan said and seeing the beast like this, away from the action, it looked as if the knights might have had a point. But why was it attacking Nulbar like this. He supposed that is just what monsters did.

"Well we can't just let the city be destroyed, can we?" Jack asked and the others mumbled. "Fine, I'll take care of this problem," Grace said in a huff. "Well how generous of you. Send the girl to Cerberus station before you go," Jay replied and Grace stood up. "My name is Alexis, remember," she said and Jay laughed. "Trust me, I'll never forget you for the rest of our short lives," he replied and cut off the communication.

Grace turned and looked at her. "Thanks," she said. "Get to the teleportation room and get to Cerberus station," she said before standing up and walking away. "Okay, I can do that," she said and watched her leave the room. She couldn't help but feel in awe, she was watching for all intents and purposes, a legend.

Grace stopped. "On second thought. I want you to watch this, stay in contact with me," Grace said to Alexis. "Uh, well. Okay," Alexis replied, not knowing if she really had a choice in the matter at all. With that she walked out of the room.

Grace walked down the path she had a thousand times over, at least. "Mistress Grace. Your vitals are elevated, your stress levels are too high. Are you sure you want to activate Nanic in this condition?" Thal asked her as she walked down the path.

"No, but I know the others aren't ready yet. Nanic recharges the fastest and is ready to go. It's just a C class. I can take it. Once I get back in the machine I'll be fine. It's just been a while. Thanks," she replied to Thal.

"Grace, I know what the problem is. It's been years but I am sorry," Thal said and Grace stopped. "Ben died because of radiation poisoning. It wasn't your fault or mine. It was the world's fault. I don't blame you, I never did," Grace replied the to the voice and fought back the tears. The memories were always just below the surface.

"Grace, Nanic awaits," Thal said and snapped her out of her daze. "Right, let's go," she replied and kept walking down the path and into the elevator. The second she entered it, the doors closed and began moving. In just a few seconds they opened to the docking chamber of Nanic. Grace swallowed and moved towards it. The chamber opened and she walked through the doors only fall into the void.

She watched as the bone white body of the machine rushed past her. "Truth," she said as she fell towards the feet of the knight. Then she teleported in mid fall. Opening her eyes Grace found herself in a familiar chamber.

"Alright, all systems check," Grace said and the chamber she was in turned solid blue. "All systems are go. Welcome back, Grace," Nanic replied to her in a smooth, feminine voice and she nodded.

"Launch," Grace said and braced herself. In seconds she felt like she was on a rollercoaster ride on a fast and steep fall that was never going to end.

"I hate this part," she whispered to herself. "Flight, activate, prepare for reentry to the planet. Nulbar City is the destination," Grace said and the blue light surrounding her disappeared to turn into what Nanic was seeing.

Falling, flying down to the surface of the earth. Stars all around, fading into the blue sky. "Oh, Now I see why that thing came out of the ocean, Nulbar's under a thick cloud bank," Grace said to herself. She took a deep breath and prepared herself to get back in the swing of things. She wasn't sure why no one caught that. Maybe they were far rustier than they thought they were, she figured.

Chapter Twenty-Five

Nulbar city, self-proclaimed jewel of the eastern Atlantic coastline was under attack from a beast. General Alaya was standing on the sea wall watching the beast advance. She was fearless in the face of a truly hopeless situation.

"Sir, we can't stop it," a soldier said to her as the cannons unleashed another barrage of energy. Alaya watched those beams slam into the dark green flesh of the monster. It screamed its dreadful roar, the thing only seemed to become angrier. "I know, how's the evacuation coming along?" she asked, never taking her eyes off the thing.

"Not good, the attack was too sudden. We're working as fast as we can," the soldier replied and Alaya nodded. "I understand," she said and knew just how hopeless the situation was going to be. Everything she ever knew for her whole life was about to be ruined and there was nothing more she could do than watch as ancient cannons did next to nothing. She sighed and turned to look at her city one last time.

"Is everything we have destined to be destroyed?" she asked herself. Knowing what was coming. "Sir, we need to leave while we can," the soldier said to her and she nodded. "Prepare the second line of defense, we're leaving," Alaya replied, turning back to the walking, green shark thing that shouldn't have ever existed at all, who wouldn't stop.

However, a new noise was coming from somewhere else. A noise that was unnatural and coming from the sky. At first, she thought it was just her sanity finally taking a vacation. "Sir, what is that sound?"

the soldier asked her. She looked at him and realized she hadn't lost her mind quite yet. "No idea, it could be another monster coming to challenge this one. Maybe we'll get lucky," she replied.

Even the beast noticed the high pitched whistling and turned to look at the sky. From the dark gray clouds, a massive figure appeared floating down. "Oh my," Alaya said and was stunned. Everyone who saw it was as well.

A bone white figure that had the body of a warrior angel without the wings tore from the clouds. It was smooth, sleek and almost beautiful to look at. The natural light reflected off the skin of the thing and made it look like it was glowing all on its own. "I don't believe it," Alaya managed to say. "Isn't that who I think it is?" the soldier beside her asked.

"It is," Alaya replied as the thing landed in the ocean creating geysers of sea water. "We might have a chance after all," she said and smiled. "Let's get out of here," she said and with that the two of them made their way off the wall to retreat from the coming battle.

The beast turned to look at this thing, its red eyes wild with rage, hate and pain. It stood three hundred feet tall, even so, it barely came up to the waist of Nanic. Grace looked down at the thing as it stepped forward. "This is Utrit. It has been defeated six times in the past one hundred and fifty years by Saphiel, Nanic, and Azagon," the voice said to her.

"Good to know," Grace said and scanned it. Immediately she knew why it was attacking and acting like it was. "Patch me in to Dylath station," Grace said. "I'm here," Alexis said to her. "This thing is going to destroy the city if I don't stop it. So, I'm going to ask you what I should do with it. Make the choice," Grace said and slid her right leg back. As she did the knight followed her every move. "Yes, kill it," Alexis said without hesitation.

Grace looked at the beast. "Kill it. Have you learned nothing?" she asked and as Utrit charged her she quickly danced around it, watching it sail past. "Why not kill it. It would kill everyone in the city. Kill it before it can," Alexis said, anger in her voice.

"Allow me to teach you a lesson, watch," Grace said raised her left hand as the beast turned around. The thing began to advance again. Nanic's left palm exploded with bright white light. Utrit screamed in pain and covered its eyes as it spun around protecting his eyes. As it did Grace saw exactly why the thing was in such a rage. She walked forward, reached down and grabbed the end of a large thorn sticking out of its back.

Grace pulled it out with ease and held the thing in her hand like it was a blade. The shark beast screamed less now and Grace stopped her spotlight to the thing's face. Utrit turned around, its eyes softer now and its rage almost gone. It grunted and shook its head a little. Then it turned and began to walk back into the ocean.

"Alexis. The monsters learn. If you kill them they will come back to life. They will remember what you did. They aren't like us but they do remember. Knights don't just kill the monsters, sometimes we have to do what's right," Grace said as she watched the monster drift back into the sea, its wound healing.

"Oh," Alexis said as she watched the battle end on the screen. Alexis watched as the long spike in Nanic's hand slowly dissolve away, turn into steam and blow away with the wind. "Yeah, immortal monsters have more drawbacks than you might think, but balance with humanity is something they've managed to keep ever since the A classes were sealed," Grace said and turned to look at the city again. "Nulbar suffered no damage. Nanic Knight at one hundred percent. Mission accomplished," a voice said to Grace.

Grace took a look around to see if whatever injured the beast was still here. However, there was no sign of it. "Scan for alien lifeforms," Grace said as she looked. "One detected, moving into the deep water," Nanic replied to her and she nodded. "Let's go home," Grace said and Nanic floated into the air. "Alexis, get to Cerberus station, I want you there before I get back. You have three minutes," Grace said into the communicator.

Alexis stood up right then. She didn't want to find out what happened when you didn't listen and didn't bother replying, time was already wasting away and the panic set in. “Get me to the teleporting room,” Alexis said in a hurry. “Yes, follow the green lights. I won’t let you down,” Thal replied and the green lights did appear in the direction. She rushed towards them, trying to count the seconds in her head as she ran.

Those green lights twisted and turned through the station until finally they lead to a door that swung open slowly. “Get inside. I’ll get you where you need to be,” Thal said to her and Alexis stepped inside the chamber.

“Thanks, I’m sure we’ll talk again,” she replied, still feeling a little bit weird about doing this. Alexis smiled as she disappeared in a flash of white light. She had plenty of time, Alexis didn’t know it but Grace was taking her time getting back to the station and never would have made it back in the three-minute time limit.

“Nice show, Grace,” Jack said through the communicator. “Yeah, you don’t have to kill them all the time,” she replied. “Well yeah, it was just a little guy, too. But still. Now everyone is going to know we’re back,” Jack replied and she smiled. “Good,” Grace said as her station came into view.

“They aren’t really concerned about us being back. I don’t think they are going to change their plans,” Grace said and flew to the docking chamber. As she spun around, as it had always been, she could get a glimpse of the ugly, broken moon. If only for a second it reminded her of how everything got started.

“Docking in process,” Nanic said to her and the image chamber she was in turned blue once more as the procedure finished. “Welcome back do Dylath Station, Grace,” the voice said as she disappeared.

Grace found herself back in the docking chamber, face to face with the angelic Nanic and she smiled. “We were able to do a little good today, old friend,” she said to it. Then she turned and walked away. She felt lucky it was such an easy mission. It could have been worse and she wasn’t sure that she was prepared enough for a big battle after all these years of being away from the fight.

"Thal, prepare the training chamber," Grace said as she walked away. "Yes, mistress, I will," Thal replied to her.

Chapter Twenty-Six

Alexis appeared in the black chamber lined with green lights. Then the door opened. Ryan was standing there and he was smiling. "Welcome to Cerberus station," he said and she looked around. "This place is depressing," she said and didn't like how dark it was.

"Yeah well, what isn't depressing anymore? Come on, I'll introduce you to Jack," Ryan said and still shuddered. The guy was a maniac and for the life of him couldn't understand how he was ever considered to be a knight of any kind.

"Okay, let's go," she replied and the two of them walked out of the teleportation room. The two of them only made it a few steps down the hall when Jack stepped around the corner ahead of them. "Welcome to my home, kids. I am sure you'll like it here," he said to them with a smile, a smile that felt fake to both of them.

"My name is Jack Red-Eye. I suppose you can see why they call me Red eye. My eyes are red, you see," he said and pointed. "Yeah, we see that," Alexis said and Jack's smile faded. He wasn't used to people talking to him like that so openly.

"My enemies call me Sepsis eye Jack. They think it's an infection of some kind. A disease. But you know, do you really want to know why my eyes are red?" Jack asked and his voice started to get deeper as he spoke.

He didn't wait for them to ask. "It's the Saphiel Knight. There is something wrong with it, it gives off a bit too much radiation. Not enough to kill mind you, but disfigure, oh yes. That it does do," he said to them and took another step forward. "And now you know why my eyes are red, because I am a hero of the wastelands. Killing monsters and protecting people, the knightly business," Jack said to them and tilted his head a little bit.

"Jack, I need you to remember you're not on Nogra island anymore. You're on the station," Ryan said carefully, as if he were talking to some kind of beast more than a man. "Of course, I know where I am. I'm not insane or that forgetful," Jack said with a hiss.

"But right now, we need to prepare you. To get you ready for the last thing you'll ever do. Follow me, rookies, follow me to the chamber of fun," Jack said, his red eyes wide as he spun around and turned the corner he came from.

"Oh, wonderful. He's completely insane. How do we know he isn't just leading us into a death trap?" Alexis asked and Ryan shrugged. "We don't," Ryan replied and was increasingly nervous about being here.

The two of them didn't waste any more time and walked towards the direction Jack went, when they turned the corner however there was no sign of him anywhere. "What?" Alexis asked as she looked around. "He wasn't that far ahead of us, where did he go?" Ryan asked, he too was confused.

"Hey, I'm over here, this way, people. This way," Jack said and he was standing in the hall behind them. They both jumped and turned around to see him standing at the end of the hall, waving at them. "Come on," Ryan said as he started walking down the opposite hall. The two of them walked, but Jack, once again disappeared around the corner. This time the two of them hurried, when they made it to the turn, they found him there waiting for him.

"The most important rule about stealth, obviously, is to not be seen," Jack said and nodded to someone in front of him, someone only he could see. "So, once you realize that, the rest is going to be easy," Jack said, pushed himself off the wall and walked down the hall. "The training room is here, right here," Jack said and pointed at a door. "It will train you in the ways of stealth, killing, destruction. Anything you might need to know is inside," Jack said and smiled.

"Killing. I'm not entirely good with killing," Alexis said and stepped back however, she wanted revenge on Hadoth for almost having her killed at the same time. "Girl, the wasteland is nothing but violence, murder and pain. You've lived there your whole life and managed to avoid all that? Pretty impressive if you ask me," Jack replied and his smile faded.

"No one likes killing, no one with a mind left to lose. The only things who do are just mindless things. Man, or beast, just a thing, a parasite that needs to be burned away," Jack said and shook his head.

"No, killing is not to be enjoyed or cherished. It's to be hated, feared, despised. Also, when needed, necessary. Not everything can or should be saved. And if something is going to kill not only you, but everything you know? It is needed. You don't need to like it, but you need to learn how to do it," Jack said and his red eyes stared deep into some invisible world.

Alexis understood this, actually. She hated the idea of killing anything but, now it might be the only option they had. "Fine, I guess we'll get started," she said and Ryan nodded. "Our time is short but we'll do the best we can," he said as Jack opened the sliding door.

"Go inside," Jack said to them and the inside of the room was black as if something physical was covering the entrance. They hesitated for a second, it looked like stepping in here was stepping right into space itself. "Well, go," Jack said and the two of them walked forward.

To their relief the floor on the inside was solid and they didn't fall into a void. The door behind them closed a second after they stepped inside and at once, lights in the room came on. In the middle of the room were two pedestals with bracelets that were identical.

"Step to the center of the room and please put the armlets on," a mechanical voice said to them. They looked around for the source of the voice. "Do it now," the voice ordered them both. "Geeze, alright already," Ryan replied and walked to the center of the room.

The silver armlet was light when Ryan picked it up. It felt weird against his skin. He put It on his left arm and the thing shrank to tighten itself against his arm. He winced at first but realized that it didn't hurt. Alexis's did the same thing.

"The Cerberus Stealth Armlet is the very latest in infiltration technology. In the year 2150, stealth is the most important ability any army can have. You have been chosen to be that special person the bleeding edge. This program will teach, will teach, teach—" The voice from the walls sputtered out.

"So much for ancient tech," Ryan said as he looked around. The room then began to shift. Then they weren't in the room anymore. Now they were in a grey hallway with running lights moving in both directions, and they could hear voices in the distance.

"I guess, we need to do something?" Alexis said. "Yeah, my guess would be we don't get caught," Ryan replied and looked at his now black armlet. There was only one button on it, so he pressed it. Alexis watched as he just disappeared before her eyes, mostly. If she looked hard enough she could still see a faint outline of him, as if the light was distorted. She pushed the button too and disappeared just as two people came walking down the hall.

Now she could see Ryan, he was in black and white, as if all the color had been drained out of him. He looked at her and pressed against the wall and she followed his lead. They held their breath and watched as the strange people in white long coats just walked past them and disappeared at the end of the hall.

"Good job. Soldiers. You understand the basics. Now we will move to the next level," the voice said to them and the wall they leaned on disappeared. Everything shifted and now they were in an underground tunnel. Silence was replaced with sounds of explosions and dirt falling from above with each one. "Your objective is to recover the intelligence, find it without being detected," the same voice said to them.

"Any ideas?" Ryan asked and Alexis just shrugged. She still saw him in the gray color so it was safe to assume they were still mostly invisible. "We should split up and look for it," Alexis said, Ryan didn't like the idea but nodded. "Fine, good luck," he said and looked left. "I'll go this way," Ryan said she nodded.

Ryan took a breath and started to walk the path. There wasn't anyone here to stop him and so far, this training seemed to be pretty easy. He had no idea what exactly it was he was supposed to be looking for, but he was sure he could find it in a short amount of time. He looked back but Alexis was already gone. "Good luck," he said and looked back and focused on the task at hand.

He came to a cross path. Ryan needed to make a choice, there were no indicators, worse he didn't have any feelings or even instincts on what to do. Usually at times like these he had a good sense of where to go, but in an environment like this it felt impossible to choose. "Oh, to hell with it," Ryan said and turned to take the right path.

He didn't listen, didn't crouch or even be very careful about it. He stepped around the corner and came face to face with a soldier. The man acted as if he saw a ghost and thrust his rifle forward. Ryan looked down to see the silver bayonet stab him in the chest. He felt it, the cold, even the pain. Everything around him was bathed in red light. "Mission failure, you were caught. Try again," the voice said and Ryan turned around to see Alexis standing not too far away.

"Man, did you do something stupid?" she asked him. "No, maybe," he replied and shook his head. "Take this a little more seriously, will you?" she asked him. "Yeah, sure," he said and sighed. He didn't want to fail but it was hard for him to take a game seriously. Even if he knew the stakes something in his mind just wasn't connecting with the reality of the situation.

"Return to staring posts, simulation restarting in fifteen seconds," the voice said to them. Alexis and Ryan quickly ran back to the center of the room with plenty of time to spare. "Maybe this time we shouldn't split up?" Ryan asked. "No, maybe this time you shouldn't be such an idiot. The sooner we can get this thing beaten, the sooner we can—" she trailed off.

"The sooner we can try to sneak aboard an enemy space station and try to be heroes, or get killed fighting someone else's battle," Ryan suggested. Alexis looked away, there wasn't an answer for that but it was true.

"The world has to stand up for itself. We'll represent it the best we can. Depending on the knights for everything is a stupid plan anyway," she said and smiled. Just then the simulation restarted and the tunnels reappeared around them again.

"I'm sure we'll get this down, you'll see," Ryan said and hoped for the best, but he didn't believe in himself that much but there was nothing new about that.

Chapter Twenty-Seven

Jack watched the lack of progress and was disappointed. He figured people from the wasteland would be better at avoiding trouble. He had been watching for the past three hours and realized that this was making him tired. He pushed a red button.

"Alright, you two newbies, you've been at this for three hours and you're getting sloppy. It's time for a break," he said with a yawn and watched as the hologram around the two of them disappeared and the exit door opened. He was just above the training room so he could hear the door.

Jack stood up and made his way down to the entrance, he managed to make it there before they even got out of the room. He looked at the two of them and could tell that they were angry at one another, their eyes told him all he needed to know.

"Before you two start digging into one another like I know you want to do, you should know that this program was designed to be the final step for people who trained for years," Jack said to them and kept going. "You're doing fine. Go get something to eat, take a nap and we can start again," Jack said to them, doing his best to contain their anger.

"You know, if you would just stop rushing into—" Jack cut Alexis off with a hard glare. "Do what I said. Go eat, go take a nap. We'll start again when you're refreshed. None of that kind of talk is going to help anyone. Trust me, okay?" Jack asked her and she narrowed her eyes. She wanted to say a lot of things.

"Fine," she said and walked off. Ryan shook his head and started to follow her. "Hold up a minute," Jack said to him and Ryan stopped. Here it was, the scolding, Ryan tensed up as he expected the worst. "She's right. I know you're trying to rush it. I know there are people down there you care about and you are just trying to get past this part," Jack said and Ryan was about to talk.

"Shut up, I'm not done," he said. "Use your head, think, breathe and plan ahead. This is serious. This plan depends on you two not screwing up. I'd say no pressure but I'd be lying," Jack said to him. "I know, I get it. Two nobodies from the wasteland are going to stop the bad guys," Ryan said and his voice was filled with self-doubt.

"Pretty much. We'll just be shiny distractions while you do all the work. And when the world finds out. No one is going to give the six-hundred-foot metal knights any credit at all," Jack said with a smiled. Ryan shook his head. "Well, alright. I'll feel better with rest and food I guess, thanks," Ryan said and almost smiled.

"Yeah, I sure hope so. The alternative really will destroy the world," Jack said to himself and closed the training room door, watched the two of them walk away. Then he started to walk down the same hall they went down. He was tired too and the first thing on his mind since he got here was having a stiff drink and sleep.

Alexis made it into the mess hall first and sat down at a table near the entrance. The place was massive, it was clearly meant for lots of people and being this empty just made the room feel weird, lonely and sad. "What will you have?" a voice came out of the table.

"I don't know, what's on the menu?" Alexis asked and a holographic menu appeared. She pushed the breakfast menu and hit the first meal option on the menu. It disappeared.

Ryan came into the room a few minutes later and sat next to Alexis. "Hey," he said and she rolled her eyes. "Sorry," he said and she was curious as to what changed. "About what?" she asked and he shook his head.

"Being an idiot. I can do better," Ryan said and Alexis nodded. "Damn right you can," she said and looked away. "I suppose I can do better too," she thought about the past three hours.

"The system is screwing with us," Alexis said and Ryan was picking his food off the holographic menu. "This whole time we've been splitting up, because the place is so big, maybe that's stupid," Alexis said and Ryan shrugged.

"Maybe," Ryan knew where this was going and wasn't sure he liked it. "I think we should, you know, work together next time we try that stupid thing," she suggested and there it was. Ryan wasn't exactly too eager to this, but on the other hand. "I guess that's the whole point after all," he said.

"When we do whatever it is we are going to do on the space station, it will be as a team, even if I have to work with a girl," he said and the way he said it made Alexis draw back. "Really?" she asked and wasn't sure what to think about that.

"Damn right. Once a month some girl from our village goes missing from our village. Sometimes we find them in an Inkit cave, sometimes alive. Sometimes we don't find them at all. So, sorry for saying it but yeah, working with you isn't exactly filling me with confidence or anything," he replied to her.

Alexis drew back as her food appeared on the table. "Well, there isn't much I can do about that but I'm all you have so, I guess you're just going to have to get over it," Alexis said, and that was all she could think of to say about it. Ryan just shook his head.

He didn't like the idea at all and was afraid it was going to get him killed. Even if he failed so much it was better than teaming up with a girl, he thought. But just kept his mouth shut about the whole ordeal.

"No choice I guess," Ryan said quietly and Alexis nodded. "If you die, I guess you were right after all," she said and almost laughed about it. Ryan didn't find it very funny. His food appeared and all of the sudden he didn't feel too hungry. "Jack said something about a Katy almost tearing you to pieces. I bet you'd work with her," Alexis replied. Ryan shook his head. "That wasn't human, that was a monster," he replied doing his best to suppress that memory.

As he looked at it he remembered from before. "Alexis, stop eating," Ryan said in a hurry. "Remember what Jay said, eating stuff will make us sick if we eat too much of it too fast," he said and Alexis put her fork down. The first bite made her feel all warm and it tasted so good.

"I just had one bite, I'm not going to die, am I?" she asked and started to feel the panic attack set in. "No, just, take it slow," Ryan replied and Alexis looked at her eggs and bacon on the plate. "Screw it," she said and despite the warnings, picked up her fork and started to eat once more.

Ryan looked at his food and shrugged. "I guess I can have a little bit," he said and started to pick it a part. Trying not to think about being forced to work with a girl in the quickly approaching future. He never actually had done it before.

Jack let the two of them be on their own, first because he didn't really care what they did and second, he didn't have anything helpful to say. They would either figure it out or die on Seran station. Jack expected them to fail anyway. He leaned back in his chair, drinking the golden liquid from the bottle. Then a message popped up on his screen monitor in his quarters.

"Damn it," he said and pushed the button to answer. "What is it, I'm busy," Jack said and was shocked to see who it was. Meria was on the other side of the screen. "Well, if it isn't the commander of bad guy station. Why are you contacting me?" Jack asked, annoyed.

"Don't be like that. I'm just here to catch up a little," she replied and he narrowed his eyes. "And you had to threaten the whole world to do it. You know you could have just asked. I would have beamed up to your station at any time and we could have killed one another in private," Jack replied and took another swig. "I know, you looked busy so I just left you alone," she replied and smiled. Jack never did trust that smile.

"I'm tired, what do you want?" Jack asked and Meria just smiled again. "I want you four to give up. I figured you'd be the most reasonable one to talk to about spreading the message. I mean think about it, the world is a disaster. I think we can all bring it back to what it was before," she said and Jack laughed.

"As long as the beasts are down there, rebuilding will be impossible. Thinking you can control them all is insane. I know you can't. Also, you're taking a serious risk. You know if we disrupt the power grid you'll undo over a century and a half worth of work. Why are you doing this?" Jack asked her again. "Because my people are sure we can control them, all of them. If we can send the beasts into the far corners of the world. Humanity has a chance to live again," she said and Jack shook his head.

"You're delusional. Even if you can control them, how long does it last? A year, decade, fifty years. Long enough for people just to begin to forget about the nightmares? Eventually something is going to break and everything is going to be worse than when you started. When it breaks, and it will, you'll not only release the monsters, but the A-class nightmares too. The world will be destroyed and you and I both know it. Whatever your people are telling you, they are lying," Jack replied.

Meria was quiet. "Listen, if we have a chance to fix the world, don't you think we should take it, at least try?" she asked. "Nothing's broken, the world is the way it's going to be until we can find a way to kill the monsters for good, nothing is going to change. The only thing you're going to do is break what little balance we have left," he replied again, taking another drink.

"Well, I'm disappointed in you. Jack, I thought for sure you'd see the light and stand with something that makes sense and not rush into death like you're doing," Meria sighed and Jack laughed. "Jay recorded your message, you know, the one about not worrying about if we came back or not because it wouldn't make a difference. We've all heard it. Contact all of us if you want. We might have worked together once but you've gone and betrayed all of us, that's just not going to stand," Jack replied and Meria's eyes went wide.

"That little," she said and stopped herself. "Fine, but when you're being crushed to death, remember that right now was when you could have had some mercy and didn't take it, enjoy what little amount of life you have left," she said and the communication screen went black.

"Whatever, it's time for a nap," Jack said to himself and looked over at his bed. It was looking really inviting right now.

Chapter Twenty-Eight

Nyogyth was standing in front of a control panel in the center of a circular room making adjustments to her machine when someone walked up behind her. "How's it going, Ny?" Lam asked her and she jumped, her focus broken. "Well it's fine. Aren't you glad we're finally going to save the world?" Lam asked her and Nyogyth smiled regaining her composure.

"More than glad, we've waited a long time for this moment and we are finally going to take back our world. The machine is almost ready," she said and looked around at all the people working on it.

"Good," Lam said. "How many can you control at once?" he asked and she smiled again. "With this much power, all of them on the planet," she replied. "And are you willing to use them to kill anyone who doesn't listen to our orders?" Lam asked and she stopped, turned around. "What idiot won't listen?" she asked.

"Well, we did kind of threat them with four giant monsters and the idea that if they didn't we'd crush them all. That kind of sets the tone. Also, the knights are back. One of them reappeared to defend Nulbar from an attacking C-class. This isn't random. You don't have to do this you know?" Lam asked her and Nyogyth looked down.

"Yes, I do," she replied. "But why. You know as well as I do that the knights, all they have to do is blow us out of the sky. We are completely defenseless up here," Lam said, he was worried about the obvious. "You think they'll kill five thousand people?" Nyogyth asked. "Because I don't think they will. I don't think they have it in them to do it," she replied and Lam shrugged. "Do you really want to test them?" Lam asked.

"Yes, I do. I don't believe they can beat us. I think they'll die fighting an endless army of monsters until they are ripped to pieces. Once the people see their heroes die, they'll give up, you'll see. The time of the knights is over, it's our time now. We can do this a better way. The world can come out of the century and a half long age of nightmares. I can't wait," she said and Lam shook his head.

"If you say so, but I don't think this will work," he said and looked out the window, down towards the planet. "This is our home, this space station. We've lived here our whole lives. Visiting the planet now and then is okay but to live there forever. That doesn't sound like my idea of a good time," Lam said with a slight laugh.

"Once we are done rebuilding it, it's going to be just like before the disaster, but better. We'll have unlimited resources to do anything we want. The people will adjust. I'm sure once even the most wayward village has running water, they'll be sure to follow any rules we set for them," Nyogyth said and Lam wasn't so sure about that.

"I think you and Meria are underestimating the human race, they aren't like us. They are proud and brutal. They live with the monsters, we live in a safe place. Who are we to come in and take over everything?" Lam asked mostly himself. He was questioning all of this and figured it bordered on the edge of insanity.

"We're the outlanders. The saviors of the human race. We got this," Nyogyth said and it was just then that Meria walked into the chamber, her eyes told the both of them everything they needed to know. "Is the machine ready for a test run?" she asked them. "Well. I guess it could be. It's not going to be at full power yet for a couple of days but I can fully control one or two monsters, why, what's up?" Nyogyth asked.

"It's time to show those knights just what they are up against. Locate two B-class creatures and have them attack, I don't know, Stiaburg, level the city," she said in a voice that was far too calm. "Show the world a preview of things to come," she said with a smile.

"Stiaburg, fifty thousand people live there in the walled section alone, are you sure you want to do that?" Lam asked and Meria glared at him. "It's just a bunch of stick houses. The people will run away. It'll be an attack but we'll move slow enough to make sure everyone has a chance to get away. Don't worry so much," Meria said and Lam didn't like this plan.

"Sure, I can find a couple, just give me a few seconds," she said and walked to the control panel again, pushed a few buttons. The thing came to life and she started to use the map to find what Meria had ordered. "I found two B class creatures. One is in the sea in Stiaburg bay and the other is in the mountains to the west, give me a few moments," Nyogyth said and started to turn a dial on the console as she targeted them. "Activating Delta Waves, now," she said and smiled.

"Congratulations. Two B-class monsters are approaching Stiaburg as we speak. They'll be there in about an hour at this rate," Nyogyth said but never took her eyes off the control console. Lam started to feel sick as to what was about to happen. "Are you sure we need to do this?" Lam asked and Meria looked at him. "Guards, throw this one in the brig until he can cool off," Meria said and immediately two men in silver armor walked up from the main door.

"Come with us," one guard said to him. "You can't do this for asking a question, can you?" Lam asked. "I'm the commander, I can do what I want. Take him away," she replied and the guards grabbed him and started to lead him out of the room.

Lam wondered, as he walked away if the two of them didn't go insane with power. He also wondered how many other people on this station knew what was going on. He didn't bother to resist arrest because they'd just break a bone if they had to calm him down. He'd seen it happen before to others and didn't want to end up that way. He looked back one last time at the people he thought he knew. All he saw now were monsters in human form.

Chapter Twenty-Nine

Mithlon sat in the conference room, at the head of a table with three people on both sides of the old thing. After getting Alexis out of her death sentence he made haste back to Stiaburg without telling anyone the things he set in motion. Right now, however, he was wishing he was back in Hadoth where it was quieter.

"We should fight the outlanders," John said loudly, Mithlon knew he was going to say that but couldn't wait to hear just what his idea was. "We can fight the monsters with the cannons, they've worked in the past and they'll work now," he said, the chief of what functioned as an army in this city was clearly over confident.

"You're an idiot. Those cannons won't do anything to those monsters. We haven't been attacked by a B class monster in fifty years, I was there and it was horrible," Megan said with the strongest voice she could muster against John's youth. She wasn't done. "We need to evacuate, it's the only choice we have if the threat is real," she said and Mithlon nodded.

He agreed with her, and at seventy years old, one of the oldest in the city and possibly the world at this point. Megan's insight was always valuable to him. The woman next to her nodded her head. "I agree. Cities can be rebuilt. We should take the things we can and get out of here," Christine said and Mithlon was happy to listen to that.

It was then Daniel slammed his fist on the table. "Women will always be the first to run away, if we stand and fight we can win. I know it. Don't listen to these people," he said, his anger growing by the second. "I agree with him, we can beat the monsters. I know we can," Daniel said, he was John's partner in crime, a warhawk and general pain in Mithlon's neck. But the people elected him to the council so there wasn't much he could do about it but deal with it.

"Guys, listen to you. Fight or run away?" Tim asked and laughed at them. "We have shelters for a reason. We can rebuild the city, hide all the tech. The monsters will go away and the attack will end. Why don't we just let the outlanders do their worst," Tim suggested.

"Hiding, you want us to hide like rats, we are men and we should die like them if we have to. Not hide," Daniel replied to him and glared. "And what good are any of us dead?" Sonia finally spoke up, newest member of the council. "We shouldn't run because there is nowhere to go. If we fight, we die. And the shelters haven't been used in twenty years. Who knows how much food is down there. Did anyone check? For all we know it could be an Inkit nest," she said, trying her best to shoot down all the ideas.

"I am sure that the outlanders are willing to talk. Let's negotiate with them and maybe, just maybe we can all benefit from one another," she said, barely twenty years old, the others scoffed at her idealistic views.

"You think that the space people care about us? If they did, why didn't they help out in the past century. They abandoned us. There is no reason to believe that they had a change of heart now," Tim said and John smiled. "Finally, something we can agree on," he said.

"The outlanders had every chance to help us, the world. I don't believe they've changed," Megan said, her ancient eyes seemed to be hiding something else but she refused to talk. "I agree, but we can't fight them. Those monsters have left us alone for fifty years. We can't beat them and the shelters are not a good option. We can move inland and move into the broken city," Christine suggested again and Megan nodded slightly.

"The shelters are good, we have them checked once a week and you all know that," Tim said and the others weren't exactly sure if that was true or not. "For fifty thousand people?" John asked. "Who do we choose to let in, and who remains outside?" he asked him and Tim looked away. "Lottery system, anyone who contributes the most. We can't save everyone but do we need to?" Tim said and no one at the table agreed with that, the looks in their eyes told Mithlon everything he needed to know and now it was time to make a choice.

"Or we surrender," Mithlon said and the others couldn't believe what they were hearing. "I have a contact in Nulbar, they said that Nanic reappeared to fight off a monster. If the Nuclear Knights have returned I am sure they have some kind of a plan," Mithlon said. "If we do anything other than give up they will kill us all," he said.

Megan laughed. "The knights, you're putting your faith in the knights. I know they are real but, where have they been the past five years. How do we know they aren't helping the outlanders?" she asked and Mithlon shook his head.

"We have to believe that they stand with the people like they always have, and in our time of need, they will help us when we need it. When the Outlanders come down from space. I will be glad to save everyone by letting them have the city. They won't have it for very long. If we fight they'll kill us. If we run they'll chase us and if we hide they will find us. Resistance is not the right choice right now. We have to believe in the knights. They are the only chance we have," Mithlon said.

"And if your so-called contact was wrong?" John asked. "What if people are just making up stories?" he asked and Mithlon leaned back in his old chair. "Then I guess we live by a new set of rules and do what any oppressed people do if they don't like the change. Rebel, resist. If they own the city they might be a whole lot less inclined to destroy it with monsters than they would before they occupied it," Mithlon said and the others didn't like it.

"Fine," Tim said and looked away.

"This meeting is over," Mithlon said and the others knew that he had the final say. Mithlon didn't like any of the options they had and could only see them leading to the same result. "I'm ordering the city to go into conservation status. Heavy rationing and make sure everyone has plenty of weapons and supplies. Keep everything hidden, just in case. Also, remember that under the bed doesn't count as hiding. The outlanders are, well, special so tell people to get creative. We are running out of time and war might be here sooner than we think," Mithlon said and looked at the others.

"This isn't mandatory, though. If anyone wants to run, they do so at their own risk. If they want to hide in the shelters, they are welcome to do that. But let them know that anyone who abandons their city in a time of need they won't be allowed to return, so choose wisely," Mithlon said his eyes grew serious. The other council members didn't bother argue to argue with him. One by one they got up and left the room.

He swiveled on his chair and looked out of the window from his building. It was the tallest, and oldest building in the city and he looked out towards the ocean. Sometimes he could see long necked beasts in the distance and things that flew in the air lazily with the wind. Today the sea was calm and the sunlight reflected off the green water.

Mithlon often tried to imagine that the ocean looked like before it was bright green, the world before it was destroyed. It was easy to do sometimes, the people, the lives they lived. All that remained of the past were broken buildings, century old technology that was getting rarer by the year. Then he looked in the distance. A shadow was moving under the green water, a massive shadow. At first, he thought it was an illusion so he rolled closer to the window to get a better look.

Picking up his binoculars sitting on the ledge he peered through them and gazed at the sea shadow. "No," he said, realizing what it was at once. He stood up, turned and ran to the door. "A beast is coming, sound the alarms get to the shelters, now," Mithlon said to the council who was still walking away. "Go, now, there isn't much time," he said again and the six of them looked as shocked as he was. None of this was making any sense but the six of them increased their pace, the alarms had to be sounded.

"Damn it, what happened. There are still two days left why are they attacking now?" he asked himself but this and all the other questions were pointless right now. He ran back into his office and slammed the red button on the wall. The buildings internal alarms began to blare for the first time in six years. He watched as people started to come out of their offices, confused at what was going on.

"Monster attack, not a drill. Get out of the building, get to the shelters," he yelled at all of them. The men and women felt the panic begin to grow and they started to run. "Hey, people. Don't trample anyone trying to get out of here. Use your heads," he said to them, and could only hope that they listened and didn't do the monster's work for them.

Mithlon ran back to his office that was beside the conference room and opened the second drawer in his desk. There was a sliver box, a communicator. He picked it up and pressed the button on the side. "Jay, buddy, I hate to be a pain in the neck but I hope to hell you're up there. We have a monster coming at us and It's a B-class, for sure it's too big to be anything else, come on Jay," he said into the thing, but there was no response.

"Damn it," he said and put the communicator down. There was no reason to believe that the knights would return anyway. The people of this city were on their own.

He turned to look out his window and was just in time to see the horrible thing rise out of the sea. Its skin was blood red, it had to be at least five hundred feet tall as the thing dwarfed any structure in the city. It was shaped like so many others, a reptile, dinosaur. Its eyes were bright yellow and glowed with their own unnatural fire. Its long tail splashed up and out of the water behind it. Mithlon couldn't tell if this thing was being controlled or it just happened to show up today on its own and was just bad luck.

The thing let loose a horrific, high pitched scream that rattled the old building he was in. As if the structure was afraid of what was coming. He grabbed the communicator, turned, ran out of the office as fast as he could go. Even if the beast was still in the water, there was no time to waste. Down the stairs and out the front door. He looked to his left and felt his blood freeze.

Approaching the city was yet another beast. A long brown haired ape thing was standing there, its eyes blazed with pure red light. Long, thick arms hung limp at its side and it was just as tall as the thing from the sea. "Are, are they going to fight?" Mithlon asked. It wasn't unheard of. Although neither of these things were reported around the city in a long time.

"Jay buddy, we have two monsters down here. I don't know if they are going to fight or what. We need help, now, come on pick up the damned phone," Mithlon said into the communicator as he stood stunned before the horrible beast that stood before him. Then to his horror, the thing started to run in his direction. Each fall of the massive foot sent shockwaves through the earth and sent screams up from all directions and all sides.

"Damn it people get to the shelters," he said to no one. Then the Klaxon alarms began to blare their dreadful, long tone through the city that scared anyone who heard it. Living in fear was no way to live at all. Right now, however, he wasn't sure how much life or time any of them had left. He looked towards the sea and the red lizard thing was just reaching land. It was clear to him now that the only target they had was this city and nothing else.

Mithlon watched as the attack began. The buildings and homes just collapsed on impact as the beasts just waded through them, as if a child were knocking down card houses. "What did we do deserve this?" he asked, watched the beasts move straight towards the center of the city from opposite directions, mindlessly. He had seen and lived through monster attacks before, this was similar, but the behavior of the things was, yes. He realized it now that they were controlled. This attack was meant to be a message to the whole world of what was coming if they didn't surrender.

"You could have picked any other city," Mithlon said, he had no idea if this was his fault. Maybe it was. Maybe his messengers got captured and this was punishment. He cursed his luck. "Sorry," he whispered to no one. Mithlon took a breath and was about to change the frequency on the communicator. As he put his fingers on the side dial. "Don't despair, we're on our way. Get to a shelter. We need to talk," a voice came from it.

Mithlon smiled. "Don't take too long," he replied to the voice and with that he ran to find the closest shelter he could find and hope for the best.

Chapter Thirty

“What in the hell is going on down there?” Jack asked as alarms started to go off in his room. “Two B class creatures are approaching Stiaburg. Delta Waves detected, behavior modification detected,” a mechanical voice said to him. “Awesome, shut off those stupid alarms. I’m on my way. If Jay is up someone should tell him that his boy is under attack and he might want to come along,” he replied and got out of bed still in the clothes he went there with.

Jack walked down the hall, turned a corner and ran right into Alexis and Ryan who were looking for him. “What is going on?” Alexis asked and Jack shook his head. “Monster attack on earth. One of the main reasons I quit being a knight was all the damn alarms,” he said, still trying get the echo of the blaring thing out of his head.

“If you want to waste time asking questions that’s fine but you should be focusing on your training. It’s not like anything important depends on you two not messing up,” Jack said and walked around them without another word.

“I suppose watching the surface wouldn’t hurt for a little while,” Ryan said and Alexis smiled. “Nah, I suppose not,” she replied and the two of them quickly made their way to the command center.

Jay was on Oriab station when the alarms went off on his ship at the same time. “Report, and kill the alarms,” he said at once. He, like the rest of them, hated the alarms. “Jay buddy, we have two monsters down here. I don’t know if they are going to fight or what. We need help, now, come on pick up the damned phone," Mithlon said through the speakers. "We're not friends," Jay said to himself and seriously regretted having anything to do with him in the past.

"Don't despair, we're on our way. Get to a shelter. We need to talk," Jay replied the first thing that came to his head. "Don't despair?" he asked himself. "I'll never tell anyone I said that," he said and stood up and started to run towards Valzin's holding chamber.

"Who's with me on this?" Jay asked no one. "Saphiel is to accompany you," Thon replied to him and Jay sighed. "Wonderful," he replied and turned a corner and entered an elevator. Immediately the thing came to life and started to take him where he needed to go. Jay wasn't sure how the systems chose what knights to activate depending on the threats that arose, not in the past, not now. The old computer systems confused him.

Sure, they could activate the knights if they felt it was needed, but the computer had always made the best suggestions. The elevator opened and here he was once again. He walked to the empty void and the same thought always came to mind when he stood on the edge. What if he fell into this void, and nothing happened. Jay figured he would die, but all the same stepped off the edge. "Courage," he said to himself, he always thought it was an unusual password.

Jay vanished and reappeared in the pilot chamber. "Welcome, Jay Bauman," a voice said to him, he knew it wasn't Thon. "Thanks, Valzin. Now's let's go," he replied and immediately the both of them fell out of the chamber. He hated this part, always the fall. The blue room around him disappeared and he could see the planet, stars and everything else as they fell, as he fell into space. The second there was no gravity the thrusters took over and he shot towards the Earth below.

"Jay, what's the situation down there?" Jack asked, it sounded as if he were right next to him. Jay waved his right hand and a menu came up. "We have two monsters. According to the records it's um, let me see," Jay said and trailed off.

"Come on man, don't hold out on me," Jack replied. "Right. It's Warga and Venodon," Jay replied. "Cerberus detected delta waves. It's the only way these two would be near one another. I've seen them fight for days normally," Jack replied and Jay nodded. "I remember, is there any way we can block the waves?" Jay asked.

"Not from the planet. The only real way to get rid of them is to blow up the source, and we can't do that," Jack said as the both of them hit the atmosphere. "Alright, after this is over I need to talk to Mithlon, too, so remind me to do that once we're done," Jay said. "Will do," Jack replied.

The two knights flew side by side, like dual comets over the ocean. Speeding towards Stiaburg at eight hundred miles an hour cutting through what little cloud cover there was in the sky. "I'll take the lizard," Jay said. "Oh man, that means I have to fight the mop. Do you know how long it takes for the nanosystem to clean out all the hair?" Jack complained.

"Fine. You take the lizard and I'll take the walking mop. I don't care," Jay replied, annoyed. He knew full well any biological matter left from the fight was cleaned up in just a few hours. "That's more like it. Let's get this done quick and send a message to Meria that this won't be as easy as she thinks," Jack replied.

Stiaburg came into view in the distance. Smoke rose from the city as two massive beasts were in the process of smashing everything that was close to them into rubble as if they were puppets or machines. Something about seeing the giant monsters like this made Jay feel bad. Sure, he didn't like them, but nothing deserved to be controlled like this. "Good luck," Jay said and focused on Warga, the giant red eyed ape like creature.

The Valzin Knight was pitch black and had jagged and thick body, its eyes burned bright yellow and it flew like a missile through the sky. Warga didn't even notice it, as if nothing else existed in the world but what it was focused on. Valzin swooped out of the sky at full speed, wrapped its black arms around Warga's torso and flew straight down and over the path of destruction it had created. In less than a minute the both of them had landed outside of the city limits. Valzin pushed Warga into the dirt as It landed on his feet.

The Saphiel knight was shining gold, its eyes burned bright blue. It was massive, thick and powerful. The golden machine landed behind Venodon and grabbed its thick red tail. In the same moment Saphiel took off into the air with a powerful blast, took the beast into the air by the tail and flew the opposite direction back to the ocean. Venodon screamed in pain as it was spun around and tossed into the ocean. The impact created a large splash of sea water in all directions. Saphiel landed in the ocean as well, waiting to see what was going to happen next.

Jay watched as the ape creature laid on the ground, as if the person controlling it had to react to what just happened. Warga started to move slowly and pick itself up off the ground with a rough grumbling voice. Jay wondered, maybe the impact knocked whatever mind control was on it had been broken. He didn't want to fight the monster to the death. Warga's dust covered body stood there quietly for a second, then like a machine it moved forward, left foot, right foot with that creepy lifeless expression on his face and its dead red eyes.

"I'll make them pay for what they did to you," Jay said to Warga, he couldn't help but feel something that resembled sadness for this creature. It hadn't attacked anything in at least ten years. Warga was a peaceful being by nature. Jay knew this to be true and slid his right foot back, prepared for battle.

Venodon recovered and rose straight out of the sea, gallons of ocean poured off of his red body. "Alright you hacked beast, time to put you down," Jack said and prepared to fight. He knew that there was only one way to break the mind control, but he didn't want to do it. Not really, it wasn't like the creature wanted to be here. The saurian lizard lumbered forward, its yellow eyes gazing at Saphiel and right through its pilot. Jack feels that gaze and it made him shudder just a little bit, he wasn't sure why.

Venodon opened its gaping mouth and fired a deep, blood red beam of energy at the golden knight. Saphiel raised his left arm and an energy shield appeared, the blood red energy impacted the shield and spread out in a thousand different directions. Rays of energy slammed into the bright green ocean and created steam geysers on impact. The attack only lasts for a few seconds but Jack's shield took a lot of damage. "Okay, lizard. My turn," Jack said to no one.

Warga rushed Valzin in a blind rage. Its large fist swung at Valzin who slid back and dodged the attack with ease. Valzin's black, long sword materialized in its left hand. Valzin spun and stabbed the monster in the back.

Warga screamed in pain as the point of the blade tore through its chest. Valzin tore the blade back out and watched the hairy thing fall to the ground. Steam poured out of the wound only for a few seconds, then it stopped. Warga's wound closed and the beast was already standing up again, facing his enemy with the same dead expression.

"You leave me no choice," Jay said and prepared for the next attack, whatever it was going to be, he wasn't too concerned about it. Jay was sure he had this fight won already but being careless was a good way to snatch defeat from the jaws of victory in a hurry.

Saphiel's bright, blue eyes began to burn, then two bright, dark blue rays fired from the knight's eyes and slammed into Venodon's chest and knocked him back. He slid back through the water and screamed in pain, as much pain as the thing could feel, but it didn't fall over. Saphiel wasn't finished, the second the attack was over the golden knight rushed through the bright green waves. It put its massive right fist into the lower jaw of the beast with so much force that Venodon was pulled off his feet and into the sea.

Jack looked and realized that he just made his situation worse. Now he couldn't see the beast. "Start scanning for it," Jack said and the process started. Every second he couldn't see the thing made him nervous, on the other hand, maybe it was knocked out of whatever control it was under and swam away.

Warga slammed his left foot into the ground with so much force that the earth cracked under Valzin's feet. The ground opened up and Valzin's left leg fell into the hole that was created. "Damn it," Jay said in surprise as this happened. He looked back up just in time to see a big hairy foot coming at his head. Jay didn't have time to say anything.

The impact of the monster's foot knocked Jay back into the image chamber. He grit his teeth when he hit. Thankfully the walls were designed for stuff like this and most of the energy of the blow was absorbed.

Valzin reeled back on impact and sparks flew off its body. Jay wasn't about to give it another chance. He jumped straight out of the hole. Warga threw its right fist in the knight's direction. Valzin spun out of the way and used its sword at the same time to slice open the beast's side in the process. Jay watched as red steam poured out of the wound and the creature stumbled away from the fight. "Sorry," Jay said and took his blade in both hands.

Valzin rushed forward as Warga turned around. The beast roared only once more as the blade carved through the neck of the beast separating its head from the body. Jay watched as the body fell to its knees, then slammed forward into the ground.

Venodon burst out of the water and grabbed Saphiel by its metal neck. The deep red beast twisted around and used its leverage to throw the golden knight into the sea. "Damn it," Jack said as the water covered him. He slammed his shield into the monster's face once, twice, three times. Venodon held fast, each time the taking the blow, still in his trance. "Come on you stupid monster, let go already," Jack said as they sank deeper into the sea.

Venodon was unaware that the machine, was in fact a machine. The creature was trying to drown its enemy by swimming deeper into the sea. "Well, if you won't let go, I'm taking you for a ride," Jack said and wrapped the golden arms around the monster. Saphiel's boosters kicked on and immediately the both of them shot straight up out of the water.

They flew high into the air, over the ocean. Jack was planning on dropping the creature. "Delta waves no longer detected," Saphiel said to Jack. Immediately he felt Venodon's grip tighten and his tail wrap around his left leg. It was clear that the monster was terrified, confused. "Alright big guy don't freak out. I got you," Jack whispered and stopped the ascent at once. Venodon stared into Saphiel's eyes and in turn right at Jack. He hated being this close to any monster.

The golden knight descended slowly and in just a few minutes landed in the sea. Saphiel released the monster, and Venodon, despite being in prime position to attack released the machine and backed off slowly. Venodon looked around, still lost as to what was going on. It grunted, turned and quickly slid under the waves with hardly a splash left behind it. Jack was thankful that he didn't have to drag this out any more. He turned to look at Valzin and was sad to see Warga's body lying at his feet.

"Sorry," Jack said through the communicator. "It's alright. Will you do me a favor and get the body out of here. I need to have a chat with Mithlon," Jay replied. "Clean up duty, fine, but you owe me," Jack replied and him and Saphiel flew out of the water, over the city and landed next to him. Saphiel picked up the severed head with his left hand and grabbed the right arm of the beast. Then he started to walk away.

"Venzin, equip the armor, I need to take a walk outside," Jay said and held out his arms. Immediately a grid of light appeared around him and black armor materialized around him that resembled Valzin himself. "Sentry mode," Jay said and disappeared in a flash of white light.

Jay reappeared outside of a thick metal door. It was an entrance to a shelter. He grabbed the handle on the outside and pulled the thing open with one hand. It was impossible for any normal human to do. Inside was a crowd of people who were scared out of there mind. Jay didn't even look at them as he walked forward and pointed at Mithlon.

The man walked to the black armored figure. Jay put his hand on their leader's shoulder and they both disappeared.

They reappeared on the top of Mithlon's old building and Jay took his helmet off. "Give me one reason not to throw you off this building right now," he said to him and Mithlon felt his blood go cold. "You sent two waste landers out to find me. You set all of this in motion. You are the direct reason your city is in ruins right now," Jay said to him, turned to face him, his eyes filled with rage.

"What are you talking about?" Mithlon asked and Jay shook his head. "You had a damn communicator the whole time. All you had to do was pick it up and ask what was going on," Jay said and continued. "Then we could have got things started from there. Let the nutjobs do whatever it was they were going to do and infiltrate the station and take care of this nonsense in five minutes. But you forced our hand. My hand. Look around you. Look at your city," Jay said and turned back. Mithlon looked and there were twin paths of devastation running through it with fire on the ground, smoke rising high in the sky.

"I didn't do it for me," Mithlon said and looked back at him. "I knew that Alexis was going to die, and you know. Watching that butchery continue has made me sick. I can't live with it. I needed to stop it and once I saw she was from Narvoi I needed to try to save her, get her out," Mithlon said and Jay shook his head.

"Okay, I see your point," he replied. "But now they know we're back. Now they are going to make all of this much harder than it had to be. I know Meria, once she gets it in her head to save the world by killing everyone on it, she'll do it. This, all of this you see around you is just a preview. They are still getting their method down but it won't be long before they have the army they promised," Jay said and Mithlon shuddered.

He couldn't imagine a real army of giant monsters like that, it seemed impossible, even now. "Well, you have a plan, right?" Mithlon asked and Jay nodded. "Of course, but don't feel too upset if I don't tell you what it is. What you need to do, right now, is get your people out of the city in case they come back," Jay said, then disappeared in a flash of white light.

Jay reappeared in Valzin's imaging chamber. "Did you get everything sorted out?" Jack asked through the communicator. "Yeah, you?" Jay asked back. "Old shaggy is going to have one hell of a neckache when it wakes up but I'm sure it won't come back. I put it in a quiet place," Jack replied and Jay nodded. "Alright, let's get out of here," he said and with that the two massive weapons took off straight up into the sky together, disappearing into the deep blue sky.

Chapter Thirty-One

Grace sat in her chair in the command center. Monitoring the surface world for radiation spikes and anything else that might be a potential threat. When suddenly on her monitor something began to flash. At first, she thought it was a glitch of some kind. "Mike, are you at your monitor right now?" she asked, pressing the communication button. "No, Grace. I'm not like you, I don't obsess with the surface all the time," Mike replied, Grace rolled her eyes.

"I think I found a beacon," she said and there was silence on the other end. "Not possible, nothing down there is still active. We checked and rechecked for years. And one shows up now, out of nowhere?" Mike asked. "Okay hold on, just let me get to the command center and I'll have a look," Mike said and Grace was happy she didn't have to convince him to go look. A few minutes later Mike returned.

"Alright, send me the location of your beacon so I can take a look," he said and Grace quickly sent him the location. "Let's see here," Mike said to himself through the communicator as he focused into the area. "The only thing in the area is some small out of the way village, there isn't anything around here besides—" Mike paused as Grace's screen lit up again. "Well I'll be, there is something there but it's impossible to know what it is," Mike replied.

"Yeah, I knew I wasn't losing my mind. There hasn't been a beacon on earth in fifty years, why now?" Grace asked, Mike didn't answer. "Grace, I hate to tell you this but this could be a trap, in fact I'm willing to bet this is exactly that. While Jay and Jack are fighting the monsters, this was made just for us," Mike said. "Maybe, but what if some old piece of tech was, I don't know, reactivated by some monster on accident. Trap or not, we need to check it out," Grace said and Mike sighed.

"Only one of us can go," Mike said and Grace already knew that. "I'll go down there," she said and thought about it for a few seconds. "How are you going to do it. Armored up or in stealth?" Mike asked and Grace thought about it. Both ways had their advantages, and drawbacks. "It might be a trap but it it's not I'm going to attract lots of attention going down there in a complete suit of armor. Attention we don't need," Grace said.

"What are you talking about. Go with the armor. Who cares about attention?" Mike asked her and wasn't comfortable with this approach. "I'm not detecting any life down there anyway. This should only be about five minutes," she replied, just then she could feel Mike rolling his eyes at her from the other side of the communicator.

"Alright. Just be careful," Mike said and tried to sound as sure about this as he could. "Don't worry, I'll be fine," she said and cut off the communication. Grace quickly downloaded the location to her armlet and stood up. It was time to go.

"Thal, get the transport room ready. I'll be there in a few minutes," Grace said to no one. "Yes, Grace," Thal replied to her. She made her way out of the command center and to the armory. The trip wasn't very far, the doors to the room slid open. She walked inside. There was a belt hanging on the hook with two empty holsters. She put the belt the around her waist, tightened and hooked it together. She walked over to two high powered blasters hanging on the wall, picked them up and slid them in her holsters.

She checked her armlet just to make sure it was fully charged before leaving. It was, just as it should have been. Grace was satisfied and walked out. She made her way to the transport room. She walked forward and stepped on to the platform. Taking one last look at herself, she figured that blending in, if needed, wouldn't be a problem.

"Transport to the location," Grace said and disappeared with a flash of white light.

Grace appeared in the dimly lit depths of a broken city. She was alone and coming to this places like this had always made her uncomfortable. There were a thousand ways to die out here, at least that was the best way to think. Most waste landers had grown comfortable with the horror and rarely paid attention to it. Grace supposed you could get used to anything after being in it long enough, she preferred the surroundings of basic civilization, now, however.

Grace looked at her armlet and a holographic screen popped up, the beacon wasn't too far away, but the distance wasn't the problem. The direction was straight to the east and the only thing she could see there was a collapsed ruin of a skyscraper. "Wonderful," she said to herself and walked forward.

She expected an ambush at any second, but the only sound she could hear right now was the wind blowing through the rubble. Creating a low moan over and through the ruins that sounded a lot like a screaming crowd of victims. Grace did her best to ignore it and walked forward to her destination.

There was no way inside the rubble that she could see, still the armlet said this was the right direction. "Damn it, it's underground," Grace said as she realized the situation that faced her now. "Three-dimensional scan," she said, just to be sure, and sure enough the beacon was located far under the ground.

There was no telling what kinds of things were down there and the only way to find out was to go look. The access points the map showed was not too far away. She smiled a little bit and walked to the left. The ancient rubble formed pathways, Grace didn't know if people made these narrow paths over the past century and a half or this was just how it fell.

After a few minutes of maneuvering through the rubble paths she came to a clearing. There was a rusty manhole cover. However, there was an arrow painted in faded yellow on the ground next to it pointing at the cover. Grace didn't like what this implied, however it looked old.

She walked to the cover, pulled out the blaster. She almost pulled the trigger, but stopped. Normally, these covers were extremely heavy, but this had an arrow and people were meant to move this.

Grace stepped closer and pushed her left foot into the side of the cover, sure enough the thing popped open with ease. She slid it out of the way. For some place people would go to, it didn't look all that inviting. It was as if the light disappeared into a void that went down forever. "Awesome," she said to herself, took a deep breath before beginning her decent down the ladder.

The path down was narrow, the shaft of light came down around her but all she could see were the grey, metal rungs of the ladder in front of her. For all she knew she could be descending straight into an Inkit nest. She stopped every few feet to listen to anything that might be lurking below but couldn't hear anything each time she did.

Finally, her foot hit something solid, the shaft of light above her looked as if it were miles away now. She turned around and turned her wrist light on. She expected to see a sewer or something like it, but instead her light reflected white tiles and a tunnel that stretched on past the edge of her flashlight. The beacon, whatever it might be, was ahead of her. Grace started to walk into the unknown.

Chapter Thirty-Two

The tunnel was abandoned for ten minutes with no indication of what it might have been. Not until she came to words, painted in yellow on the wall. 'All are welcome here' it read and Grace knew what this was immediately. It was an old shelter when the disaster first occurred. Grace knew places like this existed and for a while worked out for people. Until the Inkit showed up, at least.

She kept walking down the hall and froze. There, laying on the ground was a shattered skeleton across the floor. Something had pulled it apart. She looked around but didn't see sign of what might have done it. It was weird how the bones were scattered however. They didn't look as if it was natural, actually they looked like they were made to be some kind of primitive art project the more she looked at it. Then it made sense.

"Sand raiders," she said to herself, they were fond of using human remains as some kind art, it meant something to them and only them. To everyone else it was nothing more than a warning sign. She turned away from the morbid picture and kept walking down the tunnel. It wasn't long before she came to a steel door that had nothing more than a metal bar across it. It was locked from the outside, what kind of place was this?

Grace walked to the door, put her hands on the locking bar. She lifted it, it was heavy but thankfully not stuck in place. The bar wasn't on a hinge or anything, it was just resting there. She put the thing up on its end and leaned it on the wall. Grace carefully opened the door and immediately the smell of smoke hit her nose long before she could see the haze illuminated by a dull orange light from the wall.

Grace slid the door closed behind her. The last thing she needed was someone coming up from behind in a tight space like this. She checked the location again and sure enough, the beacon was dead ahead. She turned off her flashlight and walked forward into the smoke, the heat was increasing with every step.

Then the sounds of people, cheering, screaming. Grace didn't like this at all and she considered turning back.

"Hey, hey you," a voice said to her as she walked one step too far into a clearing. She turned and covered her armlet under her sleeve. "What?" Grace asked and turned. "What are you doing back here, no one is supposed to be back here. If you get caught you'll be food, come with me quick," the voice said. Grace saw a teenage girl, dressed in what amounted to rags. Her hair was black and tangled.

"Yeah. I'm new. I got lost," Grace said and hoped she bought it, she seemed to. "Come, this way," she said and walked down a hall, took a left an Grace froze. She didn't know what this place used to be, shelter or not, now it was an arena of carnage. There were screaming people on all sides, behind a circular fence. In the middle was a man dressed in something that was supposed to be armor. Made out of scrap metal with spikes and tied together with rope. In his left hand was a long pipe with a curved metal blade at the end.

His opponent was an Inkit. It was huge, black and supported by its eight, long and dull yellow legs. The giant spider leaped at the raider in the cage. Grace watched the man swing his weapon and the blade hit the floor. The spider jumped over him and latched on to the cage wall. Then it spun around on the wall and jumped off. It had so much force that it hit the man and knocked him to the ground. In an instant the spider opened its mouth and fired a barb into the man's back.

The crowd went quiet as the Inkit injected its venom into the fighter. The man screamed only for a few moments before his body convulsed, froze and dropped dead. Grace watched as the spider ripped off the armor with its legs as if it were ripping through tinfoil. Its hideous mouth opened wide and it was full of teeth. Grace winced as the thing began to feast. The crowd screamed and cheered.

"Jolar wasn't worthy of the prize. Is there anyone else who wants to face my champion for the prize?" A man shouted and the second he did, the screaming mass went quiet and paid attention to the man on the upper deck. He looked like any raider she had ever seen. Wearing black leather, his pale skin was scarred where it could be seen. The man looked hungry, just like the rest of them.

"What is the prize, this is the fourth sacrifice we've had and we've never even seen it," someone in the crowd shouted out. The man on the upper deck smiled, pulled out his blaster and shot the man who asked without a second thought. "Someone didn't follow the rules," the upper deck man screamed and the crowd cheered, Grace did too, just to play along with the crowd.

"You know the prize when you win the prize, so who wants it, who wants it really bad, bad enough to die?" the man said and the crowd wasn't so eager to step up anymore. Grace knew what the prize had to be so if she wanted it, there was only one thing left to do. She had to fight the giant spider in the cage.

Grace took one step forward when a hand grabbed onto her cloak sleeve. "No, are you crazy. The prize isn't worth it," the girl who lead her here said quickly and had a scared look in her green eyes. "I might be a little bit crazy, but I can handle a spider," Grace replied and the girl let her go. "What is a spider?" she asked, confused. Grace forgot. "Oh, it's just a way smaller version of the thing in there, no worries," Grace replied with a half smile, turned to face the thing still feasting on the raider in the cage.

She stepped forward through the crowd. "I want the prize," Grace shouted as loud as she could. The man in the upper deck turned his head to stare. "Who are you?" the man asked. "My name is Grace, and I want the prize. Are you going to bore the crowd to death with stupid questions or are we going to do this?" she asked and the man smiled. "Enter the cage," the man said. Just then a divider came down to separate her from the spider and a guard in leather armor stood at the iron door and swung it open.

For a quick minute Grace was worried that they were going to check her for weapons but the crowd started to scream and there was no indication that that anyone cared. Grace walked passed the guard and stepped into the cage. The iron door closed and she watched. "A new challenger arrived. Let the Inkit feast once more," the man screamed to the crowd. He might have been their leader of just some kind of a show runner. She didn't know or care.

The inkit spun around and hissed at her from behind the bars, its eight black eyes, as lifeless as they were, they looked hungry to her. The iron gate raised from the ground with and awful groan, then the spider attacked. It was fast as it skittered across the bloody ground. Grace pulled her two blasters and pulled the trigger on each weapon, once. The red beams cut through the spider's body in an instant and it fell dead and smoke rose from its body.

Grace turned around. "My prize?" she said and the man was just as shocked, maybe horrified, as the crowd. Without hesitation the man slammed a red button on the wall beside him and the whole cage she was standing inside became electrified. Grace's whole body tensed up and the last thing she saw was the man smiling, then everything went black as she hit the bloody floor.

Chapter Thirty-Three

Grace woke up in a cage. It was smaller than the one she was in. It was made for large dogs, maybe. She was in someone's room, the first thing she did was reach for her blasters but they were gone. Her armlet was still there, thankfully. "I was wondering how long it would take you to wake up," a voice said and she looked in the direction. "These shiny new weapons are going to be nice in my collection," he said and she narrowed her eyes but didn't say anything.

"Where'd you get such nice toys?" he asked and she smiled. "Let me out and I can bring you to a place where those are nothing but literal toys," she said and the man stepped into the light. "And how does someone like you get access to something like that?" he asked and she smiled. "I'm a knight. I figured the arm piece here would have a big clue. You know the average person doesn't have one," she replied and the man didn't quite believe it.

"How did a woman get to be a god damned Nuclear Knight?" the man asked and didn't believe a word she was saying. "You know, one knight dies, someone else takes their place. I didn't exactly ask for this job. It has something to do with DNA. I know as much as you do really. There is a giant shiny thing in outer space where I can get you all the weapons you'd ever want," she said again, "but you'll have to let me out," she finished.

"These two blasters will give me enough power to become the undisputed king of the wasteland. You, you're not leaving that cage until the next auction. You'll be a nice slave, or someone's meal. I don't care. But they'll pay a lot of zops for you," he said and Grace groaned at the thought of either outcome.

"Okay you raider idiot. I know you think you have the upper hand right now, but did you forget when I told you that I am a Knight. This armlet constantly transmits my location. I'm not alone. Two. I have this armlet and I can get out of here at any time I want," she said. "So, you can let me out on your own like a good little boy. Or I can just teleport out and have an orbital strike kill you and everyone in here," she replied.

The man thought about it for a couple of seconds. He walked to the cage and unlocked it, opened the door. Then he took a step back and he was a little afraid now. "What's your name?" Grace asked him. "I am Groul," he replied and walked away from her. Grace crawled out, stood up.

"Of course it is. I'm here because of the beacon, I assume it's your precious prize you kept talking about. Let me see it," she said and Groul looked at her. "Some of my guys found this thing a couple of days ago in the tunnels. I don't know what it is but it's shiny and shiny things from the old world are always valuable to someone," Groul said and walked to the back and pulled out a silver cylinder that was on a wagon.

Grace walked to it and scanned it with her armlet. "This is a nano water filter, built around 2149. This filters all contaminates out of water," her armlet said and she rolled her eyes. "This is a really powerful water cleaner but it wasn't worth all this trouble," she said and kneeled down. She pressed the green button on the side of the case and it opened up, revealing the filter inside.

"Groul, this will make you the king of the raiders if you can keep it. Charge people to run their water through this and you'll have an unlimited source of water. Perfect, clean water. No more radiation poisoning. No more disease," she said to him and sighed. Hoping it would have been something better.

"This might not mean much to you, but to my people it's the world," Groul said to her, she nodded. "Things are going to get bad," Grace said as she looked at him. "Since you've shown me relative kindness. I'm going to tell you to get your people and stay underground for a few days," she said and he looked at her.

"The space people are going to destroy all of you, raider, city dweller, everyone. The only thing that can stand a chance to stop them, is us," she said and watched the color drain out of Groul's face. "So, it's true," he replied in shock. "Keep the blasters, I don't need them," she said and prepared to leave when all of the sudden another man broke into the room.

"The Claws, they are attacking, they're at the gates," he said, out of breath. "Damn it," Groul said under his breath and turned to the door. Grace shook her head. "Who are the claws?" she asked. "The scary raiders, the ones who'll eat you. They live on the surface and they want everything they can get," Groul replied. "And you don't?" she asked.

"Well, we do, but we aren't going to go out and kill for it. We mostly use the whole Raider thing as a cover, people don't come looking for us and we get left alone. The claws, on the other hand, they'll eat you. They are the real deal," Groul replied to her. Grace nodded. "Fine, I'll help you fight them," she said and wasn't sure why she offered her help, but then again, wasn't it her job as a Knight to help people, Grace thought and knew that it was time to get to work.

"You, really, you will?" Groul asked, shocked. He didn't expect this, especially after what he did to her. "I guess I don't have a choice. You electrocuted me and took my stuff, not to mention killed a guy just for asking a question," she replied and Groul shook his head.

"You, well, we have rules. Without the rules we might as well be monsters. Besides, he's not really dead," Groul said and Grace was confused. "Just stunned. You don't question the leader, that's rule number one. Not without making an appointment," he said, she just shook her head. "Well, whatever, let's go see what the Claws want," she said.

"All they want is to kill us, that's easy," he replied. "We might die, but the Aklo won't go down without a fight," Groul said. Grace didn't care what they were called, really. Groul pointed to an elevator.

"This will take us to the gates," he said as he looked at the man who was still standing there. "Dude, what the hell, get out of here, get a weapon and get to the lines. Tell the men I am on my way, keep her a secret," he said and glared. The man nodded and ran back out of the room.

Groul walked to the elevator doors, there was a white, crude, skull and crossbones painted on it and it split open down the middle. Grace was surprised that the elevator still worked in a place like this. "How long have you been here?" Grace asked as she carefully stepped inside the thing.

"Since the fall, our people moved into the shelter and we never left. Made it home," he replied, it was clear by his eyes alone that he really didn't know more than that. He stepped inside and pressed the only button that was still lit up on the panel.

The old thing creaked and groaned but it did begin to move, and it moved much quicker than she anticipated. "The claws, they are annoying but they've never come to the gates before. It's an unwritten law, we don't attack one another. Something changed," Groul said mostly to himself. Grace didn't bother answering. The elevator seemed to move up for just a few seconds when the doors open and the natural sunlight poured in.

Grace was thankful to see it again and stepped out on to the balcony. She realized now what this place used to be in the past seeing it from this point of view. It was a stadium. The far side had been knocked out but the walls were intact as they curved inwards and high into the sky.

Groul walked forward and she did too. In the large clearing below them, it was filled people. Vicious and terrible looking people, not to mention the smell. It was the smell of rotten blood more than anything else and it made her feel like she was going to throw up despite being this far away.

"Groul of the Aklo, we will take what you have. If you give up, we only promise to eat half of your number," a man screamed out, he was in the middle of the crowd standing on a large, mobile stage. Grace figured it was some kind of old hovercraft. "What's this idiot's name?" Grace asked Groul as she listened to him screaming.

"That guy is new. Anyone can be the leader of this group. If they win, and eat the heart of the former leader. They can be the leader," Groul said. Grace didn't like that idea. "You could have just stopped at he's new," she said and continued on. "Alright, well. Let me see if I can talk some sense into him," she replied and stepped to the railing, but didn't dare lean against it because it looked as if it could give way at any second. Groul tried to stop her but was too slow. He wasn't expecting her do more than show up.

"Hello down there. You have a great offer, but here's my counteroffer. You take your gross group of inbred psychopaths out of here, and I won't kill you all," she shouted back. The leader of the raiders shook his head and he laughed. It was a shrill laugh that echoed off the old walls.

"Groul, a woman speaks for you, well, in that case we will just have to eat all of you. Prepare yourself," he said and Grace slowly began to reach for her bracelet when from behind the crowd something began to rise out of the rubble.

"What in the hell?" Groul asked no one. Grace expected the raiders on the ground to scatter, but they didn't. Then she saw the man behind the leader holding a silver box. "Delta waves detected," the armlet said and Grace knew what was going on. "Does everyone have their own monster under control today or what?" Grace asked as the thing rose out of the ground.

It was four hundred feet tall as all the rubble cleared away, its skin was bright orange and its eyes were blue. It had a long, slender body, as if it were a snake with skinny legs and arms. The thing had one long horn on its nose. However, it just stood there. Those blue eyes were dead. The shadow of the beast blotted out the sun.

"A silver space lady came down to me. Told me that if I promised to kill you all. I'd get to control this unstoppable monster to do it, I said yes," the man said and spread his arms. The crowd that followed him cheered, screamed as he said it. The look in his eyes, even from here, told Grace all she needed to know.

"Can I use one of your blasters really quick?" she asked Groul and he handed one to her. She took it in her hands, pushed a button on the left side. A scope popped out of the top and she took aim. She pulled the trigger. A deep red beam fired from the gun and hit the sliver box. The thing exploded with a shower of sparks. The man holding it dropped it, screamed in pain. "Delta waves no longer detected," the armlet said to her.

The orange beast stood in his trance state still, however. "You have about two minutes to run. That C-class monster is going to wake up at any moment and it's going to start eating everyone closest to it. That means you," Grace screamed down to the Claw leader with a smile. "Get your people inside, quick," she said to Groul just as fast.

The leader of the Aklo waved his arm around and anyone who saw it on the top of the gate knew to retreat, and in a hurry. They stared to make their retreat when the beast started realize where it was and look around, as if it was waking up from a dream.

"That's not fair. That's not how this was supposed to be. You miserable little—" Grace watched as the orange beast leaned down and slammed its hand down on the ground. Ten of the claws were covered as the scaly hand closed shut around them. Grace watched the monster lift the members of the claw to its tooth filled mouth and dropped them in. They died screaming, Grace couldn't help but smile as they died this way. Who knows how many hundreds of people they killed and eaten over the past century and a half.

Still, this thing, as distracted as it was right now, she knew it would turn its sights on the people here, too.

Chapter Thirty-Four

Grace touched a button on her armlet. “Emergency situation, send Nanic to my location,” she said into it. “One minute until arrival,” the armlet replied to her. “One minute. Lots can happen in one minute,” she said to herself and watched as the beast kept looking down at the people and swiping handfuls of them as they tried to flee.

Even if these freaks deserved it, the crunching sounds of bones and the blood staining its mouth was getting sickening to watch and listen to. The screams were the worst part, however. The beast swung its head and its blue eyes narrowed in on the one person who was just standing there. Everyone else was running and this one was defiant and that enraged the beast.

No human was going to behave like this, they were food, nothing more. The giant beast lumbered forward, Grace still didn’t move. She was counting the seconds in her head.

The orange beast opened its maw wide and all Grace could see now was the inside of its throat. She swallowed her fear and counted the seconds down. “Come and get me,” she said and waited, stood fast against the deadly jaws that threatened to swallow her up. The beast’s jaws closed down around her and where she stood seconds later and disappeared.

The beast had a mouth full of rubble, but it tasted nothing but metal and old, crumbling concrete and rusty iron. The second it attempted to lift its head back up a large metal fist ran into the back of his neck.

The beast was slammed into the ground face first. Grace was in Nanic's imaging chamber. "This C-class monster is Volgun. It was named by Alice Granger, the first Nanic Knight in 2151," the voice said to her.

"Nice, I don't care. Weaknesses, give me a readout," Grace demanded as she backed away from the monster as it stood up, she kept backing away from the stadium and Volgun was more than eager to follow her. This was something his reptile brain remembered. He hated this enemy. Despite being twice as big as he was, he hated it all the same.

Volgun didn't wait. It lunged again, sending its long, slender body into the machine. He latched on to the monster's neck with his jaws, his long claws raked against the white chest armor sending sparks in all directions.

"Damn it," Grace said, she hated C-class monsters and was pretty sure everyone did. She punched the beast in the side of the head with so much force that it fell to the side and through a bunch of ancient rubble. "Read out, now," she demanded again.

"Volgun has the power of acid mist breath, it also has—" Grace jumped back as the orange beast lunged at her. "Weaknesses," Grace said. "Get to the weaknesses," she finished saying as she landed. The ground shook and ruins collapsed around her. "Volgun is sensitive to water," Thal finally said to her and Grace looked around. There wasn't any water around here. "Damn it," she said and the beast roared in anger, it jumped in her direction.

Grace flinched and stepped back. Volgun sailed right past her, however its long tail wrapped around Nanic's left leg and tore it from under her. Grace and Nanic fell straight back and landed on ground together.

"Well, this is embarrassing," Grace said, turned her head just in time to see the orange monster open its mouth wide and shoot out a sickly shade of green mist in her direction. Grace also watched as the cement of old buildings melt away as it was enveloped in the mist.

"No," Grace said, fired her boosters. Nanic flew out of the way just as the green mist enveloped where she was just at. Volgun watched as she flew away, he immediately gave chase running on all fours leaving a trail of dust in his wake.

Nanic spun in the air and landed on her feet a good distance away. "A doctor shouldn't have to do things like this," she said to herself and knew that this was a fight to the death. Most struggles with C-class monsters like this usually ended up this way. Volgun rush didn't slow down for a second and jumped at her again. "Is this all this thing knows?" Grace asked herself, stepped forward to meet the monster.

Nanic grabbed Volgun, put her steel hands around the mouth, twisted around and slammed the monster into the ground in one motion. It screamed and thrashed violently. Its claws dug into Nanic's arms. Grace couldn't risk letting this thing open its mouth again. "All power to the eye beams," Grace commanded. Nanic's eyes burned white. Volgun struggled, then its own eyes grew wide. Nanic fired her white-hot eye beams directly into Volgun's blue eyes.

The lizard screeched in pain only for a few seconds before Nanic's beams fried his brain inside his skull. Volgun went limp, the screeching stopped. Grace sighed and stood up, looking down on the beast's body. "Where is the nearest source of water?" Grace asked. "Twenty miles to the north. Lake seventy three," the computer replied and she reached down, grabbed the corpse of the monster. She lifted it in both arms as its limbs dangled to the side.

Nanic took off into the sky with Volgun, flying to the north. "Estimated time of resurrection, two hours," the computer said to her as they left the earth. "Plenty of time," Grace said as they flew. She hated flying through the air like this. She increased her speed to a low one hundred and fifty miles an hour, making a straight path to the lake.

At this speed, and nothing in her way Nanic made the trip in about ten minutes. The lake, like all the other water on the planet it was bright green now. From the sky she could see the other side of the lake, but it was big enough. Grace flew to the center of the lake and dropped the bright orange corpse into the lake. She watched as it fell, hit the water to make a splash. "Maybe that'll keep you down for a few years you overgrown salamander," Grace said and watched it disappear under the waves.

Then a thought occurred to her. “Scan for settlements near the lake,” she ordered. “None detected, the area is over run with Vor,” the computer replied. Grace let out a sigh of relief. “Good,” she said with a sigh of relief. “No beasts detected in the area,” the computer said and Grace was satisfied with the job. “Alright, let’s go home,” Grace said, activated the boosters. Nanic shot off into the sky.

She’d be spending enough time on the planet in the future. Leaving the earth behind in a rapid pace, she almost smiled when the alarms began to blare. “What the hell?” she asked. “Incoming energy attack,” the computer said and showed it on a screen.

“Oh my god,” Grace said, whatever the reason her scanners didn’t detect it until it was far too late. “Brace for impact,” the computer said and Grace did so.

Two seconds later the energy slammed into Nanic’s back and everything in the image chamber went black. Grace ran to the protective chamber just before Nanic began to fall. She managed to get inside and slam the doors shut. She strapped herself in as the machine began to fall back to earth. There was only one entity capable of such an attack, and if she lived through the fall, she was going to make them pay for this. All she could do now is hold on and be at gravity’s mercy.

Chapter Thirty-Five

"Those stupid raiders couldn't even use a simple tool right, I can't believe they stood there and talked like they did," Meria said. "Don't worry, commander. Our cannon blasted her right out of the sky," Nyogyth said and smiled, taking her hand off the console. "Worried, I know they won't attack us, not this station anyway. But the knights are pretty creative. Attacking one of them directly was a bold move, but I suggest we prepare for the counter attack. They tend to be on the vengeful side when one of their own goes down," Meria said as she watched Nanic fall to earth.

"it was only a quarter blast. She should survive the fall," Nyogyth said, she hoped that the Knight would live anyway. If not, they might risk attacking the station outright in their anger. "Commander, I have a question," she said and Meria turned to look at her.

"Why can't we just use the A class monsters and take over world with them?" Nyogyth asked and Meria cringed. "Oh, child. Trust me. It's not worth it. Those things, those things are true monsters. I've seen one, and I know all the stories, we'll stick with the original plan. Don't bother looking for the A class beasts, alright?" Meria replied to her and Nyogyth shook her head. "Fine, I just think you're scared, but okay," she replied.

"You're damn right I'm scared," she replied and watched as the Nanic knight disappeared from their screen. "Someday, when you're a higher rank I'll let you see the records for yourself, so you can know the truth of what happened to our world," she said and continued. "I'm going to retire to my quarters, I'll expect an angry message or two so if they show up, give them directly to me, okay," she said and Nyogyth nodded. "Don't worry, it'll be done," she replied, Meria turned and walked out of the bridge.

Nyogyth looked down on the earth, she had the same questions that she always did, but now there was a chance the commander didn't see and she didn't bring it up in conversation. Nyogyth had the chance to capture a Knight, she was down there. Her machine was broken, at least for now. She waited a few minutes to make sure that the commander wasn't going to come back. When Nyogyth was confident she was alone, she turned to the person next to her. "You have the bridge. I have something I need to take care of," she said to the man.

"Yes sir," he replied. Nyogyth turned and walked out without another word. She walked to the armory, slid her badge through the card reader and the door opened. She walked in and grabbed two blasters. They magnetically sealed to her belt as she had them close. "Alright. Let's go catch a knight," she said to herself and walked out, down the hall and made her way to the teleporting room.

"Miss Nyogyth, where are you going?" the operator asked. "Earth, tell no one," she replied as she stepped onto the platform. "I mean it. Tell no one," she repeated and the operator nodded. "Any particular place on earth or, just any old place?" the man asked. Nyogyth was growing frustrated.

"Send me close to lake seventy-three. I'll do the rest," she replied and the man nodded. "As you wish," he replied, pushed a few buttons on the console and Nyogyth was gone in a bright white light.

Nyogyth reappeared near the shoreline of the lake. She looked around and saw that the water was still quite agitated from the beast being thrown in it. Other than the noise of the violent waves, there was no other sound here.

A black plume of smoke was rising from the west and, it was obvious that the only thing that could have made that all the way out here. She began walking through the trees, into that direction where her prize awaited her.

Grace hit the ground and the protective chamber did its job. She quickly moved her fingers, toes and did her best to make sure nothing was broken. Once she felt okay enough to move. She undid the straps and pulled herself to the door, and pulled it open. "Damage report," she said. "Nanic is fifty percent damaged, estimated time to repair, three hours," the computer replied and Grace groaned.

"Alright, send an emergency signal to the other stations when you can," Grace said as she stepped out. Despite being on its back, the imaging chamber was designed to always be in an upright position at all times.

"Is there anything I can do to help?" Grace asked and there was a moment of silence. "No, the nanite repair systems will take care of everything," the computer replied. "What kind of energy hit us? Grace asked, she knew already but needed to be sure. "Ion energy cannon from a low orbit," the computer said and Grace shook her head. "Yeah, I figured that's what it was. I just had to be sure," she replied.

Grace pressed the button on her armlet. "Anyone awake out there?" she asked, and for a bit there was no reply. "Yeah, I'm here," Jay replied. "Seran station knocked me out of the sky on the return trip home. Nanic's damaged, I'm okay," she replied. "Yeah, I saw them shooting at something, thought it was just a test fire or something. I guess not. Man, I wish we could just blast those people right out of the sky sometimes," Jay said and Grace agreed.

"How are the trainees doing?" Grace asked him. 'I have no idea, I've just been doing my best to try and forget what I had to do to Warga," Jay replied and Grace nodded. "Yeah, I hear you," she replied.

"Human life form detected, approaching," the computer said and a holographic map appeared on its own. There was a little red dot slowly making its way to the crash site. "No idea who it is, I'm going to have to call you back," Grace said to Jay and cut off the communications before he could reply.

"Any identification?" Grace asked. "None detected, will arrive in ten minutes at current speeds," the computer replied to her. "Do I have access to the internal armor or any weapons?" Grace asked. "The damage is too great to activate the internal armor, however, the emergency set of blasters is available to you," the computer said and a black panel slid back quickly.

Grace walked to them and stared. "I wonder when the last time these were used?" she asked herself, the computer didn't bother to reply to that question. Maybe that meant they had never been. Grace grabbed them off the rack, they were cold to the touch. She put them in the holsters and took a breath. The one approaching could have been anyone. If she was lucky it was just a random traveler curious about the giant that fell out of the sky.

Grace walked over to the far side of the chamber, opened the exit and looked up, the situation was disorienting for a few seconds. She grabbed on to the ladder and began to climb to the emergency exit. The path up was thankfully easy. Grace got to the hatch above, twisted the lock open and with a hiss the door swung open to the left.

Grace was disoriented again when she discovered that she stepped out into the ground. Something about that whole trip didn't make a whole lot of sense to her but, she tried not to think about it. She didn't understand everything about these machines and how they worked.

The land she was surrounded by, besides the damaged parts, was all forest. Tall trees in every direction she could see. "Well, I can see why this is Vor land," she said to herself, listened for any sounds, but there wasn't anything obvious, not yet. They weren't going to appreciate a giant metal weapon in their forest and would come to at least investigate what it might be.

Grace took a breath and started to walk as quietly as she could in the direction of the one coming her way. The farther away she got from Nanic, the worse this idea began to feel. For all she knew this place hasn't seen a human in over seventy-five years or more, many of the places were like that now on the planet, it was a wonder how humanity even managed to hang on this long.

It didn't take too long before she heard the soft crunching coming in her direction. It was too soft to be a Vor. "Don't move," Grace said before she even saw who it was, the footsteps stopped. "Whoever you are, it's dangerous out here. Go back to where you came from," Grace said into the distance. Then the footsteps began again, no reply. Grace was sure that any normal person would have said something, but she wasn't quite sure what normal was.

"You're right, it is dangerous out here. For you," a female voice finally replied and immediately Grace knew who it was. She hid behind a tree. "Nyogyth, what are you doing down here?" she asked and pulled her blasters out. "I'm here to bring you back to my station and capture you, what else, I mean I did shoot you down. It's pretty hard to miss a six hundred foot tall robot," she replied and Grace tried to listen to where she was coming from, but couldn't quite pin it down yet.

"This is Vor country, they'll be here soon and we shouldn't be when they get here. Come on let's do this later," Grace said. Nyogyth she wasn't worried about. The Vor were a different story. "We'll both be long gone before they get here. Unless you're scared to face me, then, well, maybe not," Nyogyth replied and Grace could hear the smile in her voice when she said it.

"Scared of you. I've never been scared of you. You're a spoiled brat that lived her whole life in a space station, I bet your tired already from the walk it took to get here," Grace replied and almost laughed because it might have been true. "Not quite, but guess what?" Nyogyth asked and Grace narrowed her eyes. "What?" she asked. "I see you," Nyogyth said and Grace turned her head to see her in the distance, just before she pulled the trigger.

Grace dived out of the way as the deep red beam smashed against the tree she was standing beside causing it to explode. "Damn it," Grace said as she kept her footing and ran forward into the trees.

The last thing she wanted to do right now was get into a fire fight with the crazy one in a dangerous forest so she started to run back towards Nanic as fast as she could. Turning her back to someone like this was equally as dangerous, however.

"You can't get away from me. You might as well stop now," Nyogyth yelled out from behind and fired again. "Geeze," Grace said and she could feel the heat before the blast even got there. She dove to the ground and watched as the beam sailed over head and hit something in the distance and explode in a shower of sparks. That was more than enough motivation to shoot back.

Grace turned around, pulled out her blasters. Took aim and fired. The blasters shot twin blue beam, thin, but accurate. "Son of a," Nyogyth was cut off as the twin beam sailed past both of her shoulders. "That was a warning shot, the next one goes through your head," Grace said and hated killing anyone if she could help it, but if it had to be done it would be.

"Kill me, you'd really kill me?" Nyogyth asked her. "If you don't give me a choice," Grace replied and there was silence. "Well, I'm not giving you a choice, then. You're going to have to kill me if you want to save yourself today," Nyogyth said. Grace groaned and took aim.

"Fine, if that's how you really want it," she said and prepared to pull the triggers when suddenly she screamed. The footsteps were running in her direction, panic filled now.

"Vor, run for it," Nyogyth screamed as she came into view from the general direction Grace was sure she was in. "Damn it," Grace said as Nyogyth ran past her. Grace got to her feet and ran behind Nyogyth. Then she heard it. The roar behind the both of them. It only sounded like one had shown up but one was enough.

"Get to Nanic, we'll be safe inside," Grace said and she couldn't believe what she was saying. "I could just teleport out of here," Nyogyth said. "But you're coming with me once I deactivate your stupid armlet," she said and Grace knew that the maniac was serious about this whole capturing thing. Grace also knew that right this second, she could have shot her in the back, too. But she didn't have the heart to do that.

Nyogyth was about to say something else when a large humanoid shape came out of the shadows up in front of them. The both of them stopped in their tracks. "Well, don't just stand there, shoot," Nyogyth said, aimed at the thing and fired. The deep red beam flew into the beast's chest sending sparks in all directions, it screamed in pain and stumbled backwards as the smoke rose. "This way," Grace said as it fell back, turned to the right and ran. Nyogyth followed.

The trees became thicker this way and it was getting harder to get through them. Grace turned to look for a clear path when a thick, hairy hand grabbed the back of her neck and picked her up. With ease the Vor tossed her into a tree. Grace hit the tree hard and felt something inside of her break. "Damn it," she said as she rolled on her back. Nyogyth was thrown across her vision and landed on the ground.

"Did you know?" Nyogyth asked as the Vor seemed to melt out of the shadows around them. "I tried to tell you, but you're an idiot. And now we're both going to die," Grace said as she tried not to make eye contact with the Vor that was surrounding them. "No," Nyogyth said, pulled up her blaster and was just about to fire. Grace shot her a look.

"If you want to live maybe, just maybe you shouldn't shoot at the thing when we're surrounded. That might be a good idea," she said and did her best to hold her pain back at the same time.

The Vor were hairy, seven feet tall and bigger than any human. In the past they were called by a hundred different names, but the most famous was Bigfoot. "Why do you come here?" one of them said as he stepped forward. His eyes seemed to glow in the sunlight, what little of broke through down here. "Just an accident. Didn't plan to stay long. Just let me get back to my ship and you'll never see me again," Grace replied to the Vor who must have been the leader.

"Don't listen to her, she lies. She was going to use that giant knight thing to burn the forest down," Nyogyth hissed. "I shot that thing down and I came to capture her so she couldn't hurt anything else," she added and Grace turned her head in disgust. The Vor grunted in annoyance.

"This is our land. We saw the white machine drop the beast into our lake. It looked dead, its body will make the water toxic for decades, we know you are a knight, you can't be anything else," the Vor said and Grace didn't know what to think.

"For all the good you've done, you've only done it for humanity's sake and not the earth. But this woman here would capture you and you'd do no good for anyone. However, you violated our land and you must pay for that," the Vor said and motioned to the two beside them. "Take them to the camp. We will deal with them there," he said, turned and walked away.

"No, you don't understand. I have to go back to my ship. Bad things are coming and—" Grace was cut off as the Vor beside her picked her up with ease whatever was broken inside shifted and she screamed. Nyogyth couldn't help but smile at that scream.

She didn't plan on going quietly but now that she knew these things could talk and might be reasoned with, she stood up with their help. A large Vor carried Grace and Nyogyth was forced to walk.

The trek through the woods was a blur to Grace. The pain inside was tearing into her with every step the giant took and all she could do was hope it wasn't much longer and do her best not to let them know just how much pain she was actually in.

Nyogyth was seconds away from attempting to shoot her way out of this, when she noticed a black mark on the chest was walking beside her. If the thing could live through that, shooting wasn't going to help her at all. So, for now she had to see what these things wanted to do with them. She hated the thought of having to team up with her after all of this.

Chapter Thirty-Six

Grace looked around as they entered the Vor village. It was a strange mix between primitive and almost modern. The buildings looked sturdy as if they were built by human hands. Yet they had all been modified by the Vor to be more in line with the nature around them.

"Okay, I'll be honest with you," she said. "I'm not doing so well, I'm pretty sure something's broken on the inside. You wouldn't happen to have a healer or something, around would you?" she asked quietly, trying to not let Nyogyth in on the conversation.

"Yes, I will bring you," the Vor replied to her and Grace smiled. "Put the other one in a cage and make sure to take her stuff. I'm sure she'll try to escape, even without me I imagine," Grace said. "Do not worry, she will be secured. We've dealt with your kind many times before and know how handle you," it replied in a gruff voice as he stopped and turned to the right.

"Hey, where are you taking her, she's mine you over grown mops," Nyogyth said as the Vor beside her lifted its fist. "If you like your head where it is, you'll learn to keep quiet. This is your only warning," it said to her and its fist was bigger than her head was. Nyogyth rolled her eyes and decided that keeping quiet would keep her alive a little longer.

Grace did her best to keep her eyes open as they passed through a wide doorway. The inside wasn't as dark as she expected, actually nothing about this was what she thought it was going to be like. It didn't even smell bad, just like wood and something else she couldn't quite place. She was sure the Vor were just animals. All of this was very surprising to her. The Vor laid her down on a table that made her feel like a kid it was so big.

"A human, you expect me to heal a human now? They are as fragile as spiderweb, they aren't worth fixing," a higher, but much more annoyed voice said. Grace supposed she understood where the mood came from.

"This is no normal human, she pilots the great sky knight that fell," the Vor said and the healer crossed her arms. "What's your point, a human is a human. Just because she can drive a walking piece of metal doesn't make her any more special," she said and Grace have enough strength to reply anymore.

"Well, the chief wants her alive, so she stays alive. You know how it is," the Vor said to her and the healer grunted. "Fine, I'll fix her," she said Grace was beginning to worry about how this was going to happen. "I'll wait here," the Vor said. "Whatever, this won't take long," she replied.

"What's your name human?" the healer asked, towering over her. "Grace," she replied quietly. "Great, Grace. This is going to sting a bit, but a tough sky walker like you should be able to handle it, right?" the healer asked her. Grace just tried to smile. "Sure, whatever. Let's get this done," she replied and prepared for whatever might happen next.

The healer turned and walked to a shelf nearby. She looked through a few items before finding what she needed. "This isn't strong enough for one of us, but for you, should be just about right," she said and turned around with a small syringe filled with orange liquid.

Grace had no idea what that was and really didn't want to be injected with anything. Before she could protest, even in the slightest. The Vor doctor stuck the needle in her arm and pumped the fluid in.

Grace didn't feel any different at first as the needle was pulled out. Then she remembered what that stuff was just before it began to take effect. She felt her ribs crack back into place, she suppressed the pain well enough.

"Where in the hell did you get nano-health from?" Grace asked as the pain faded away. "We scavenge your old cities. You left so much behind. We find it," she said and Grace shrugged. She'd only ever saw that on the station, but only in the history records. It was deemed unstable in most cases. She was surprised that this dose worked and didn't make her explode.

"What's your name?" Grace asked. "I am called Bryn," she replied. "Is she healed?" the Vor asked, impatiently. "Yeah, she'll be fine," Bryn replied. "Get up human, you're going to the cage," the Vor said to her.

Grace thought that things might be getting better from here, then everything went right back to how it started. "Damn it, I need to get out of here. I only came down to," Grace paused. Had that much actually happened in this short amount of time.

"I came to fight the monster, that's all," she said. "I need to get back, there is a bad thing that will happen, you don't understand," Grace pleaded with him. "Take it up with the chief, he wants you in the cage so in the cage you go," he said and Grace knew she could teleport out of here at any time. But Nyogyth had access to an orbital cannon and this location.

"Fine," Grace said, sat up and got off the table. She slid on to the floor and it was farther away than she expected, she kept her balance anyway and walked towards the door. "Don't worry, I won't run," she said to him. "Yeah, I know," the Vor said. "My name's Grace, what's yours?" she asked him. "I am Necom," he replied as they walked out the door.

The cage was a literal cage just down the road. Nyogyth was sitting on a bench along the back. "Get inside," Necom said as another Vor opened the large door. Grace shook her head but stepped inside the cage. The door shut behind her. "Well. I guess neither of us saw it turning out this way," Nyogyth said to her.

"Shut up, the only reason I'm not gone yet is because I can't leave you behind. I know you'll blast this place just like you did to me once you get home," Grace replied. "And you're coming with me, now," Grace finished. Nyogyth didn't like where this conversation was heading as she stepped forward. "Come on now, you know I won't blast this place. You have my word," she pleaded.

Grace shook her head. "No, you can't be trusted, ever," Grace replied and walked towards her. She intended to teleport the two of them right back to her station when suddenly a voice came from behind them.

"A knight and an outlander come to our village on the same day. To what do we owe the pleasure of entertaining such elaborate guests," the said to them, Grace turned around. "Just disposing of a monster in a lake, I can find a different lake," Grace said and then she looked over her shoulder. "Then this one shot me down and here we are," Grace finished.

"Yeah. I shot her down because there is a plan in motion and her and her idiot friends are going to stop us. I'm going to make the world normal again. For everyone. Monster free," Nyogyth said. "So, I thought I could make my mission a little easier," she finished. The massive, grey haired Vor nodded. "I see. What to do with you two. What to do," he said to himself, crossed his arms.

"It's clear you two are nothing. A world without giant monsters in it does sound like a better place to live. However, the beasts seem to keep themselves in balance. They don't bother too many unless provoked, not since the fall of the big four ones," the Chief Vor said and seemed to drift off. "I know what to do," he said and nodded.

Grace didn't like where this was going. "You two will fight to the death. It is clear that both options are not bad, but only one can prevail. You will prove your convictions to your cause, now," the chief said to them. Grace knew this was coming, or something like it.

"I don't want to kill her, I don't want to kill anyone unless I don't have a choice. I am a healer by trade, not a killer," Grace said and the Vor looked at her with his dull blue eyes.

"But you do kill, right?" he asked. "When I have no choice," Grace said and looked away. "Well consider this one of those times where you have no choice, because either one of you dies here. Or we'll kill both of you. But honestly, I hope you win, Knight. Then at least you can get that undying corpse out of our lake and put it elsewhere," the chief said.

"Hey, no favorites you hairy jerk, I'm right here," Nyogyth shouted and crossed her arms. Neither of them bothered to look back at her. "Fine, let's just get this over with," Grace replied and the chief nodded. "I'll be back," the chief said, turned and walked away.

"A fight to the death, really?" Nyogyth asked and Grace turned around. "Don't worry, you're not worth killing but I have a plan," she said and sat down on the bench next to her. "Do you mind telling me what your plan is?" she asked and Grace shook her head. "No," she answered, "you're just going to have to trust me," she finished. Nyogyth narrowed her eyes in suspicion. Grace ignored it.

Neither Grace or Nyogyth liked being here. The Vor walked past them staring at them as if they were some kind of animal in a cage. To them, they were, Grace figured. She'd always thought the Vor were mindless, vicious things. After all people who went into the woods, the deep parts anyway, tended to disappear without a trace.

Of course, they might not be violent or mindless, they sure had violent ways of problem solving. A fight to the death was right out of the pages of history files, tales of ancient earth culture. She wasn't sure she liked that idea very much the more she sat here and thought about it.

Grace watched the sun, she sure that she could see it moving through the trees, she wondered what the others were up to and if they were going to come looking for her or not. She supposed not, or at the very least she imagined them debating if it were a trap or not. That was a nice thought, anyway. It almost made her smile, even here stuck in a cage.

Time was being wasted down here. This was supposed to be a simple mission. Nyogyth didn't know how she ended up here. She wasn't too interested in killing the knight, however, in the new world they were going to make. The knights weren't going to be needed anymore, but still. Killing was the last resort. Now some hairy talking ape thing was going to make her kill. She'd do it, she supposed. What worried her the most was how she was going to explain her disappearance to the commander.

They didn't know how long they sat there, it felt like much longer than it really was, as the sun was still pretty high in the sky, but it was on the downward slide. Then the chief returned to them. "Stand up, warriors. Follow me to the pit. The time to see what cause is better has arrived," he said and was overly too cheery about this whole situation.

The two of them stood up, but still refused to talk to one another. "I see you're getting along, great, I like that in future combat matches. A good, well-tempered hate always makes the battles much better to watch," he said with a big smile, turned and began to walk. Grace had no idea what was up with this guy but she supposed he had a point with all of it.

They walked and they could feel the eyes of the Vor looking down on them as they did. "So, this is how it feels going to an execution," Nyogyth said mostly to herself. "Shut up, this is all your fault. All of it. If you hadn't shot me down neither of us would be here right now," Grace said, the anger she felt was real and killing her was starting to feel like a better idea all the time.

"Don't worry. I'll make it quick. The new world isn't going to need any of you once we're done with it," Nyogyth said to her and Grace narrowed her eyes. "it's a pipe dream, even if you win, you'll lose more than you can ever imagine," Grace replied as the chief turned a corner. There in front of them was a tall, wooden wall with a door in the middle of it that was big enough for five people to walk through side by side at a time.

Chapter Thirty-Seven

"Welcome to the pit, two beings enter, only one leaves. The ultimate decider of all things," the chief said with too much pride in his voice as they walked forward towards the building. The three of them passed through and before them was nothing but a bare, dirt clearing with two metal swords in the center, stabbed in to the ground. "No rules in here, may the best human win," the Chief said as he stepped back beyond the doors as they closed.

"Damn it," Grace said and took off running towards the sword. Nyogyth did the same. She was faster than Grace and passed her, at the same time put her right elbow into Grace's face knocking her back. She grunted in pain and watched as Nyogyth made it to the weapons, pulling both of them out of the dirt.

Grace was positive that right now, Nyogyth didn't trust her at all and fully intended to kill her. "Scared?" Grace asked and backed off. "No," Nyogyth replied, but it didn't convince Grace. "You're forgetting one thing," Grace said and smiled. Nyogyth wasn't sure what that might have been.

Grace pulled her blasters from her holsters. In all the chaos, no one bothered to take them from her, or maybe it was on purpose. Grace wasn't going to say anything and Nyogyth seemed too nervous to notice being in a cage. "Oh hell," she said once she saw the weapons. Now that there were no more rules in this fight, she was sure no one was going to come in and take them.

However, this wasn't part of Grace's overall plan and the space dweller was messing everything up. If she told Nyogyth the plan, someone might have heard it, or worse the idiot would have used the information to try and gain favor with the Vor and escape or something like that.

"I'll make you a deal, I'll throw my blasters down if you give me a sword," Grace said and Nyogyth didn't trust any of this. But the idea of getting shot didn't sound that great either. Nyogyth tossed the blade and it landed at Grace's feet. She put the blasters away and reached down to pick up the blade. It was half way down when she heard her enemy running right at her.

Grace grabbed the hilt and immediately raised the blade just in time to block the sword coming in her direction. The sharp sound of clashing metal rang out. Grace lost her balance and fell back into the dirt. "Fine," she said and pushed her back with all the strength she had. Despite being at a disadvantage, managed to push her away.

It was then that Grace heard the roar of the audience as she stood up. The Vor screamed wildly as the combat began. Their deep roars shook the air around both of them. It was nearly as loud as a beast's roar up close. Grace winced at the sound, it was causing her pain. Nyogyth winced too, she was even less used to all the racket the things were making and covered her ears without thinking about it what she was doing.

Grace rushed forward through the sand, Nyogyth widened her eyes once she realized what she did. Grace leapt forward and tackled Nyogyth into the dirt. She knocked her blade out of her hand. Grace landed on top of her and raised the blade high over her heart. "I've always hated you," Grace said as she straddled her. Nyogyth didn't read the look in her eyes, panicked and raised her left knee into her back, "What in the hell are you doing?" Grace said as she tumbled forward and off her.

"Stopping you from killing me," Nyogyth said, rolled to grab on the blade's hilt. Nyogyth swung the blade, Grace rolled right into it with her left leg. The tip of the blade ripped through her skin. The pain burned through her body. Grace winced in pain, she knew It felt worse than it was but that wasn't making it any better. She pushed her way back through the dirt just in time to avoid another wild swing.

If they thought the crowd was wild before, the sight of the blood intensified it. Grace used her sword as leverage to stand up. She could feel the blood running down from the wound just below her knee, it burned and she hated to think about all the sand, bacteria and who knows what else infecting it right now.

Nyogyth was standing too, her silver clothes covered in the dirt, too. "Seriously. What part of trust me do you not get. I was going to make it look good then teleport us both out of here," Grace said and Nyogyth still didn't believe her. "Or, I kill you and get out of here all the same. I like my chances," she replied and ran forward. Grace didn't mind killing her, but she was afraid of what Meria might do while seeking revenge.

Grace held the blade close to her and steadied herself for what was coming next. Nyogyth ran at her again, trying to take advantage of Grace's injuries. "Stupid girl," Grace muttered to herself as she watched her run. Nyogyth swung the blade at Grace's neck in hopes that she would get in a lucky strike, wouldn't see it coming. Grace did and turned into the attack. Her blade collided with the other. Grace didn't stop moving, instead slid down the blade guiding it away from her.

Nyogyth lost control of her momentum, sliding forward and away. Grace immediately spun around as she got to the hilt of the blade. For one brief moment her deep purple eyes meet with Grace's gray eyes. The moment was brief. Grace completes her move and the blade slices the across the width of Nyogyth's back. The fabric and skin are torn all the same. The blood explodes from the wound as Nyogyth falls face first into the dirt, screaming.

She caught her breath, both surprised that actually worked and glad at the same time. Grace didn't drop the blade as she stumbled forward, the blade in her left hand dropped so she was dragging it through the sand behind her as she walked.

Nyogyth might be dead now, she didn't care. The closer she got the easier it was to tell that her enemy was still breathing, but for how much longer she wasn't sure. "Knight, remember?" Grace said in between breaths, like Nyogyth should have known better than to try something like this.

She raised the blade over Nyogyth's back, held the hilt in both hands and prepared to thrust the blade down. For a second, she was sure the Vor chief was going to rush in and put this to a stop. She hesitated just to be sure this wasn't going to happen. Nothing changed, however. The Vor crowd screamed for blood, death and who knows what else. "Fine," Grace said to herself and thrust the blade straight down.

At the last second, she shifted the blade and buried it deep into the dirt. In the same motion she let the blade go, put her hands on Nyogyth's back. "Recall to Nanic, now," she said and the two of them disappeared in a white light. The Vor crowd's screams of excitement changed into ones of rage as they disappeared. But the gray-haired Chief smiled as he watched them vanish. "So, the knights have some heart after all, good," he said to himself.

The two of them reappeared in the imaging chamber of the Nanic. Grace stood up. Medical attention for this one. Stop the bleeding, stabilize and throw her in the brig, knock her out, too," Grace ordered and Nyogyth disappeared in a white light. Then she limped over to the center of the room. "Stand up," she ordered.

The six hundred-foot Nanic's eyes lit up and the machine slowly got to its feet, standing up above the trees. Grace looked around and saw the lake nearby. "I should just let the Vor suffer, next time," she said to herself, considering for a split second to let Volgun stay right where it was. Grace quickly reconnected herself to the Nanic image control and took off into the sky, towards the lake.

Nanic flew over the center of the lake and fell into the water. The green water surrounded everything she could see as she sank down. The lake wasn't that deep, it was only a few seconds before she hit the bottom with a thud. It didn't take long to see the thin lizard, Volgun lying there on its side. It looked dead but Grace knew better.

She walked forward and grabbed the thing by its long and slender neck. Then, without hesitation Nanic blasted straight out of the water, clearing the surface in a few seconds. Then it curved to the east. "I need to find place to put you," she said to herself as she increased her speed to four hundred miles an hour. In a matter of seconds, the lake was behind them.

"B-Class detected to the south, three minutes at this speed," the computer said to her and Grace smiled. "Perfect, who is it?" she asked. "B class designated as Vicira," Grace heard that and shuddered a little bit. "Okay, set course," she replied and Nanic turned slightly. She watched as the ground beneath them sped by.

Two minutes later she slowed Nanic down considerably. In the distance the seven hundred foot Centipede could be seen crawling on the ground, minding its own business as most beasts tended to do. "Surprise, bug," she said to no one and spun around in the air, upon completing the spin, she let Volgun loose.

She watched as the much smaller monster flew through the air and smashed into the middle of Vicira's body. The centipede immediately curled up as Volgun caused it to crash into the ground. A high-pitched screech of surprise, mostly, rang through the air. Volgun was still dead, at least for now. The centipede quickly regained her balance and twisted around to see who or what had just run into her.

Grace watched as the giant bug poked at it a few times. When Volgun didn't respond, Vicira did the unexpected and pushed the lizard off of her. It then turned to look in Nanic's direction, only for a second.

Then the beast turned back to the direction she was going and continued on her way, not interested in either of them. "Weird," Grace said and watched it go. She expected something, well, anything really. Volgun wouldn't be causing any trouble to anyone for a while, not naturally anyway. "Let's go home, turn the shields on this time just in case they decide to try something again. The same trick won't work twice," she said and Nanic took off into the sky.

The blue sky turned black in just a few minutes once more, this time as she flew towards Dylath Station nothing happened. "Dock to the station and let's go home. Is our, um, guest, fixed up?" Grace asked. "Yes, Nyogyth is resting in the brig, her injuries are ninety percent healed," the computer replied as the knight began to slow down to begin docking procedure. This whole time she had blocked out the pain in her leg when she realized that there wasn't any.

Grace disconnected from the controls as they docked with Dylath and pulled her pant leg only to reveal that the wound had healed at some point. "It still must be in effect," she said, but she still knew that she needed to get herself checked out anyway. "Get Nyogyth to the brig, tell me when she's awake," Grace replied and the power on the Knight began to shut down.

"And make sure to get this thing back up to a hundred percent," she said. "Don't worry, captain, Nanic will be perfect for next time," the computer said and Grace almost smiled, although she knew the next time might be the last time.

Grace walked to the exit of the Knight and she could barely remember how this whole ordeal started, but all she really wanted was answers from Nyogyth and began to make her way to the brig to get them.

Chapter Thirty-Eight

Five years had been a long time. Mike honestly didn't know what the others had been up to this whole time, but him. After that last nightmare. He never wanted to see them again, never wanted to be in space again. Instead he took great advantage of his teleportation armlet on his arm. He used it to port from place to place, ringing up a hefty Zop tab at the bar, drinking himself to near blindness, then disappearing. With millions of little settlements all over the world, it was a perfect situation.

The life of the criminal, the drunk and the parasite had suited him well. Then Jay walked back in to his life. The Outlanders decided to change everything. Like it or not his lifestyle he came to enjoy was going to a come to a crashing and immediate halt.

This is why Mike was now trying to remember how to fight. Mike had just got beaten down by a level five hologram. He was breathing hard and laying on the ground. Blood trickled from his nose. The hologram was a reconstruction of a B-class monster called Savago. A beast that was bright blue, covered in spikes on its back. The thing was taller than him, stronger too. He'd fought the beast only once. Even here in its hologram form it was still violent as he remembered.

Mike pushed himself up off the floor. "Come on, you can beat this thing. What good are you if you can't even beat one monster anymore," he said to himself. The second he did, the program resumed its command to only attack while he was standing. The bipedal beast marched in his direction. As the Azagon Knight armor formed around him, another hologram.

Savago was not swayed to stop his attack. Mike held out his hands and fired twin yellow rays of power. The beams slammed into the blue creature's iron skin. He turns his head and gets pushed back a little, otherwise no real damage was done. Nor was any intended.

Mike ran forward with the attack and the second he closed the distance, Mike sent his left fist into the monster's lower jaw, killing the beams at the same time. As Savago staggered back, the attack was pressed forward and his right fist landed where he thought the beast's heart should be.

Savago's iron like scales protected him from the fatal blow, but the force of the attack sent him back again. "Any other monster and that'd be a win for me," Mike said but he didn't pick this enemy because it was going to be easy. Savago was proving his tenacity. The bright blue demon snarled and marched forward.

Mike thought of what to do next. Hesitated long enough for the beast to open his mouth and unleash a great arc of electricity. Mike couldn't avoid it at this range. The stream of blue and yellow energy slammed into his green armor. Mike felt every volt course into his body and once again he fell to his knees. At once the beast stopped its attack.

"Would you like to lower the difficulty rating?" a voice asked him, he was still in too much pain to answer. The voice was muffled by the ringing in his ears. Mike knew full well that the level five difficulty took the stats of any monster and raised them far above anything that would normally be thrown at him in the field. Still, he was sure that he could have done better than this. Once the ringing stopped he could hear the computer.

"No, I'm fine. Keep everything just like it is," Mike replied and forced himself to stand up again. Savago wasted no time in starting the attack again. He had no time to react as the beast's long tail swing. The thing hit Mike in the chest, knocked him off his feet and into the wall. He heard something snap, maybe it was something inside of him.

Mike was done, he knew it as he slid down the wall, he crumpled to his side in defeat. "End program," he said softly and watched as the blue monster disappeared. "Medical bay, please," Mike said and the computer teleported him. Mike found himself laying on a cold table in a bleak white room, he shut his eyes.

"Your injuries are 62% internal. I can treat the flesh wounds, but you will require the assistance of a human, shall I call a doctor?" the computer asked and Mike groaned in pain. In his head he was sure he said yes, but right in reality it was meaningless mumbling.

"Yes, I agree. I'll call Grace," the computer replied. "This is Atador calling Dylath station. Come in," the computer sent the message. "I'm busy right now, computer, call back later," Grace replied. "It's Mike. He just went two hours in the training room at level five. He's bleeding internally and its beyond my power to fix. He has six hours left before he's dead. But, I suppose it can wait," Atador replied.

There was no response for a few seconds. "God damn it," Grace finally replied. "Fine, I'll be there soon," she said with annoyance. "Thank you," Atador replied. Mike groaned again, he tried to move but a sharp pain from the inside caused him to stop.

"Don't move Mike, you're making it worse," Atador said and could do nothing more than watch. It knew that treating the flesh wounds would just cause more harm than good right now.

Grace was half way to the brig when she got the call. She almost thought about calling one of the others to take over for her, but knowing them they were more likely to just kill Mike instead of helping him at all. "I guess there is still some time," Grace said to herself, turned around and began to make her way to the teleportation room to see if Mike was going to live or not.

Chapter Thirty-Nine

Jack had only been on board Cerberus station for just a few hours now, but he was bored already. Everyone had gone off to do their own thing and just left him here to babysit. He thought about it as he was going through files and then it occurred to him. "Oh, crap," he said to himself and got up to make his way to the training room of the station.

"How are our trainees doing?" Jack asked as he walked. "They are doing fine. They have made no progress and refuse to work together as a team. Other than that, they are doing just fine. Mission success rate at this point is at three percent," the computer replied to him and Jack narrowed his eyes. "What in the hell?" he asked no one "They should have figured it out by now," he finished and quickened his pace.

Jack made his way into an elevator, he pushed a button and the thing started to move as quietly as ever. It was only a few seconds until the doors opened again and he stepped out. Jack made his way to the training room's observation deck. In the past there was always someone here watching, now in this ghost station, that wasn't the case anymore.

He turned on the screen just in time to watch Alexis get caught by the back of the neck by holographic military person, get lifted up into the air. Then the scene faded away.

"How did you get caught, you're practically invisible. What did you do?" Ryan yelled at her and Alexis shrugged. "I don't know maybe this thing is unwinnable. One of us should have been able to do it by now," she yelled back. "It's not like you did any better than me," she yelled back at him, frustrated.

Jack watched the two of them. "Computer, run rec program three," Jack said and walked away.

Ryan and Alexis prepared to start the mission over again as the familiar hum of the hologram started to power up around them and immediately realized that something had changed. The sky turned blue and large buildings materialized around them. They found themselves standing on the side of a street and people just materialized out of thin air.

"What in the world?" Ryan asked. He'd never seen anything like it, or this many people. But the place he recognized. It was the broken city or at least one of them he had come to know. "This is the before time, it has to be," Ryan said and Alexis looked at him. "Yeah, I know. I'm not blind," she replied but didn't understand why this happened.

"This is a place they used to call Atlanta. Or, at least I think so. This was made to simulate life on Earth for the people who got, what they called, cabin fever," Jack said as he came walking out. The two of them took notice right away. "Yeah, it's a nice place. It's also hard to imagine that they thought that this would never end and took it for granted," Jack said as he looked around.

"I used to spend lots of time in this place back when I was on the job. Used to pretend the people were real. One quick mod and we can make them practically real, you know. Right now, they are just walking up and down this road," Jack said. "So, I thought I could give you two a break," Jack said. Alexis's eyes widened.

"A break, we don't have time for one of them. If we don't succeed the world as we know it is going to be destroyed, again," she said and Jack shook his head. "Maybe, do you even care about the world? I mean the outlanders have their own station. They could make the world whole again. Are you really so sure you want to succeed?" Jack asked them straight out as someone walked right through him.

"This is our world now. They outlanders don't want to just fix it. They want to take over, too. So yeah, I'm ready to do whatever I need to do," Ryan said, thinking about his house, his friends who he just realized he had no idea if they ever made it home or not. He also imagined them being slaves to the Outlanders who wanted to rebuild the world using their hands. He didn't like what came to mind.

Jack smiled. "Computer, history file one. Level Five," he said and the sky went from bright blue to black. "Kids, this simulation can and will kill you if you aren't smart. Are you ready to test out your skills because we don't have much time. That low level training session just isn't pushing you hard enough," Jack said, the both of them knew it wasn't a question.

"What is history file one?" Alexis asked and Jack's smile faded. "It's the first day of the end of the world. The stations recorded a lot of things. This is one of them, and numbered them on level of importance just in case future generations might forget," he said and as soon as he said it the sound of an explosion shattered the quiet. Neither of them could see the source from here.

"This is the night of the fall. All over the world this was happening. All of that information is pointless. All you need to do is live through the night. In the simulation time is sped up a bit but to you, it'll feel like a whole night. If you come out the other end in one piece. You'll be more than ready. If not. It was nice knowing you. Get your act together, this is your last chance," Jack said to them, then he turned walked towards a wall. The hidden door opened up and he walked right out of the virtual world, the doors closed behind him, remaking the illusion.

Another explosion echoed through the skyscraper canyons and this time the windows shook a little, the ground did too. "What are we going to do?" Ryan asked. "Well I don't think standing in the middle of the street with all these tall buildings around us is a good idea. Let's get the hell out of here," she answered.

Ryan, beginning to panic was brought back to the situation at hand. Then he remembered the mountains of rubble that made up the broken city in a hurry. "Right," Ryan agreed in a hurry.

Neither of them knew where to go. Any direction but towards the explosion was good enough for them, at least right now. It wasn't very long before the eerie and all too familiar sounds of the klaxon sirens began to echo through the night air.

"Come on, we need to keep moving," Alexis said. "Where are we going, I know, survive the night. But where are we going?" Ryan asked. Just then a car sped around the corner. It's back end sliding and the tires making a screaming sound neither of them had ever heard before.

Worse, they were standing in the middle of the road and the thing was coming right at them. Ryan snapped out of it and pulled Alexis to the other side. Seconds later the black car sped past them with no hint that it even saw them. "It's only going to get worse. I have a feeling this isn't exactly how it happened," Alexis said as Ryan let go of her hand. "Doesn't matter how it happened. Let's stay off the street," he replied and she agreed with a nod.

The city sprawled in all directions and none of them looked like a very good way out of danger. Then a new noise started to fill the sound around them. The sound of screaming. They turned to look in that direction and people could be seen, running.

Ryan looked up. The tallest skyscraper started to wave back and forth gently. Then all the windows shattered sending sparkling shards of glass falling in the night and shattering against the ground on the crowd unlucky enough to get away. Alexis watched the people fall to the ground, transfixed by the sight until something else demanded their attention.

A black hand grasped the side, it's long fingers wrapped around the front of the building. They had seen beasts before, lots of them. But none had ever been this big. Then they looked up, above the buildings. Looking down at them, all they could see were two red eyes peering down on them and not much else. "Oh my god, let's get out of here," Ryan said and the two of them started to run from the thing with the rest of the crowd.

Chapter Forty

Grace walked into the medical room and shook her head. "What did you do?" Grace asked. "He went into a level—" Grace cut the computer off. "I mean, I know what he did, I just don't understand why," she said, pushed a button on the side of the table. "You can't do chemical surgery?" Grace asked, annoyed. "No, I am an assistant. Not qualified for anything over level four treatment. This qualifies as level seven," the computer replied.

"You should have just transported him to Dylath. Thal could have taken care of this in a few minutes," she said and pulled out a syringe filled with blue liquid. She lifted up his shirt and saw all the bruises. "It must hurt to be that stupid," she said to herself and stabbed the needle into his chest.

Mike let out a small scream of pain, but Grace smiled. "Serves you right for being such an idiot, level five, really?" she asked him, frustrated at his stupidity.

"Why did you do that?" she asked him. He groaned. Grace knew he was going to be fine so she punched him in the side. "Talk, why did you do something like this and almost get killed, more importantly why did you feel the need to waste my time?" Grace asked again. Mike coughed. "I needed to get ready for the fight. It's been five years. Figured I was out of practice," he replied. It wasn't that convincing.

"If you needed practice all you really had to do was get in the machine and go find some rampaging monster to fight. That's all. You know the level five simulations are practically suicide unless," Grace paused. "Unless that was your whole plan," she said but her tone didn't soften at all. Actually, she expected one of them to pull something like this, but Jack was the one to do it in her mind.

"No, nothing so dramatic as that. I just wanted to see if I could win is all," he replied, already feeling a little better, but it was still hard to breathe. "Yeah. Well, knock it off. We're going to need all hands on deck in just a couple of days so if you need practice. Take Azagon down to the surface and go play the hero to some village who needs it. Don't just die up here, uselessly," she said and was upset. She punched him in the side again.

Mike recoiled and grit his teeth through the pain. "What was that for?" he asked her. "Just a reminder of what happens when you're stupid. Now. I captured Nyogyth, she's in the brig on my station. I have questions that need answers so if you'll excuse me I have work to do," she said and started to walk away.

"Wait, let me come too," Mike said and tried to sit up, but the second he did there was nothing but pain on the inside and his eagerness to come with disappeared. "You're not going anywhere for at least three hours. Get comfortable," she said to him and he rolled his eyes in response. Even that small action hurt.

"Yeah, I think I will," he said as she walked out. Mike had plenty of time to think about just how stupid he was. Grace didn't have time for this nonsense. "Thal, get me to the brig, now," she said into her armlet, and disappeared in a white flash. She reappeared outside of Nyogyth's cell. She was sitting there, still covered in dirt from their battle in the Vor arena.

"What took you so long. Did you have someone more important than me help. Maybe another primitive excuse for civilized society needed to be saved from the natural order of things?" she asked. Grace narrowed her eyes.

"First off, everyone's more important than you. Secondly, silver pants, how did you discover the way to control the beasts?" she asked.

Grace knew how it was done. She'd always known that and it was a secret, one Meria would have known, too.

"It was easy once I knew what to look for. The commander put me on a special research project. Monitor the progress of society incognito, you know, boring work. Put me to work around islands, villages out in the middle of nowhere, even for you primitive screwheads. In my research, studying the poor excuse you have for water down here. I picked something up," Nyogyth said.

"Strange, slow waves coming from the ocean. I didn't know what to call them. After a couple years. I saw that there were no monsters anywhere near the places of origin in the sea. Like, they were afraid. I thought that this could be the answer to the problem. I thought that the waves repelled the beasts. So, I created a device to mimic the wave output. Imagine my surprise when instead of driving the monsters away, it turned them into puppets," Nyogyth said and laughed. "I am such a genius to discover that," she added.

Grace crossed her arms. "Meria knew about the Delta waves. She knew you'd find them. Don't you remember how the Knights, we sealed the A-class monsters away?" Grace asked her. "No, you're making that up," she replied.

"No, I'm not. It's a secret. Meria knew it. The four of us knew it. The A-class monsters controlled with the others using the same waves. The places the waves are the strongest, if you haven't noticed they are under our stations," Grace said and Nyogyth shook her head.

Nyogyth never connected the dots and the revelation of that shocked her. She couldn't believe that she never noticed that. "So what? Even if it's true. I figured out how to do it all on my own, all me," Nyogyth said and Grace shook her head.

"Stop being stupid. Meria doesn't care about you. She's using you, if this whole plan falls apart, and it will, guess who's to blame for it. She'll take responsibility for your actions like a good leader should, but you're the one who's going to be punished for it. Likely sentenced to death for putting the whole world at risk," Grace said.

The color ran out of Nyogyth's face. She didn't want to believe it, but everything Grace was saying sounded accurate enough. "And how do you know it's going to fail?" she asked and Grace shook her head. "Lady you're playing with fire. The Delta waves control the monsters, sure. But you know what you don't know. That's going to get us all killed," Grace said and continued.

"Each of the stations are holding an A-class in place using a modified delta wave. It's worked for a century, or more. The world is saved. The beasts, without the A-class, settled into a natural balance. They don't attack much anymore unless provoked. Sure, there are some bad ones, but that's just like anything. We take out the bad ones when needed," Grace said then she got to her point. "if Seran station floods the world with your corrupted waves, you risk undoing one hundred and fifty years of effort, sacrifice and suffering," Grace said.

Nyogyth laughed. "You're trying to scare me into thinking that controlling the monsters runs the risk, a chance. A small chance, that it will free the Apex class monsters. Are you insane? That's literally impossible. The amount of Delta waves we'd need to make would have to be three times the amount, more than we need to even faze those things. They won't wake up. Not as long as your precious stations remain over them, I'm not nearly as worried as you are. Nice try, though. You almost had me," Nyogyth replied and smiled.

Grace knew she was right. This plan didn't have a chance to wake the A class monsters up.

"Well, even if your plan works, you'll never get to see it. You're not leaving here until you're old and wasted," Grace said and Nyogyth's smile disappeared.

"What, you can't keep me locked up like this. I'll be rescued, you'll see," she said, but didn't get up. "Yeah, maybe. But I'll make sure to give anyone who tries hell, you're not worth the effort," Grace said. "You destroyed towns, killed people to test out your theories. You deserve worse," Grace finished and started to walk away.

Nyogyth rushed to the forcefield and slammed her fist against it sending waves of yellow energy in all directions. "When I get out of here. I'm going to kill you do you hear me, you're dead," she screamed. Grace heard her, but decided that replying was pointless. "Lights off, turn back on in three hours," Grace said to the computer. The lights clicked off.

"Damn you to hell, Knight!" Nyogyth screamed in the dark as the doors closed behind Grace leaving Nyogyth in complete darkness. She carefully walked backwards until she reached the bench and sat back down, thinking of what to do next. She really wished the Vor hadn't been so good at searching, they took everything away from her. All she could do now is wait for the lights to come back on and think.

Chapter Forty-One

Jay was monitoring the Earth. Nothing changed. If the outlanders were going to do something, anything, they hadn't shown any signs. Even the beasts were on the quiet side. All in all, it was a good day on planet Earth and here on Oriab station. It was just how Jay liked it, too. So, while he had nothing to do he decided to contact Jack.

"Calling Cerberus Station, you there, Jack?" Jay asked into the communicator. "I'm here,' Jack replied. "Don't sound so cheerful, so how is the training coming along?" Jay asked. Then, silence. "Jack?" Jay asked again.

"I got sick of their whiny approach to it so I put them in a level five sim, history file one," Jack replied and Jay felt his blood freeze. "What the hell did you do that for, that's insane, you're going to kill them," Jay replied, worried. "Yeah. I suppose. But that's just two more mouths who can't tell the world who we are anyway. Besides, they didn't take any of this seriously. They'll either live or die. It's up to them," Jack replied.

"No, I doubt you could live through that. Get them out, now," Jay replied. He was angry at Jack for two reasons. First for throwing the newbies into a suicidal mission and secondly for ruining what was looking to be an almost perfect day with this pointless stress.

"Out, they just got in. Readouts say they are both still alive. Let's give them a couple more hours," Jack replied. "You idiot, don't you remember how history file one ends? You need to end the program, now," Jay said again and Jack thought about it.

"Oh yeah, I did forget. I only watched it once and that was many years ago. Fine. I guess I'll get them out. Eventually," Jack said with no sense of urgency and Jay widened his eyes. "No, you need to do it now, right now. Go," Jay said and he was beginning to panic. "Calm down, sparky. I'll get them out if your little pets mean that much to you," Jack replied.

"They aren't pets, but they know too much to just let loose. They can still be useful," Jay said and just after he said it, he realized how harsh it actually sounded. "I mean, not, you know what I mean," Jay said.

"Not really, but I'm going to get them now. They should be fine. Maybe," Jack said and stood up from his chair. Jay didn't say anything, or, at least if he did Jack didn't hear it.

He truly forgot how that simulation file ended, and at level five they didn't have a chance. Sometimes Jack wondered why the people that built this place made it so the holograms could actually kill you. There were no answers but he knew that the people of the past weren't that much different than the people of right now.

It didn't take long for Jack to get back to the imaging chamber. He opened the door and stepped inside. The sky was red with fire, the ground shook. "Yeah, it's all coming back to me now," Jack said. "Computer, find Ryan and Alexis," he said. "They are in section eight," the computer replied. Jack could have just shut it all off right now, but there was something that he wanted them to see. Jack took a breath and walked into the disaster.

Ryan was out of breath. Alexis wasn't doing much better. The two of them had run as fast as they could. The room didn't seem to have any kind of boundaries. "Where do we go?" Ryan asked and leaned against a car. The metal was warm to the touch. "I don't know, we just need to live through the night, that's all," she replied.

Ryan looked. The beast was there, it was wading through the buildings, knocking them over as if they were nothing. "That thing is so," Ryan said and trailed off. He still couldn't get over how big it was, towering over the tallest buildings with ease, the ones that still stood. "Yeah, you're impressed. I get it, now let's go," she replied and kept walking.

He pushed himself off the car and followed her. People were walking around them. Bleeding and limping in the same direction. Most of them in shock doing everything they could to keep going.

They were all covered in dust, too. It reminded Ryan of old pictures he saw and the rare recordings they would find sometimes of the first attack. He never imagined that he would actually be in one. Even if it was just a very good simulation.

Someone screamed behind them. "Run," the voice cried out. Ryan and Alexis turned around. The beast had slammed its left fist into the side of a building. To the horror of the crowd the force of the attack had sent the skyscraper falling in their direction. It looked like it was too far away to be a threat. However, no one was taking the chance. "Come on," Alexis said, grabbed his hand and they took off running.

"Always with the running," Ryan complained, but did it anyway. He looked to his left to see a large chunk of a wall come crashing down on three people, he heard their bones crack on impact. He cringed at the sight and even if it wasn't real, it was something he wouldn't be forgetting anytime soon. Then he felt a sharp pain in his right shoulder. He fell to the ground on impact. Alexis turned around and gasped.

Ryan had a long, narrow metal rod sticking out his shoulder and was bleeding badly. "Damn it," she said but this was random. This wasn't anyone's fault. "Are you alive?" she asked him. He groaned a little and tried to move. Alexis looked up. "Sorry about this," she said, ran to him and picked him up. He screamed as she rushed to the left. Seconds later another hulk of a building crashed where they stood.

"Thanks," Ryan said in between breaths. "Come on, let's get out of here," she said and helped him stand up. "If we take it out, you'll bleed to death, sorry man," she said. "I can make it. Come on," Ryan replied. He wanted to complain, scream, do anything. But he walked instead.

The two of them walked forward once more. It was endless, in front of them, houses, civilization and the world that was. Behind them, the new world was being created one step at a time from a monster that they had never seen before and because it was so dark, still have yet to fully see. They didn't want to think too much on what was going on around them.

Alexis screamed as a hand fell on her shoulder. "Oh, you've been hurt already," Jack said and Alexis relaxed. Ryan didn't say anything, kept his head looking down, blood dripping onto the cement. "We need to get out of here, now," Alexis said and Jack nodded. "Yeah, I know. But I want you to see something before we go," Jack said to them.

Before they had a chance to protest the ground underneath them cracked and lifted into the air. "Thanks for the lift but can we please just get out of here?" Ryan finally asked. "Yes, we will. But I want you to see how the world ended. How it ended and who the true enemy really was, and is," Ryan said and groaned. With a wave of Jack's hand, the metal spike in his shoulder disappeared. It was immediately replaced with bandages. "It'll hold for now," he said.

Ryan didn't feel much better, but it was nice not being impaled anymore. "That thing you're looking at is an A-class beast. One of four," Jack said as they watched it rampage through the city. "How did humanity beat this thing?" Ryan asked. Seeing it like this, it seemed that beating such a thing was impossible.

"Do you see that building its head is above now? That's a thousand feet tall, just to put some perspective on the matter," Jack ignored his question, the answer should have been obvious to him by now. "That thing is thirteen hundred feet tall?" Alexis asked. "Yeah, at least. Scientists were too busy amazed with how something like that could even stand up on the planet. But yeah, that's right the first one was the smallest one," Jack said, talking in a mechanical tone, seeing this thing seemed to be bringing bad memories back to him, but he did not look away. None of them did.

A different sound filled the air. To Jack, this was nothing more than a fancy version of a rerun on television. He knew what was coming next. "The Nuclear Knight program was not intended to fight giant monsters or, anything really. After the last great war, they were built as safeguards, guardians of peace I guess. They turned into the world's best chance to fight the monsters that invaded our world," Jack said it as if he was reading it off a board, like he was a tour guide.

Just then the five massive machines sailed over head towards the rampaging beast, who in turn, didn't even appear to notice them. The two of them watched the machines fly through the sky. The difference in size quickly became apparent. The monster was twice their size, at least.

Jack smiled as Knight Saphiel opened fire first. Bright blue beams launched from its eyes and slammed into the neck of the beast. "That's my favorite part," he said mostly to himself.

The knights flew into the distance. The three of them watched as multiple colored beams struck the beast. "Simulation to level one," Jack said at once. Neither Ryan or Alexis heard him say it. The beast finally took notice of the knights, then it's body started on fire. It resembled a burning mountain now.

"And this is when the world ended," Jack said as the burning mountain exploded. Red and gold fire exploded in every direction. Jack stood motionless as the wall of flame consumed everything. Alexis and Ryan threw up their hands as if that would protect them from the incoming wall. "Relax," Jack said as he noticed them.

They lowered their hands just as the gold and red fire covered everything they could see. "The A class monster, this one, could do this once a month, generally. The entire city of Atlanta was destroyed along with a ten-mile radius. The other ones had their own special tricks. Ironically, the only ones that survived were the knights. The moon fall started out with the lesser class beasts, then these demons appeared," Jack said, then the fire disappeared, revealing the empty simulation room. They were standing on the floor.

Ryan collapsed as the blood from the wound began to flow onto the ground. "Oh, I forgot about that," Jack said, but didn't feel too worried about it. "Take your bleeding friend to the sick bay and get him patched up. Then take a break. I don't think we have much time left and whatever the plan is going to be, I guess you're just going to have to wing it," he said, still annoyed with them.

Alexis quickly put pressure on the wound and Ryan grunted in pain. "Come on, you can make it," she said to him and he concentrated on moving. One foot moved in front of the other, leaving a trail of blood behind them.

Jack pushed a button on his armlet. "Jay, you'll be happy to know what I saved your pet projects. They are a little banged up but they'll live. You can relax now," he said as the two of them left the room.

"Wish I could buddy but while you were playing God, Meria made an announcement, you should get to the bridge and check it out," Jay said and Jack could hear the groan in his voice even if he didn't express it. "I'm on my way," Jack replied and walked out of the imaging room to make his way towards the bridge.

Chapter Forty-Two

Jack walked into the bridge of Cerberus station. His screen was already on, divided into three sections. "What took you so long?" Grace asked. Jack shrugged. "I had to babysit the kids, they were going to be burned alive in a nasty simulation, but we avoided that," Jack said with a smile, his red eyes told a different story, however.

"Whatever, someone bring him up to speed," Mike said, trying to break up the nonsense. "Yeah, sure, I'll replay the message," Jay said, pushed a button and the screen flashed to someone else. It was Meria's face.

"Hours ago, one of my people went down to the surface and disappeared. Maybe she's dead, captured, I don't know. However, citizens of the wasteland. The time is now. Every beast you fear living under the sea, under the ground and every nasty thing you fear flying through the air at night is going to come to every excuse for a city that you have and kill everyone you know. Unless, of course, you surrender to me. If you surrender. I want you to light a large fire in front of your town's main gate. You will be spared. You have three hours to comply. Any who do not surrender, well, you know what happens next," she said and the screen switched back.

Grace couldn't help but notice that the offer to return Nyogyth was never mentioned. She wondered how old purple eyes would react to that bit of information. Then she knew that this was all her fault, well maybe not. She wasn't going to worry about it right now.

"Well, I do have to say I like a lady who knows what she wants and just how to get it," Jack said but his sarcasm didn't translate well and the others rolled their eyes. "That was twenty minutes ago. What's the plan?" Jay asked and the others didn't have one.

"Even if she can do what she says, we can't stop all of them," Mike said and they all knew it was true. "We don't have to. All we have to do is stop what we can for as long as we can. We'll let the two you almost killed infiltrate Seran station and do what needs to be done," Jay said.

"Oh, and what needs to be done, does anyone actually know?" Grace asked and shook her head. "If we send them in there, all that's going to happen is they are going to get caught, then thrown in the brig. Or killed," she finished.

Mike rolled his eyes. "You're supposed to have a little faith. All we need to do is get them wave readers. With their stealth units they'll follow the thing to the source of the waves and break it. They aren't helpless kids after all," Mike said and the others weren't so sure it would go as smoothly as that.

"Look at it this way, if we said no, they would likely find a way to try and sneak over there anyway and try to play hero. I think the only real training they needed is knowing their everything is about to be wiped out. I think there won't be any shortage of motivation," Jack said just trying to get past this part so they could actually make a real plan instead of talking about other people.

"Fine, whatever. So, I have an actual idea," Jay said, picking up on Jack's hint. "It'll be tough but we'll need to do mobile strikes. Scan as much as we can and fight monsters off where ever they show up. We won't be able to save everyone but I think between the four of us, we can put up a pretty good defense," Jay said and the other three thought about it.

"Well, it sounds good to me," Grace said "Yeah, me too," Mike agreed with her.

Jack just nodded. "I can't help but feel this is a trap," he added and the other three laughed, it was clear they all felt the same way. "Alright. I'll get the other two ready. I'll see you on the surface, but not too soon," Jack said and turned off the screen, turned and started to make his way towards sick bay to see how they were doing.

It didn't take him long to get there from the bridge.

Ryan was sitting on the edge of the long table and Alexis was there in the chair. "How'd it go?" Jack asked when he stepped inside. She looked at him first. "The, well, all is fine. Although he didn't trust the machine, we made it work," she said and he just shook his head.

"Alright, well the timetable has been sped up. Someone did a thing and Meria decided to let her monsters loose, oh, in about two hours from now. So, that means I need to make some minor adjustments to your stealth bands you have and get you ready to do what you need to do," Jack said and the two of them looked up at him.

Before they could say anything, he shook his head. "You have to understand. She's going to attack as many places as possible. Anything you knew down there is at risk. You understand right?" Jack asked them.

"I need to protect my friends," Ryan spoke up. "What do we need?" he asked. Jack looked at them. "First, you're going to need to blend in. The people of Seran station haven't had a fashion update in the past hundred and fifty years. Follow me. We'll get you situated," Jack said, turned and walked right out of the room. The other two followed him out of the room.

It wasn't long before Jack walked into what Alexis could only describe as a walk-in closet. However, there were no clothes inside of it, instead to large pods that had a blue glow to them. "Inside, both of you. One each as if it wasn't obvious," he said to them. Ryan and Alexis each entered a pod. Jack looked to a panel on the wall and pushed a few buttons. "There, that should do it," he said to mostly himself.

The lights of the pod increased for a few seconds and over their bodies, silver suits appeared that were very similar in appearance. "This is what the weird one wore when she tried to kill me," Ryan said and Jack shook his head. "Yeah, genius. It's standard uniform for the space stations, or was, anyway," he said and continued. "You're going to have to blend in, so wearing what you were wasn't an option. Now come with me, we have one more thing to do," he said and walked away.

Their new, silver suits made an annoying crinkling sound as they took each step. "Don't worry, that goes away in a little while. Besides the people on the station are so used to hearing that noise that they actually don't anymore. Second, you still have your stealth bands so stop complaining already," Jack said, even if they hadn't said anything at all.

"Okay listen. Cerberus station has a secret. The guys want you both to go to Seran station to try and destroy the wave emitter. However, I don't think both of you need to go. One of you needs to stay here and operate the Orbital Ion Cannon in case we need some back up. This is going to get insane and I don't like it. So, who wants to go and who wants to stay here?" Jack asked them.

The two of them looked at one another. They both had reasons to go, but, maybe Jack was making sense here. "I'll stay here," Alexis said and Ryan's eyes widened. He didn't want to go by himself and he didn't really want to go at all. But now, if he said that he didn't want to go and try to make her do it. He might never live it down. Especially after all of the complaining he did about how women were nothing but trouble.

"I wouldn't want to, you know, get in your way or anything," she said to Ryan and he rolled his eyes, swallowed his fear. "I wouldn't have it any other way," he replied as loudly as he could. Jack looked between them.

He knew what was going on between them, typical waste lander drama. "Come on. Alexis, you go to the bridge, wait there. Ryan you come with me," Jack replied. Alexis looked at Ryan, for what might have been the last time. She thought she could see a hint of terror in his eyes, but he smiled anyway. "You got it, see you soon," she said, turned and walked away.

"Alright tough guy, let's go," Jack said. The second they turned the corner and Ryan was sure she couldn't hear anymore. "Man, you gotta hit me or something. I can't do this," he said and Jack smiled. "I know, but you had to be tough and take the job. So, you're doing it," Jack replied to him as they walked.

"Damn it," Ryan said and Jack cut him off. "You're going to the station. Chances are very good you're going to get caught, and even die. So, some pointers I want you to remember," Jack said and continued. "First, destroy the wave emitter if you can manage it, but don't destroy the whole station," Jack finished.

"Why not, wouldn't it be better to just solve this and any future problems. That makes more sense to me," Ryan replied, not really thinking about the bigger picture. "Sure, it makes sense, but there is a power grid. I call it a terrible design flaw in the plan, but the plan went something like this," Jack said as they walked.

"The five space stations are connected and enhance one another. The four stations, each one, holds an A-class beast in stasis. So, if one station goes down, the power supply will be disrupted and the monsters will return. Undoing lots of progress, really ending the world. This is why we haven't just attacked them directly. It's the same reason they haven't attacked us. No one is willing to risk it, that's the basic jist of the situation and I'm sick of explaining it," Jack finished all in one breath. Ryan wasn't sure he heard it from him even once, or anyone up until now.

Ryan didn't need any reminders of those things. He only saw one for a few minutes, that was more than enough. The two of them made into a room. It was bleak in here, one table in the middle of the room and four gray walls. "What is this place?" Ryan asked at once, already starting to feel a little bit nervous. "Engineering. I just need to modify your stealth armband to track the waves. You can find the machine, unless you get caught, arm please," Jack said as a panel opened up on the wall.

Ryan put his arm on the table with the black stealth armlet on it. "Don't worry I've done this at least, I don't know, twice. I'm pretty sure it won't blow up or anything," Jack said as he pulled a tool that looked like a screwdriver without the metal piece attached, but just as long.

"It's all about the frequencies. Just need to make a little adjustment here. Hold still," Jack said and pushed the button. The device made a strange sound and Ryan had no idea what was going on or how this was changing anything.

After a few seconds of waving the buzzing, weird sounding tool over Ryan's stealth armlet and it beeped. Thankfully it didn't explode or anything like that. Jack turned the machine off and smiled. "You're good to go. Is there anything else you might need before heading over there?" Jack asked and Ryan thought about it. "A weapon, something to use and blow up the, whatever it is I'm looking for," Ryan said. Jack shook his head. "Of course, how could I forget something as important as that," he said, but then his eyes locked on to Ryan's.

"If you bring any weapons on that ship, it'll detect you immediately. You're going to have to get creative," Jack informed him. Ryan hated every part of this and had no idea what he was going to do now. "Well, kid. I hate to do this but you need to go, and so do I. Let's just keep this whole you going on your own thing between us, okay?" Jack asked him.

Ryan just nodded in response. Of all the thoughts running through his mind right, the thought of ever coming back wasn't one of them. "Well. Time to go. Remember, don't get caught and don't do anything stupid, let's get to the transport room," Jack said, he thought he was being helpful. Ryan didn't think so, but didn't bother to say anything. The two of them left the gray room and walked a short distance to one of the various transport rooms on the station.

"Good luck, kid," Jack said as he stepped on to the platform. "I'm sending you to level B, it's the least populated and hopefully no one will notice your arrival. Don't forget to turn your stealth on when you get there," Jack reminded him. Ryan looked at his armlet and nodded. With that being said Jack pressed the button on the console and Ryan disappeared in a flash of white light.

"Yeah, this is never going to work," Jack said to himself and started to make his way to the bridge.

Chapter Forty-Three

Jay was hovering in his knight, about nine miles above the surface of the planet. "I'm over sector six and everything is quiet," Jay said into the communicator. "Yeah, it's quiet but we're early so keep an eye out for anything, you know, weird," Grace replied and Jay rolled his eyes.

"It is a trap but we still need to be here. As long as we keep the stealth shields up we won't be shot out of the sky like I was," Grace said to them. "You got shot down. That was such a rookie move," Jay replied to her and laughed. Grace didn't bother to reply to that. Jay was going to keep talking when suddenly a red dot appeared on his radar. "Alright, I have incoming on sector six. Just south of Stiaburg, looks like it's just one B class monster but I'm not sure what it is. There is no signal fire. Stiaburg has decided to make a stand," Jay said and almost smiled.

"Too bad. If Meria keeps her word anyone who did would have been safe. Just would have meant less targets for us to worry about looking after," Mike said and that was something none of them wanted to think about because it was true. The defiance of the cities and towns was going to make this a lot harder than it needed to be.

"Oh well, we'll be fine, maybe," Jay said as three more dots appeared on his radar all moving towards the city in every direction. Jay was about to say something. "Yeah, I just got contacts in my section too. Alright everyone. If you need help, ask, but do the best you can," Grace said.

"Good hunting," Jack replied to them but no one bothered to reply to him. "Well, okay then. I guess I don't matter," he said to himself. He knew that wasn't true and wasn't sure why he said it to begin with. Seconds later three red dots appeared on his radar too. "And here we go," he said to himself.

Valzin landed outside of Stiaburg sending a large cloud of dust into the air as it did. The city was far enough away to be safe for now. Jay hoped that anyone who was going to leave did a long time ago because it was too late now. The ground began to shake. Even in the insulated imaging chamber he could feel the vibration through the metal.

"Who are we dealing with?" Jay asked. "Pridor, Shadora, Vicru, and Talor," the computer said and Jay took deep breath. "Crap," he said to himself. "She's really pulling monsters from the past," Jay said. "Correct, they haven't been reported in twenty years. Shadora, thirty-five years ago," the computer said and Jay had another problem.

He didn't know how to fight these monsters but how hard could it be. They were mind wiped behemoths. Jay waited for them to show up. He was sure that they knew he was there already so there wouldn't have been any point in trying to keep it a secret.

A few minutes later, the things arrived. Two of them on the ground and the other two lazily wading through the air, barely flapping their wings to do so. One looked like a Dragon from picture books and was five hundred feet long at least. He was surprised that Pridor could fly at all. The other flying one was a much smaller brown bat and lizard mix but didn't belong to either, Talor was clearly a C class beast. The two on the ground looked much worse.

Shador was pitch black from head to toe and it was easy to see where he got his name from, worse he was as tall as Valzin, standing at six hundred feet tall. The other thing on the ground was more like a giant gecko, it had white spikes running down its back and dark green skin.

Then a message came on to his screen, interrupting what he was seeing. It was Meria.

"Jay, you don't need to do this. Go back to the station. When this is all over we can get a drink or something. You don't owe these people anything. Come home, take a nap and we can talk all about it later, what do you say?" she asked him. Jay thought about it and just before he realized what was going on the message shut off at the same time the flying beast slammed into him, knocking him straight to the ground.

"Damn it," Jay said and figured that he should have known better than to be distracted. The room shifted back to normal. In his face was the flying thing, half bat and lizard. He grabbed the neck of the monster and tossed it to the right, doing his best to keep the fight away from the city.

Wasting no time, he used his boosters to return to a standing position. The other three had surrounded him already. They looked like Warga did earlier, all puppets. Dead eyes and lifeless. Jay felt really bad about being forced to do this.

Valzin jumped out of the crude circle the monsters tried to trap him inside. He spun around in the air and blasted Shadora in the back with red lasers from the palms of his hands, sent him stumbling forward into Vicru. This was barely a challenge, Jay couldn't believe they were worried as he easily escaped the two in the air.

Jay smiled just as the pitch-black dinosaur known as Shadora recovered. It opened its mouth and fired an equally black beam from its mouth. Jay was glad this wasn't happening at night but he was too slow to avoid It entirely. He twisted away from the attack and the black energy glanced off his left shoulder. The beam splintered into a thousand tiny bolts of dark energy.

The impact knocked him out of the air. He hit the ground and ignored the pressure the imaging chamber was giving him. If there was one thing he wished he could change about this was the sensor systems. Shadora turned and marched towards the fallen machine. Vicru ran forward resembling a large dog more than a lizard.

The oversized, long lizard leapt forward and put its jaws around the machine's neck and began to shake from side to side. Jay felt the pressure around his neck at the same time and he couldn't breathe. Immediately his hands went to the hologram of the monster around his neck and he tried to move its jaws apart, but they might as well have been a vice. With no time to waste Valzin fired red beams of energy into Vicru's left eye.

The impact of the beams caused the beast to scream in pain. Jay was thankful in its controlled state it could still feel pain. The second it let go he rolled away as fast as he could and got back to his feet. He was ready to go on the offensive when a deep roar was the only warning he would get. Then he was bathed in deep red fire from the top down.

Jay could feel the intense heat like it was the worst sunburn he'd ever gotten. It dropped him to his left knee. Every part of Valzin was burning and Jay knew that whatever this half-baked plan of his he had going on in his head wasn't going to work. It was time to show some force in this fight.

Valzin's boosters erupted and it took off into the sky. The red fire streaming off it as Jay rose into a sky like a comet in reverse. Jay looked over his shoulder and saw that the dragon was following him through the sky behind him. "Two flying things at once, my lucky day," Jay said to himself.

Talor was flying in his direction, no longer lazily flying through the air. Jay was seconds away from attacking when Talor let out a horrible screech of compressed soundwaves. The second Valzin crossed into the sound the whole structure of the machine began shake violently.

"Alert, sonic attack detected," the computer said to Jay. "No, you don't say?" Jay asked sarcastically and shut the boosters off. Valzin fell out of the sky and escaped the attack. The second it was free of the attack the boosters turned back on. Jay stretched his arms out as he flew and blasted Talor in the face with red energy beams from Valzin's palms. The attack slammed into Talor's face and the screeching stopped at once. Smoke rose from the monster's face as it veered away.

Pridor shot another burst of red flame at Valzin who twisted out of the way in the air. "Never thought I'd kill an actual dragon," Jay said to himself as he dodged the attack. He clenched his teeth as he spun around and came to a stop in midair, facing the beast that was flying in his direction. With a thought formed his curved blade in his left hand and his shield in his right.

Pridor was not afraid, in this state it didn't know how to be afraid. "Damn you Meria," Jay said to himself and got ready to charge the monster head on when another black beam cut through the air between them. Jay looked down and what he saw was weird. Shadora was acting as if it was fighting the control. Then Jay understood what was going on but had no time to act on it.

Pridor was too close and Jay spun out of the way, changing his plans on the fly he dropped out of the monster's path seconds before it made impact. Then he flew back down towards the others. Both of them now were acting strange, irritated as if something was buzzing in their heads. Pridor wasn't showing any signs of being distracted, however, and screamed in annoyance.

Valzin flew down, at the last minute pulled up and sailed just over Shadorah's head. Pridor, on the other hand wasn't nearly as agile. The two of them collided into one another. The both of them disappeared into a massive cloud of black and brown dust kicked up from the impact. Jay had no time to see what was going to happen next.

Talor slammed into him from behind. Jay was thrust forward and a second later it felt as if his head was going to explode as that same hypersonic screech came from the monsters' mouth. The attack itself was harmless to Valzin, but Jay, on the hand felt like his insides were going to explode.

"Electric barrier," he managed to say. Valzin's body was charged at once with more than enough electric current to knock the flying monster off him. The shrieking stopped but he still felt terrible on the inside. Jay knew that if he had to put up with any more of that sound it was going to kill him. He looked at Talor who was already recovered and coming in for the second attack.

Jay tightened his grip on the blade. He hated the idea of killing these monsters, especially when they did nothing to deserve it. But this thing, now it had it coming. Jay still had a little time, more maybe a lot, he didn't know how long it was going to take the other two to get sorted out. This time he turned his thrusters and sped towards the giant lizard bat thing his sword and shield raised.

Talor opened its mouth. It was going to scream again. Jay picked up on this and wasn't about to let it happen again. He wasted no time and threw his blade as hard as the knight, and himself could manage to do it.

The black blade sailed through the air, Talor was really good at flying straight, but turning, not so much. It turned to the side and the long end of the blade sliced through its underside. Like all the other monsters, instead of blood, steam burst out of the wound. Bright green steam trailed behind the beast as it veered off. Valzin's black blade returned to its hand, but Jay wasn't finished. He spun around and threw his shield. The black disk sailed through the air and lodged itself Talor's back. This time the monster screamed and dropped out of the sky, crashed into the earth.

Valzin wasted no time in flying to Talor's side. The beast's essence was spilling out into the air, it was moaning in pain as the bright green vapor disappeared into the air. Jay looked down at the thing, into its eyes. They were full of sadness, confusion. The thing didn't understand why it was in the condition it was. Jay hated himself right now. This wasn't what he was meant to do. He knew the beast would live, they always did. But they remembered, too.

Jay kneeled down. "It'll be okay big guy. I'll get you out of here," he said, picked the bat up, folded its wings in, too. Then he lifted into the air. Valzin left the other three monsters behind. Talor's control was broken by the pain. Jay knew he couldn't go far, however. He flew over the mountains, at these speeds it didn't take too long. He found a nice place, isolated. He landed and set Talor down. "Remember this, you stupid monster," Jay said, knowing that it couldn't hear him anyway.

The beast's wings spread out over the ground, taking in the sunlight. It stopped growling in pain. Jay wasn't sure if it died or not, but didn't have time to stick around and find out. He took off into the sky and headed back to the fight.

The other three monsters had fallen back under the control of the delta waves and were heading towards the city again. They were already halfway to the city. He was sure he could handle this situation when three more red dots appeared on his radar, at a farther distance out. "Oh, come on," he said to himself.

"Guys. I have six of them coming towards Stiaburg. They seem to be easier to deal with than normal but six might be a little much. Is anyone free?" Jay asked as he flew to intercept them.

Chapter Forty-Four

Jay's plea for help came over Mike's speaker. "Sorry buddy. I'm a little busy right now," Mike replied. It was true. Mike had a problem.

Jay's voice was replaced with Meria's own voice. "Mikey old pal. I was watching you. Especially you. I knew you'd be too stupid to step down so I got something special just for you, enjoy my gift," she said to him. Mike ignored her. He was outside Nulbar City, who had refused to surrender to the power of the Outlanders.

Only one red blip appeared on his radar. Up from the depths the thing rose. The last monster he wanted to see, but it was the only one it could have been. The eight hundred foot tall, four armed and scale covered beast towered over Azagon who stood at six hundred feet.

"This is Zloon. Azagon has faced Zloon thirty seven times. It has killed fifteen knights. You have faced it once. With the rest of the knights for backup. Good luck," Atador said to him. "Gee, thanks," Mike replied and swallowed his fear. Zloon's eyes weren't glassed over like the last time. No, Mike knew exactly what Meria did. She just guided this monster too him. No mind control was needed after that. Zloon hated this machine. It needed no more motivation, hatred was enough.

"Hey, big guy. I know we've had our differences but we can do this later, right?" Mike asked, it was pointless. Zloon couldn't hear or understand him. Mike took a step back, trying to suggest that he didn't want to fight. He was doing everything he could think of to try and stop this. Zloon took a step forward anyway.

The beast bellowed and started to walk into his direction, raising its four arms. Mike looked at them and swore that those limbs were as thick as Azagon's whole body. The city sat behind him and as soon as Zloon advanced, the coastal cannons began firing on the monster. The beams struck the thing's dark green scales that covered his chest, and did nothing. The beams spread out on impact and they looked like a more intense version of an ancient laser pointer on the beast.

Mike couldn't blame them for wanting to try and fight the monster on their own terms. "Turn on my modulator and contact Alaya," Mike said quickly. "In progress," the computer replied. Seconds later a new voice came over the speaker.

"General, thanks for the help but why aren't you running?" Mike asked and waited. "Knight, this is our city and we'll defend it, we decided not to run away," she replied to him. "Damn it, woman. Zloon isn't under mind control. This thing is going to destroy your whole city if I can't stop him. You should be running, you and everyone else," Mike replied.

"Nulbarians never run, if you die, we die with you," she replied and Mike rolled his eyes and shut off the communication. "Why does it have to be that way?" he asked himself but didn't think about it too long.

Zloon, while irritated at the deterrent cannons, quickly ignored them and focused on the machine he'd learned to hate over the long years on this planet. Mike noticed the attention had returned to him at about the same time and now he needed to try and figure out what to do now. Zloon started his advance again and Mike knew that there was only one choice. He had to save the city and to do that he needed to get the monster away from it.

"Follow me, four arms," Mike said to himself. He and Azagon took to the air. A shoulder cannon deployed and fired at Zloon's face. The blue orb of energy hit the monster between the eyes and exploded as Mike did his best to fly away.

Zloon reached out to grab the knight as it escaped but missed. Zloon had no interest in the city. He turned and followed the knight as it flew from the city. As the beast stepped away from the defenses of the city, they stopped shooting at him.

Mike had achieved his goal, one of them anyway There was no promise anywhere that if he just flew away Zloon would return to the sea and not just be mind-jacked again to destroy the city. No, Mike was sure that he had to fight this thing, at least long enough to get it to lose interest or one of them died in battle.

Azagon landed hard in the sand, it had moved far enough away from the city. Zloon was big, but it wasn't as slow as it looked and wasn't far behind. "Okay," Mike said to no one as he faced the thing. "I guess we both know what happens next," Mike finished and concentrated on the impending battle. He had no choice, this, everything about this was terrible in his mind.

Zloon never stopped walking in his direction. It was going to grab Azagon, tear him into scrap metal and kill the person inside. There was always a little shred of meat inside this thing, he wasn't exactly sure why but there always was.

Mike knew that there was only one weapon he had that could even damage the beast. Two long chainsaws extended from his wrists and turned on. The whine of spinning blades made Zloon hesitate. He knew the bite of these things well enough to avoid them. "Oh yeah, you remember these. Let's see how eager you are now," Mike said and was hoping that just maybe it was enough to convince it to leave, it wasn't.

Zloon got over his bad memories of the chainsaws and moved in for the attack. Mike moved back, blasting through the sand as he did. He was much faster than this ogre was, not that it made much of a difference in the fight. One wrong move would be all it took for everything to be over. Zloon didn't chase him down as he flew backwards, expecting some kind of a trap. He opened his mouth and let loose his own attack.

A torrent of black smoke poured from its mouth. Mike blasted up into the sky to avoid it. Everything the smoke touched began to melt. The sand liquified on contact into a soupy mess when it hit the green seawater. Mike hated that attack, he was sure just about every other living thing did too, it was too toxic. Mike watched as the black cloud quickly spread out and disappear into the air. If there was only one good thing about it, was that it didn't last very long.

Mike knew that It was far more interested in a physical battle and Mike almost felt bad for making him feel like he had to use it at all, almost. Azagon flew straight down and at the same time ran those chainsaw blades into the top of the monsters' armored head.

Zloon screamed in pain as the biting blades chewed into his head, lifted his top left arm, grabbed Azagon by the middle in one hand and tossed him to the side with ease. Mike held on tight and did his best to not fall. With great effort he spun around in the air and managed to land on his feet, dropping to his left knee as he slid back through the sand.

None of this was going according to plan. Not that there was much of a plan to begin with besides fight whatever the crazy woman threw at them until they died. Mike didn't think he would be the first one to die, but on some level, he knew he would be all along.

Not knowing what else to do, he stood up and took a breath. The four armed, towering beast waited for him to do something. Mike's heart wasn't in the fight, but he needed to try. So once more he ran right at the monster. Zloon did the same thing. Azagon flew forward and twisted to the left at the last second to avoid a fist that had swung in his direction. His right chainsaw plunged deep into Zloon's chest on contact.

The monster screamed in pain as black smoke poured out of the wound, so thick it almost looked like it was actual liquid. For reasons Mike did not understand, this smoke was harmless. Another small thing to be thankful for, he supposed. Then Azagon threw its left chainsaw into the flesh of the creature. Mike was putting all of his strength in attempting to bring the two blades together. Chunks of dark green flesh were spraying out from the wounds. Zloon screamed in pain.

At once the four armed beast grabbed Azagon and pulled the knight away from him. The chainsaws were covered in scales, flesh and smoke. Zloon held the monster in one hand, away from him. The pain it felt was already fading as those jagged wounds began to close. The beast looked at its prey and knew this was the end. It was going to crush it right here and now.

Mike felt more like a toy than a six hundred foot knight of nanosteel and power. Then he saw it. His opening. Mike wasn't sure if it was all the pressure around his chest making him light headed or just something random, but there it was. He brought those chainsaws down on the holographic wrist. One on top coming down. The other from the bottom coming up. He put all of his strength into it.

Those blades immediately tore into Zloon's wrist and in three seconds, the hand that held him fell from the arm. This was more than enough to send the beast reeling in pain. Azagon fell and hit the sand. Already the flesh of the monster was dissolving away. But those fingers were wrapped around him were still intact. Azagon quickly used his spinning blades to free himself.

The monster was in pain, and more importantly distracted. Now was his chance. His only chance to strike the thing down. Mike rushed the beast, took to the air as he did and went for the head. If he could cut the things brain to pieces, it was all over. He rushed with that one goal in mind. Zloon wasn't that distracted, this wasn't the first time he fought this thing. Ignoring the pain, he spun around and slammed its giant fist into Azagon's back putting it into the sand.

The force of the attack was so great that the metal of the knight groaned under the pressure and Mike could feel the both of them sinking deep into the sand. The green water was rushing in to fill the hole. "Damn," Mike said, realizing how stupid he really was right then. Nothing he could do about it now, however.

Zloon's hand was already beginning to reform out of the black smoke pouring out of the wound. It put its left foot into Azagon's back, sinking him deeper into quagmire of sea water and sand the impact had created.

"Warning, pressure limit critical, warning," the computer spouted out its alarm. "I know, I get it," Mike replied, it was pointless to reply to that but he did it anyway. He felt the foot lift off of him, it was going to come down for another stomp, he knew that much. But he pushed himself up with his arms. Not very far, that wasn't possible.

It was just far enough for him to allow himself to turn over. With only seconds to spare lifted both of his arms and put the chainsaws through the monster's foot as it came down for the second time. The blades chewed through the bottom of the foot and came out the top.

Zloon screamed in pain, lost his balance and fell back into the sea. The impact caused bright green seawater to spray up hundreds of feet. Azagon stood up. Mike was angry, now. A fight was one thing but being stepped on, that made him mad. Mike saw the beast there in the water. No, Mike couldn't explain to himself why that made him so mad, but it did the trick.

He ran forward, jumped through the air. He landed on the monster's chest on his knees. Mike had no more patience. Azagon began to swing his chainsaws into the monster's chest. Each swipe of the blade removed hunks of green, mangled flesh. Mike, in his mind, was going to tear out the heart of the beast and cut it into pieces while it watched.

Zloon was taken by surprise and roared in pain was the machine cut into him, sending meat and black smoke in every direction. He opened his mouth and let loose a stream of toxic smoke. Azagon's right arm was directly in the path. The smoke covered it completely and the arm began to melt on contact. Azagon jumped back before any more of the smoke could touch it.

"Ninety percent damage on right arm, repair time estimated to be at two hours," the computer said to Mike. His whole right arm felt tingly. Mike knew that he couldn't win here. "Guys. I really need some backup. This thing just melted my right arm and I don't think any of my weapons are going to do enough damage," Mike said into the communicator.

"We're all busy, you knew this could happen. Run if you feel you need to," Jack replied to him. "We both know I can't do that," Mike replied and for a few seconds there was no response. "Are you in the city or close to it?" Jack asked.

"No, I lured it away," Mike replied as he watched Zloon was already healed enough to stand. "Stand by," Jack replied to him and Mike shook his head. "What, stand by for what? How long. You can't just tell me to stand by and leave it like that," he said, worried now as Zloon started to approach him again. He looked up into its bright, glowing deep blue eyes and prepared to fight again.

Jack, if he had a plan, he was being slow about telling him what it was. It was making him nervous and he took a step back from the approaching four armed beast that was intent on tearing him apart.

"Okay, I got it, there should be a beacon on your map. Big red dot. Go there," Jack said and Mike brought up his map. "I see it, it's a mile away. I think I can manage to get the monster to follow me," Mike replied, he had no idea what was going on but not being here was better than being dismembered. Azagon took to the air and fired the shoulder cannon again. The blue orb slammed into the monster's still open chest wound and exploded. It screamed in pain and started to run after him.

It was a careful game. Mike couldn't fly far enough away to make the monster lose interest, but he couldn't get close enough to be killed either. He fired his shoulder cannon every few seconds while acting more damaged than he was. Of course, Mike had no idea what his final destination or what was going to be waiting for him when he got there.

Mike didn't know how long it took, but soon enough he was in the area. To his surprise, and horror, there was nothing here but open wilderness, burnt out trees and flat land. "Damn it, Jack. What the hell? There's nothing here. What's the point of all this?" Mike asked in a hurry, worried.

"Calm down, sparky. I need you to get away from the monster, fly. You have ten seconds," Jack replied. Mike didn't bother asking why. Azagon blasted straight up into the sky at full speed and curved away over the sea. Zloon watched his enemy suddenly fly away in confusion.

The four armed monster took one step towards the sea when a second sun appeared in the sky right above him. Zloon and Mike looked up at the same time. Mike knew right then that he was not far enough away and put his rockets on full blast.

Zloon screamed as the thick, yellow beam struck the earth. The explosion was immediate. The sand rose up in all directions as the deep red and yellow fire expanded with great speed. Azagon was hit by the shockwave, it wasn't fast enough. The knight fell through the sky and hit the bright green water seconds before the shockwave knocked him deeper into the sea.

Mike tumbled in the waves and struggled to get control again. It only took him a few seconds before he could pull up and get back into the air. The wave traveled out to sea. Mike turned back to the shore and saw a smoking crater that was half a mile wide, still filled with fire. The mushroom cloud of dust, black smoke and sand rose high into the air beyond what he could see.

Zloon's husk of a body lay at the bottom of the crater. It was in pieces, what remained of it. Mike knew the beast would walk again someday, but he wasn't sure if it had been damaged this much in the past and had no idea how long it would be before he walked again. "Orbital strike. Effective. But who operated the thing?" Mike asked.

"Not even a thank you, well, hopefully next time you don't need any help. Alexis offered to be my backup, don't tell anyone. Get back to the city," Jack said and Mike shook his head. "Yeah, I'm on my way," Mike said and flew as fast as he could in the direction of Nulbar city.

It only took him a few minutes, but when he got there three more beasts were already ravaging the city. Two C class monsters. "Figures you'd do that," Mike said to himself and revved up his remaining chainsaw before charging back into battle again.

Chapter Forty-Five

"See, I knew it was a good idea to leave you up there," Jack said to Alexis. "Yeah, I suppose it was but Mike is just lucky I didn't blast him into oblivion, too," she replied. "Oh, you were fine," Jack replied.

"The cannon needs to recharge. So, I hope you don't need it any time soon. It was just bad luck that he had to fight a monster like that," Alexis replied. "No, it wasn't luck. It was intentional. Zloon and Mike, Azagon, I should say have a very long history. She did it on purpose," Jack replied, but he changed the subject quickly.

"Alright, I need to get to work now," Jack replied. "Alright, if you need me I'll be here. I guess," she replied. She sat alone on the station. As she sat alone with her thoughts, the only thing Alexis could think about was using this cannon on the city of Hadoth and taking revenge for her and all those they have murdered in the past.

She would have three hours to think about it.

Jack was standing just beyond the gates of Hadoth. The sun was hanging lower in the sky now and he faced two beasts that were rising out of the sea to meet him. Jack expected more. He expected an army but this would have to do for now. Him and Saphiel would take all comers together. "Alright old friend. Let's show these monsters a good time," Jack said to himself.

The first to rise out of the sea was huge. The five hundred foot monster revealed itself to be Nidal. A beast that was light red, its skin was smooth. A long fin ran down it's back to the tip of its tail. It stood there in the sea, its head looking down into the churning water.

Beside Nidal, another beast rose from the depths. Comenas. A hideous sea beast that made Jack physically recoil when he saw it. She sure knew how to pick them, he thought to himself. Comenas was more octopus than monster. It stood on two legs, they looked like legs anyway. Its body was constantly twisting as the tendrils hid its true body.

"Neither of these monsters have been seen above the surface for at least ten years. However, Comenas has made his lair close to Hadoth, last reported," the computer said to him. Mike didn't care where they lived.

"Whatever. Let's just take them down before any more of them show up," Jack said and wondered if he was going to have to make the first move or if they would. Then he wondered if controlling the monsters was like a game or if it was more direct in the controls. He only thought about it for a few seconds when Nidal began to walk forward.

"Alright, you're first. I'll deal with mister squid later," Jack said to himself and realized that maybe talking to himself so much wasn't exactly healthy. He'd ask Grace what she thought about it later.

Saphiel stepped into the water to meet his enemy. It was almost a hundred feet shorter than the knight, this wasn't going to take very long. The golden fist rose up and swung forward the monster to put it down in one attack.

Nidal, with a quickness that defied it's looks, reached up and grabbed the metal fist, stopping it with one hand as it came down. Then the beast stepped forward, lifted the metal body up using its other hand.

In one swift motion he lifted the knight over his head and smashed it down into the green sea water. Jack was shocked at the turn of events as his vision in the imaging chamber flooded with water. He turned his rockets on and blasted away from the monster and back to the surface. The second he broke the surface black tendrils shot out and snaked around his wrists. "Oh, come on," Jack said as he tried to pull away from the sea monster.

The tentacles felt like thick rubber bands around Jack's arms and the more he tried to pull away the tighter they got. Saphiel activated his shock barrier. The power tore through the tentacles, they snapped away in pain. Saphiel wasted no time and flew straight into the sky away from both of them. The second he did was the same second the two monsters started to move right back towards the city, ignoring him completely once he was out of the picture.

Jack narrowed his eyes as he saw them walk away. He wasn't sure if he should be insulted or not. Normally a beast wouldn't act like this but nothing about this was normal. "Alright," he said to himself, lifted his arms and blasted the two beasts in the back with his bright blue hand beams.

The two monsters were struck and knocked off their feet, face forward in to the sea. Wasting no time Jack made his way to the shoreline. Once again standing between them and the city.

The monsters broke the surface again, unharmed by the attack. There was one hundred feet between Nidal and the shore. Jack watched the monster carefully, wondering what it was going to do. To his surprise Nidal jumped out of the water, cleared the distance between them and knocked Saphiel off his feet and into the city.

Saphiel and the monster slid through the beach side buildings smashing them to pieces as they slid through them. "So much for protecting the city," Jack said to himself and tried not to think about all of the people he might be crushing to death right now. With any luck they evacuated, but there was no way to know for sure.

As the two of them came to a stop Saphiel pushed the monster off of him to the right. Saphiel turned over and pushed himself up off the ground as Nidal did the same. The two faced one another again when a black slime covered Saphiel from behind. "Really, you just slimed me. How come all of you sea monsters are so gross?" Jack asked as the slime covered his vision.

The slime began to harden around him quickly. “What is this stuff?” Jack asked. “It’s, a chemical that includes—” Jack wasn’t smart enough to know all about the details and cut the computer off. “How do I get rid of it?” he asked the better question, the more important one. “Sea water will remove it or extreme heat. In the water this acts much like the ink of an octopus. In the air it becomes like glue,” the computer said to him.

“Thanks,” he replied and managed to point his arms down. His hands fired twin beams into the ground. Seconds later bright blue fire shot into the ground and fire shot straight up and over his body. Burning the slime away in mere seconds.

Saphiel stepped out of the fire. His body was still blazing as he did, the gold and the blue mixing around him for a few seconds. Then he clenched his fists, turned around and decided that the bigger threat right now, was the tentacle beast that could stick him to the ground.

Comenas screeched as Saphiel turned to face it. The voice the monster had was shrill and piercing. Jack cringed as he heard it, just another reason to take this thing out first. The black, tentacled beast didn’t look taller than him, but then when he took one step forward. All of the tentacles spread out in directions, hundreds of them revealing its head.

The thing had six eyes and a beak for a mouth. It looked goofy and Jack almost laughed. He prepared to attack when two powerful arms grabbed his arms and pulled them behind his back. Nidal crept up from behind and took him by surprise. “Damn it,” Jack said as the overpowering monster held him in place.

Jack struggled against the grip of the beast when suddenly the black tentacles began to slam against his chest. Sparks flew from the knight, but Jack could feel each impact as he was trapped there. The black sea beast’s tendrils were less like whips and more like thin, flexible blades.

Each time a tendril slammed into him, he could feel the gashes in the metal growing wider each time, the nano repair systems were beginning to struggle to keep up.

Jack wasn't sure what to do. He didn't expect Nidal to be that strong, it didn't make any sense to him and now he wished he would have listened to the readout of the beasts. He needed a plan, something that would work. Nidal must not have been able to feel how hot the metal was on his skin as he grabbed him.

Another tentacle strike whipped across his face. It felt like the damage cut open the skin on his face and that was enough. "Boosters to full. I'm taking this thing for a ride," Jack said to the computer and seconds later he felt the power ramp up, then the boosters exploded with bright blue fire. Him and Nidal shot straight up into the air together.

Jack turned and flew over the ocean, but he kept going up. "I can make it in space, can you?" Jack asked the monster as they continued to rise into the sky. The air around them continued to dissipate around them.

Jack wasn't sure how far in the sky they were but the city was far below them. A couple of miles, he supposed. It was then Nidal either passed out or gave up. He let go of the knight and fell through the air towards the ocean. Jack grabbed it by the tail and spun around in a circle before tossing the beast away. "Don't come back," he said as he watched the red monster disappear as it fell away and down into the sea somewhere.

He turned back towards the city and flew straight down towards the black, tentacled beast as fast as he could go. Jack was done playing with the monsters. Saphiel was approaching Mach two when he slammed on the tentacle monster feet first from above.

The impact smashed the monster into the ground, but the shockwave made buildings collapse in every direction. And it sent chunks of black flesh with thick red smoke trailing off of them far and wide over the city.

The main body of Comenas lay there, smashed into the ground, broken and dead, as dead as a monster could get on this planet. "Legs damaged eighty five percent, estimated time to repair, three hours," the computer said to him. "Can I stand?" Jack asked. "No," the computer replied and Jack shook his head, grabbed on to the black, slimy body and activated his boosters again. They barely came to life and lifted him and the body off the ground.

Saphiel barely hovered over the ground with the beast and moved back towards the ocean. The red smoke was trailing off its body in thick plumes. As soon as he was over the green water, he dropped the walking squid back into the ocean and hoped that once it regenerated it would swim back into the depths where it called home.

Jack turned back towards the beach, flew to it and landed on the sand. He faced the sea and hoped that his knight would repair itself sooner than later. He didn't bother looking back at the city he was trying to protect. He didn't want to see how much damage he did in the stunt he pulled. He was just going to watch the sun go down for a little bit and hope for the best.

"Jack, did you really give the control of an Orbital cannon to a teenager?" Grace asked through the communicator. "Yeah, why. I figured we could use the extra fire power," Jack replied and shrugged. He knew that Mike couldn't keep his mouth shut. "I hope that doesn't, you know, turn out to be a bad choice on your part later on," Grace replied and signed off.

"I'm sure everything will be just fine," he said to himself, but he couldn't help but wonder what Ryan was up to. Surely, he had to have made some progress by now at least.

Chapter Forty-Six

Ryan was holding his breath. The transport to the space station worked out perfectly. Now he found himself in a hallway, invisible and hugging the metal wall. His armlet was telling him where to go with a soft beep that he was sure that only he could hear somehow, at least he hoped that was the case.

No, Ryan's situation was fine but he was not. The stress was causing him to sweat and the fear was making it nearly impossible to move forward. He carefully put one foot in front of another. Took a step forward. He expected this stealth thing on his arm to fail at any second and some security team to come grab him. But it didn't, at least not yet.

Ryan finally let his breath out quietly and started to walk. This place reminded him very much of any of the other stations, however he could hear lots of people that felt like they were just beyond the walls. It was strange because these people didn't sound like they were in a moment of distress or planning anything and Ryan figured with everything going on down on Earth, things might be a little tenser. Unless, of course. They must not have known either.

Sure, staying on track was one thing but on the other hand he was sure that he might never be here again or anywhere else. So, he wanted to learn more about them, he supposed anyone would and it would only take a few minutes.

Ignoring the flashing light on his arm, he walked towards the sounds of the voices as carefully as he could do it and walking close to the wall the whole time. It didn't take him long before he came to a door, this is where the voices were coming from. Then he realized his problem. The door. If it opened up with no one to open it, that might give him away, and it would alert anyone on the other side in a second.

He turned around ready to leave and return to the mission, defeated, and his stealth armlet touched the wall.

"Alright, who can tell me what this is?" a voice said directly into his head and he nearly jumped out of his skin, he pulled away from the wall and the voice disappeared. Ryan moved his arm again and put it against the wall. "That's Mytlite," the crowd said, it was a crowd of children. Ryan knew immediately that there was some kind of class going on the other side of this wall.

"Very good, Mytlite is what this whole station is made out of and—" Ryan didn't care, removed his arm from the wall and kept walking down the hall. He didn't know anything about the schedules of this station or why it was so empty, but if he was near a classroom he was sure that he was in the school section of the place.

It was not where he wanted to be if class was dismissed and this whole place flooded with kids so he walked faster and looked for a sign on how to get out of here. Seconds later he came to a sign. He almost hoped to see a sign called evil secret lair with an arrow but there was nothing so helpful as that. Instead he looked at his armlet and held it to the left. The dull flash slowed down in this direction, to the right the beeping got stronger.

The decision was made for him and he started to walk in that direction but made sure keep his line of sight to what was in front of him and not just on the flashing light on his arm. Then down the hall a white door on the left slid open. A man in a silver suit stepped out and started to walk in his direction. Ryan quickly put himself against the wall as flat as he could.

The man in the silver suit walked right on by and didn't even bother to slow down. "It must work better than I thought," he whispered to himself without thinking and the man stopped. "Hello?" he asked nervously. The look on his face changed to one of almost terror. Ryan had no idea what was going on but he wasn't going to say anything else. All he could think to himself was that he hoped this guy just got out of here.

"No, seriously, is anyone there?" the man asked again, his eyes darted back and forth. Ryan was picking up that something was really wrong, maybe wrong with this whole station. Ryan got an idea. "No one's here," Ryan whispered. The man panicked. "Bob is back, someone help me," he screamed and took off running down the hall.

Ryan was shocked at the turn of events and could only wonder what any of this meant, it didn't matter. He still had a job to do and kept walking. When he got to the end of the hall there wasn't a sign of any other person there. Where ever that guy went he was nowhere to be seen, either. To the left, the light flashed slower, so Ryan moved to the right and continued on until he came to a problem.

The closed door loomed before him as if it were some unpassable barrier. On the side of it near the edge was a lock with a red light on it. No other buttons. Now Ryan had a choice to make. He could try to find a different way, or risk trying to open the door. There could have been all kinds of security here he didn't understand. Even after all of this he still didn't understand half of this stuff, but time was wasting and he was in something of a hurry.

Ryan pushed his fear aside and pushed the red light. The door slid open revealing more hallway. "Good to know," he said to himself and walked through it and kept going. Just when he was starting to get comfortable in this mission, a weird sounding drone came from nowhere. Ryan froze and waited for the security team to come get him. That didn't happen. However, he heard the sound of feet, people. Lots of people and they were all coming in his direction, from both directions.

"Oh," Ryan said and realized that now was not the best time to be in a hall like this. Thinking fast, there was only one real option. The door closest to him, he opened it and went inside without looking what was on the other side.

The door slid shut and he turned around to see a bunch of teenagers looking back in his direction. Ryan didn't move, he didn't breathe.

"Did someone mess with the door?" the teacher, well, Ryan thought it was teacher of some kind. "I didn't do it," the one closest to the door said. "Didn't touch it," another girl replied. "Remember when the door wouldn't close, I'm sure it's just broken again is all," the teacher said to them and continued. "Alright. Tammy, will you flip the light switch so we can get started?" she said and the girl nodded. Stood up and moved next to Ryan, almost close enough to touch him. Then she reached for the switch.

Ryan thought the dark would only aid his stealth, but when she hit the switch, the lights didn't turn off. Instead they turned a bright purple. Tammy instantly screamed the second she saw Ryan. The ultraviolet light was doing something to mess with his camouflage. Ryan appeared as if he were a solid black shadow person standing in front of the door.

The teacher slammed the security button under the desk immediately. An alarm began to blare. Without even thinking Ryan opened the door again and ran out. Once he was in the normal light he turned invisible again, at least he hoped he did.

Running down the hall, the alarm still blared. Ryan was sure he could find a place to hide for a while. Maybe all of this would settle down. He turned a corner and ran straight into a security team wearing strange headgear. Ryan didn't get much of a chance to see all of it because the man in the middle pulled the trigger. A thin wire fired from the weapon and hit him in the chest. The electricity flowed into him and knocked him to the ground.

He felt like he was on fire and every part of his body hurt as he lay there. The power shut his stealth armlet off. "Bring him to the brig. Report this to Meria. I don't know what's going on but we'll let her decide what to do about it. We just catch them," a man said, Ryan could barely hear them, everything in his head was ringing.

Ryan felt hand grab him by the wrists. He couldn't move, or even cry out in pain as they dragged him by his arms. He was thankful the floor was smooth at least. "Hit him with a shot of some L, just in case he snaps out of it," one guard said to another.

"Oh sure, yeah," the other guard said. Ryan felt a sharp jab in his arm a few seconds later. Then as he was pulled along the floor, the hallway started to spin and everything went black.

He woke up on another cold, metal floor. He was still spinning and felt like he was going to throw up, but that feeling was quickly fading. Then it was replaced by another. Overwhelming panic. He sat up, put his hand on his head.

"Woah there, buddy. You got a dose of L, take it easy," a voice said to him. "What, never mind, how long have I been out?" Ryan asked at once. "Just a few minutes since they threw you in here. L doesn't last that long. So, what'd you do to get locked in here?" the man asked.

"Look, I'm going to be honest. I don't belong here. I got caught," Ryan said, and even if he didn't belong, his silver uniform made him fit in. "Is that right?" the man asked. "Well no one really belongs here and yeah, it's obvious you got caught," he said and rolled his eyes.

"No, you don't understand. I'm not from here. I got caught. You people are trying to destroy my whole world with an army of monsters. I need to stop it," Ryan said, there was no point in lying about it now. Lam smiled. "Yeah, I know. I didn't like the idea and they threw me in here," he said and sighed.

"Wait, you know about it, well if you don't like it either we need to get out of here and stop it, at any cost," Ryan said and Lam nodded. "That'd be great, but you might have noticed the forcefield, and the fact we're locked up might mess up your mission," Lam replied.

"Well, do you have any ideas on how to get out of here?" Ryan asked and Lam thought about it. "No. Not one. Besides one of us dying and trying to trick the guards, but if we pretend to die these cells are equipped with incinerators. They'll just torch us, so that won't work," Lam said and Ryan shivered at the thought of being burned alive.

"The guards never took that thing off your arm. Does it still work?" Lam asked and pointed at it. Ryan looked and to his surprise it was still there. He wasn't sure why they didn't take it but now wasn't the time to worry about it. Ryan soon realized that it wasn't the only thing the guards didn't take. His weapon was still on his side too and he thought that was very strange.

"That thing looks like mine," Lam said and lifted his arm. "But I can see it's not like the ones they issue here, is it?" Lam asked. "No, I got it from another station. It's old world," Ryan replied and Lam thought for a few seconds.

"Well our problems are solved then. Just hack through the security with that thing. It's old world and so is all of this. Hasn't been upgraded since, well, you know," Lam said to him. Ryan shook his head. "And I'd know how to do that?" he asked, Lam shrugged.

"You'd better figure it out because pretty soon Meria is going to come in to say hello, and she's a whole lot smarter than those idiot security guards. Once she sees it, it's all over. You're either burned in that cell or thrown out into space. You're dead either way," Lam said.

Ryan decided to get familiar with his armlet quick after that little speech. He didn't know what he was doing. "Try talking to it. Maybe it's speech activated?" Lam asked and suggested. Ryan shrugged. "Hack security, open up the gates," Ryan said, but nothing happened. "Hack mode?" Ryan asked again, and again, nothing. "Come on, help me out here," he said and a hologram shot up from his wrist.

There was a blue menu there and infiltration mode was the selection in the middle. Ryan pushed it. This was overwhelmingly simple, but the more Ryan thought about it the more he figured the military would need things to be fast in times like this, so he didn't judge it too harshly. Ryan pushed another button, then the menu disappeared. The armlet's blue light flashed three times in a row, then went solid blue again.

The forcefields on the cells shut off too. "Come on, now's our chance to get out of here," Lam said and then something occurred to Ryan. What if this guy was some kind of a serial killer or something like that. He didn't even know his name and now he had to trust him?

"My name is Ryan, are you a serial killer?" Ryan asked him in one sentence and Lam stopped. "No. I'm not a serial killer. If I was, I wouldn't be here. Any serious crime like that is instant death. There hasn't been a murder on this station for fifty years," Lam said and continued.

"I think you meant to ask me what my name was. I'm Lam, now let's get out of here before the guards get back," Lam finished. "We met before, remember outside of the village. I didn't kill you and you were supposed to keep your mouth shut?" Lam asked and Ryan shook his head. With all that had happened he nearly forgot about that. "Oh yeah, I remember. Thanks for not killing us," Ryan replied.

Lam walked to the door and pushed the red button. He was surprised when the door slid open like it did. He figured security would be a little bit tighter here but that didn't seem to be the case. "What was your plan, anyway?" Lam asked him.

"I was going to go to the machine they are controlling the monsters from, then I was going to smash it to pieces. That's basically all I had planned," Ryan replied. "I don't know where it is but this thing here is supposed to lead me right to it," Ryan said and Lam just shook his head. "I know where it is but I don't think it's going to be that easy. Come on, follow me," Lam said and walked out the door. Ryan followed him. Still not sure if he could trust this guy but happier not to be alone anymore.

Chapter Forty-Seven

The sun was low in the sky, Grace had just finished tearing off the head of some underground C-class beast. Bright brown smoke was pouring from its neck. Nanic picked the body up and flew into the sky. The titanic lizard in her arms, smoke trailing behind her. "All clear here," she said into her communicator as she flew into the sky and away from the city. The second she was not over the city anymore she dropped the beast and didn't bother to watch it fall.

"If this is all Meria's army is made out of I don't see why we were worried, this wasn't so bad," Jay replied, the disappointment was clearly heard in his voice. "I don't know. Zloon was pretty bad. I'm just now getting back to full structure status," Mike replied, his voice still shaking from the experience and having to dispatch two other monsters with just one arm.

"Zloon was unexpected, but all the rest weren't anything special." Jack replied. "Whoa, okay hold on. I'm picking something up in the deep water," Jack said to them. "Well, what is it?" Grace asked. "Dots, lots of dots coming towards Hadoth," Jack replied.

"I'm picking something up North of you, Jack. Dots, more than I've ever seen," Jay said then. "I got a bunch too. All converging on Hadoth," Grace said. "Yeah, I think we're all seeing them now. Get here as soon as you can," Jack said, increasingly worried about was coming right at him.

The three knights blasted off into the direction Hadoth as fast as they could go before the real army of monsters arrived.

The three of them arrived on the shoreline outside of the city and stood together facing the sea. "Well, this is new," Jay said as he looked around. "How many?" Mike asked.

"There are three hundred entities approaching your direction," Atador replied to him. "Three hundred walking mountains of flesh coming in our direction," Grace said to herself in disbelief.

"I guess the space witch was serious about taking over. I don't think we can stand very long against all of this," Mike said. No one was too eager to reply to that. "Does anyone have a plan, a little bit of a plan. Helpful advice maybe?" Jack broke the silence.

"Yeah. I have some advice. We move fast and don't get bogged down. Four of us. Two hit the sky monsters and the other two hit everything else on the ground. We might lose the city but we're going to make one hell of an impression. People will talk about what happens here for generations, that's for sure," Jay said to them.

"That's a terrible plan. But I guess it's better than anything else we have. Who's going to do what?" Jay asked and again. No one wanted to volunteer in a hurry. The ground started to rumble, even in their knight suits, they could feel it. "Grace and I should take the sky, we are the fastest," Jay said and Grace groaned. "I don't think anyone is faster than anyone else," she said. "You might be right, but I just like watching you fly," Jay replied.

Grace was about to say something, then in the distance. It looked as if the whole ocean was about to boil over. It was raging as the line of horrific monsters began to break the surface before them. It was just as Grace described. Walking mountains of all kinds rising from the deep. Then things were screaming from the sky. The four of them looked up into the darkening sky and saw the it filled with a flock of flying monsters. Each of them showing off their several hundred-foot-long wingspans.

"Last as long as you can," Grace said, as used to battle as she was, the sight of all these creatures coming in their direction sent chills down her spine. She swallowed her fear, took a breath to calm her nerves the best she could. "Let's go," Jay replied and blasted off into the sky. Grace was only a second behind.

"Are you ready?" Jack asked. Mike nodded. "We both are," he replied. Jack wasn't sure if he was talking about them. Or him and his knight. He supposed it really didn't matter right now.

Saphiel and Azagon stepped forward but dare not rush into the sea to meet them. In the ocean things could turn bad in a hurry. The would wait until the army of monsters got closer to them to start the fight.

Grace and Jay were high over the city in seconds to meet the flock of monsters that screamed towards them. They flew side by side. "Have you ever seen so many in one place?" Jay asked her. "I don't think anyone has. Not even during the fall," Grace replied. "Are you scared?" Grace asked him. "Yeah. Every time I do this I always know that one of these things are going to get lucky someday," Jay replied, but he did his best to not sound worried about it.

The time for talking was over. One flying long necked beast that resembled a crane sped ahead of the flock and screeched, flew in for the attack. "I got this one," Grace said and sped forward. Nanic's sword, already in her hand, was quickly thrown forward. The pure white blade struck the beast in the chest. The thing made no attempt to avoid it like it naturally would. It screeched in pain only for a few seconds. Black smoke poured from the wound as the beast began to fall.

Nanic's blade ripped itself out of the monster's chest and returned to her hand. She grabbed it and had no time to think about what she did next. A bright purple beam of power was thrown in her direction. Nanic rolled to the right to avoid it.

Valzin raised his black shield as the purple ray was thrown against it. The energy reflected off the shield and was sent back into the flock. It struck another flying beast in the face and knocked it out of the sky and started it on fire on the way down.

Valzin wasted no time in flying straight into the floating orb shaped, one eyed monster that fired the purple beam. At the last second, he spun around and ran his long sword into the beast's eye and straight out the other side. The dark green smoke poured out of it as it fell to earth. The two knights looked at one another for a brief second, then engaged the enemy head on.

The ocean did not last long as a barrier against violence. The army of beasts from the sea had made it to the shallow water. The two defenders faced impossible odds. The first beast, a black and red skinned, six hundred foot monster was the first challenger that marched ahead of the line of beasts. It approached and Saphiel stepped forward to challenge it.

The monster didn't size up his enemy, instead it simply rushed forward to fight. Saphiel didn't have to think about what to do. He stepped forward and intercepted the monster with his right fist. The golden armored fist struck the head of the beast and knocked it to the side.

The monster didn't fall over and instead raised his hands in the golden knight's direction. The hands crackled with red and black energy a second before similar colored arcs of electricity fired at Saphiel.

The golden knight could do nothing, the energy struck him in the chest and arced around his body. Sparks flew from the metal but Saphiel did not fall. He walked forward into the attack and grabbed the wrists of the monster and pointing the hands up. The energy did not stop however, it arced into the sky in every direction and around the two of them striking the water as well.

The beast roared and forced its hands straight back down and normally, Saphiel wouldn't worry too much about any of this, but he was something of a hurry. He thrust his metal head into the beast's face as hard as he could at this close of a range. The impact caused the monster to stumble back and stop its energy attack at the same time.

Saphiel fired his eye beams at full power at point blank range. The beast's head was completely torn off and the two of them were concealed in blood red and black smoke that shot up from the wound. Saphiel tossed the body of the beast to the side just in time for another, golden skinned monster to burst through the smoke and grab him by the neck.

Azagon would have come to his partner's aid but he had both of his chainsaw hands in the stomach of a purple skinned thing that resembled a tyrannosaurus, doing his best not to get surrounded. He pulled the blades apart shredding the beast in half at the waist. It fell to pieces in the water. Wasting no time, he jumped back in order to not get surrounded. One mistake and it was all over.

Two beasts that looked similar to one another waded out of the water. Their bodies resembled stone blocks stacked on top of one another. The one on the right was bright orange, the left one was dark green. Azagon wasn't sure how to approach these two. His shoulder cannon fired at the orange stone golem. The energy blast hit the stone skin of the monster and accomplished nothing but sparks and smoke to roll off of it.

"What should I do about these two?" Mike asked, he'd never seen anything like this before. "This is Zok and Tor. Rock beasts. There are only ten in the world, known. No known weaknesses," the computer replied to him. Mike didn't care what color was assigned to each name. The only thing he paid attention to was the whole no weakness fact that kept ringing in his head.

Beasts kept moving towards the city. They were coming from all directions. These two rock monsters were may not have had a weakness, but Mike quickly thought of something that he hoped would might just work. He turned his boosters on to full power and rushed the two stone monsters that were in front of him.

Each chainsaw plunged into the chest of the stone monsters and he did not stop digging. The monsters were taken off their feet and pushed backwards. The knight didn't go very far into the sea but he didn't need to. The momentum was built up enough where he pushed the stone beasts off of their feet. Then he dug his metal feet into the sea floor and as he stopped, the two monsters were cast off the spinning blades and into the other monsters still coming their way.

The twin stone beasts never even had a chance to react before they were turned into wrecking balls that weighed one hundred thousand tons each. They crashed into, and crushed, six monsters that stood behind them. The bright green water started to fill with several different colors. Evidence the monsters he crushed had been either injured, or with any luck out right killed, at least for now.

Chapter Forty-Eight

Lam and Ryan were running down a hall. Lam was leading the way. "I need to know, is it true?" Ryan asked and Lam had no idea what he was talking about. "You're going to have to, you know, make more sense. "A time machine," Ryan said and Lam stopped in his tracks. "Uh, No. No one has a time machine," he said and shrugged. "Where did you get this idea from?" he asked.

"Someone mentioned it. It sounded like it was a cool thing and I kind of wanted to see what the past looked like" Ryan said and Lam looked around. "This is the past as far as you're concerned. This is one of the last remaining intact things that people ever made. Are you impressed?" Lam asked.

"Yeah, this is pretty cool. Too bad I couldn't be here for other reasons," he replied. Lam shook his head. "Come on, the guards should be on us at any minute," Lam said and then he realized that they should have been here already. The security wasn't this relaxed and someone should have at least discovered them missing by now.

Lam started to run again, and Ryan followed him and didn't have any idea where they were going. "We need to hurry. I don't know how long the knights can last down there," Ryan said. He had no idea what was going on the surface but all the things he imagined were bad, worse than he wanted to admit. Lam increased his speed a little bit. He knew the way to the place and it wasn't far away now. "We, you, are going to fail," Lam said then as they moved.

"We're running right into a trap. The security should have at least noticed we were gone by now," Lam said and Ryan came to a stop. "What can we do about it?" he asked and looked ate his unlikely partner. "I don't know. The chamber they are in only has one door in and out. We can't sneak in," Lam said and thought about it. "We can't, but I have an idea," Ryan said and took off his stealth armlet. "Put it on," he said and handed it to him.

"All you have to do is stay quiet, if this is a trap, then we should spring it," Ryan said to him and Lam shook his head. "I have a better plan. Keep the stealth, turn it on and follow me. This is the only chance you have," Lam said and Ryan turned it on and disappeared before his eyes.

"Okay, follow me," Lam said and took off running. Ryan followed him into the unknown. "When we get there. No matter what, you need to keep quiet," Lam said again and Ryan didn't say a word.

The two of them ran down the metal, static hall and the farther they moved, the more nervous Ryan became. The only thing he knew was that he didn't know what to do at all. Ryan wasn't used to all this running. Even in the wasteland most predators went after easy meals. He was feeling out of breath and it was going to catch up with him when Lam finally stopped. Before them was a large metal door. Ryan fought to keep his breathing under control. Once Lam couldn't hear him anymore. He pressed the button. The door slid open.

At once two guards in silver uniforms stepped out and Lam backed off. "She's been expecting you," the man on the left said and Lam swallowed. "I thought so," he said and he was lead through the door. Ryan stepped in right behind the guards, just before the door closed.

"What did you do with your waste lander friend?" Meria asked, turned around to look at him. "We made a deal. He got me out of the cage and I'd send him back home, he's gone," Lam replied and Meria shook her head. "That's a shame. I really wanted him to see the last stand of his tin soldiers and the creation of the new world. Oh well. I guess he'll have to be part of the old, soon to be dead world," she said and walked to him.

"Come on, look at this view," Meria said, put her hand on Lam's shoulder to lead him to the viewing screen. "The four red dots in the center are them, the green dots are monsters, beasts that destroyed our whole planet and way of life. Now little more than puppets of mutant flesh at my command," she said.

"And once the knights are dead, you plan to wreck the world again with these monsters, isn't there any way I can talk you out of it?" Lam asked, he knew the deaths of lots of innocent people wasn't the answer. Meria didn't seem to care. "They aren't our people. Most of them aren't even human any more. Not fully. Their genetic code has been altered by the very planet and the aliens they live with. The food, the water. The very air they breathe is toxic. The planet earth must be reclaimed," she said as the army of monsters kept moving in on the four defenders and the city.

"How, what kind of twisted science will allow you to fix the whole planet and control the monsters. Nyogyth isn't here. How do you know it's not going to explode?" Lam asked. Meria looked around.

"Don't you see all the people here monitoring the equipment. Nyogyth had them build it and showed them how to use it. I don't know how it all works, but I think it has something to do with that contraption there in the center of the room. You know. The one with all the lights on it. It kind of looks suspiciously like a weak spot in one of those games the kids like to play these days," she said and narrowed her eyes.

Lam swallowed, immediately he figured she knew something wasn't quite right. "Lam, I know why you came here. You want to save the people, the world. You've always been too soft on them. But you have to understand they were all going to die anyway. The population is on the decline. The alien beasts are over taking everything. Why keep the suffering around longer than it has to? These people are doomed. We need to do this," Meria said to him in a sad tone.

Lam glanced at the metal device in the middle of the room. "And what are we going to do? Replenish an alien world? Life has been fine here for so long and now you decide that it's up to you to change it without asking anyone and– Meria struck Lam in the back of the head. "I am the commander, the leader of all of this. Talk to me like that again and I'll send you down there in the attack. Then you can be smashed into the sand of your precious planet under the foot of one of the invaders," she said and Lam grit his teeth. The guards tensed up but she calmed them down with a nod. "Sorry. I won't bother asking again," Lam replied, rubbing the back of his head.

"And now, witness the end of the knights, once and for all," Meria said as the army of blips on the screen approached. It was hard to imagine each one was a walking mountain of death. "Yes. Witness the end," Lam said. Ryan had heard and seen all he needed to. He pulled out his blaster and pointed at the machine, the second he did however, his stealth was broken and he became visible.

Ryan had a clear shot at the thing. Meria didn't act surprised. "I knew you were there, kid," she said to him and he was confused. "Why do you think the guards didn't take your weapon, you think they are that stupid, no, hardly. I told them to let you keep it," she said with a smile.

"Even if you wreck the machine, two things are going to happen anyway. One, we can just rebuild it. Two, the monsters down there have all been chosen because they have track records with those machines. Even if you destroy it. They will know who their enemies are and fight the knights all the same. This will not change anything," Meria said to him with a smile.

Ryan figured all of that was true. He had no reason to doubt it. "What are you waiting for, shoot the thing," Lam yelled to him. "You have one chance to walk out of here alive. Don't pull the trigger and I'll let you live up here. We have the room. You can have Lam's old room," she said and smiled. "Man, you know she hates you and all of your kind. Don't listen to her. Shoot that thing. Neither of us are getting out of here alive," Lam yelled back and Meria turned to look at him. "You're half right," she replied to him.

"Sorry, most of the people I care about live down there," Ryan said and pulled the trigger. The beam from his blaster struck the machine and burned a big hole in it. Everyone working on the consoles around the room stopped as all the machines shut off at the same time. White smoke began to rise from the machines in the room.

"I'll be sure to send them your ashes," Meria said to Ryan. Lam closed his eyes, prepared for death. Ryan tensed up as well. "Put Lam back in the brig," Meria said as a guard came up from behind Ryan and took the blaster out of his hand. "Ready Robor. It's time I take care of this problem myself," Meria said. "Ryan you're coming with me," she said with a smile. Ryan didn't like where this was going and the guard lead him out of the room. Meria was right behind him.

"So, before we die. I have one question," Ryan said and Meria didn't care what it was, but she obliged him. "What?" she replied. "What's the deal with these stupid silver suits?" he asked. "I don't know, it's all I or the rest of us has ever known, so we just stuck with it. Also, it provides great radiation and energy resistance, practical but boring I guess," she replied as they walked. "I guess it makes sense to me," Ryan replied.

Chapter Forty-Nine

The four knights stood their ground. The sky was full of monsters, screeching, flying in strange patterns only people could have made. The ones in the sea were making landfall, lined up, an army. The beasts continued their mindless march but all at once, they stopped moving. "Guys, what's going on?" Mike asked as he looked around. Jack smiled. "That little bugger must have actually done it. The mind control is gone," Jack replied.

"That's great, but if you haven't noticed we're still surrounded by monsters. Giant, insanely powerful monsters who as far as I can tell, don't like us very much," Jay said. "Yeah, thanks for pointing out the obvious, attack now while the monsters are still stunned. Take out as many as you can," Grace said and she and Nanic ran forward into the monsters standing in the sea. "Damn it," Jay replied but knew there was no other choice in the matter and followed her into battle.

The stunned monsters began to realize where they were, but that was all they knew. A bright green skinned monster looked at his hands, vision began to clear. Then the heavy thuds of footsteps were apparent. He looked up and saw a massive metal machine running in his direction. Nanic, the bone white slayer. One he'd seen before and had killed him several times.

The curved blade was swinging in his direction, right at his neck. He had no idea what he had done to deserve this or be in battle. It didn't matter. He stepped forward and grabbed the wrist of the knight with his right, scaled hand. He stopped the sword cold and in a second opened his mouth, let loose a deep red beam into Nanic's chest knocking it back to the shore and to the ground.

The beast looked around and saw the other knights there too. It was hard to understand what was going on. It was clear something had taken control of their minds. This battle was one that didn't need to happen. The second the creature considered turning back to the sea a black fist struck it in the side of the face. It stumbled to the side, pain coursed through its body but falling wasn't an option.

The behemoth stood tall, taller than the knights attacking and most of the beasts here. The black knight must have wanted revenge for hitting the white one. It didn't matter. The others here were slower coming out their shocked state. The black knight rushed him. The beast stepped backward and grabbed the knight's arms. The point of his sword stabbed into his chest. White smoke poured out of his wound.

The beast pulled the sword out slowly and used the knight's momentum to spin it around and thrust it into the green sea water. His tail struck the white knight that had returned to continue the attack and knocked Nanic to the side, quite on accident. It wasn't his intention to do that.

The black knight rose out of the sea and right behind him another of his kind exploded from the sea, a turtle shaped beast with pincers for hands clamped on to the knight. Holding him in place. This was his chance.

The knights were out matched and they would be destroyed here and now. On the other hand. The knights had to be the same ones that freed them from whatever control they were under. The real monsters that controlled them like puppets. The monster narrowed his eyes at the situation.

The bright green beast made his choice and screamed into the air. His voice echoed loud and clear. The beasts were snapped out of their stupor immediately as they heard it. The crab turtle hybrid grunted but released Valzin reluctantly and backed away. It turned and started to wade off into the sea. The things that flew in the air began to scatter into the growing night sky.

"Guys, what just happened?" Mike asked, he was ready for a fight and it looked like one wasn't coming. "I think the monsters don't like being controlled and realized we didn't do it," Jack replied, he couldn't believe what was happening. Maybe kindness paid off once and awhile.

"Anset must have put a good word in for us," Jay said as he stood before the bright green beast stood before him. Jay lowered his weapon, it was all he could think of to do to say thanks for not killing him. The wound on Anset's chest closed and the white smoke was cut off. It appeared to get the message across.

"Guys. I think we won," Grace said as she stood up. The beasts were returning to the sea, to their old lairs and homes in peace. "Finally, we get a break, but what are we going to do with Meria, she's still up there," Grace added and the others weren't overly quick to respond.

Anset took a deep breath and started to walk away too. There was nothing more to be done here. Then, something caught his attention, something in the sky. He looked up and tilted his head in curiosity. "Guys, what's that?" Jack asked, the first to catch what was going on and looked up. The other three looked up as well.

In the sky was a falling star. A shiny point of light that very much appeared to be coming right at them. "No, really, what in the hell is that?" Mike asked.

"It appears to be Rabor. The knight of Seran station," Atador replied to him. "Oh, I almost forgot they even had a knight up there," Mike replied.

"It looks like we don't need to find her. She's coming to us. Will Anset fight with us, do you think?" Jay asked, none of them were sure they wanted to team up with a monster. They all watched as the star in the sky fell towards them. The longer they watched the thing the less it looked like a star and the more it looked like one of them.

Chapter Fifty

Meria was enraged. Her plan was ruined by some wastelander and one of her own people. The rage of the beasts she depended on had all but fizzled out. "If you want something done right, you have to do it yourself," she said to herself, eyes focused on the enemy below her.

It wouldn't be long now before she would tear them apart one by one. "You don't have to, you know," Ryan said, chained to a railing as they both fell. "Shut up, you're going to watch all of your friends be torn apart," she replied.

Rabor landed in the sea, the splash of the green sea water exploded high into the air around her. Immediately the four knights surrounded her, but there was a problem. Rabor was seven hundred and fifty feet tall. It was bright red. Her eyes burned with yellow fire.

"What the hell, seriously, what the hell?" Grace asked. "How is that thing so big?" Mike asked as the four of them backed off.

"Does it really matter, we are the only things standing in the way. Nothing has changed. We need to fight her," Jack replied. "Well, we could try talking to it first. I mean, that's always an option. We do know the pilot," Jay said and no one responded to him. "Fine. I'll do it," Jay finished and opened up a channel. Or, he tried to. He wasn't sure that he could actually do this.

"Meria, can you hear me, long time no see. What, uh, what seems to be the problem today?" he asked and there was no response. Not at first. Her voice came through, seconds later a holographic image followed.

"Problem is your little maggot of a spy over there wrecked my machine to start reclaiming the earth from those mutant alien things, clean the place up and make sure that humanity had a chance. Now I have to start over. I decided to take care of the only problem I have so that when next time comes it won't have any issues. If it means anything, I will miss you after you're gone," she replied to him and the image shut off.

"Yeah, I'll miss you too," Jay replied. "Alright guys. Let's take this monstrosity apart but be aware, Ryan is on that thing too," Jay said to the others. "It would be like her to hold a hostage, but it doesn't matter. We have to take her down. Ryan or no, don't hold anything back," Mike replied, the other three agreed with that.

Rabor was looking down at the enemies before her. The four knights and the monster that refused to leave. Meria smiled. "Let's get this over with quick. Activate all weapons. Lock on to their joints, heads, then fire," she said. "Yes, Commander, in progress," a mechanical voice replied to her.

The red giant's shoulders lifted up revealing batteries of missiles, waiting to be fired. The eyes started to burn with energy. Her arms bent and her hand started to crackle with bright blue electric light. The message was clear.

"Guys, we need to scatter, now," Jay said to them, no one bothered to tell him he was pointing out the obvious. Anset even took the hint and wasted no time in jumping into the water. The four knights blasted off into the sky. The second they did, Rabor's weapons let loose. A thousand shoulder mounted missiles launched into the sky. Twin burning bright blue rays tore through the air from her hands and equally bright yellow beams from her eyes.

"What in the hell are these missiles, I can't lose them," Mike said as he shot off into the sky. He looked behind him and there appeared to be at least a hundred tiny points of light behind him. "Heat seekers, composition unknown, recommended course of action. Blast them out of the sky before they do the same to you," Atador replied to him. Mike shook his head. "Yeah, sure" he replied and rolled his eyes.

Azagon spun around in the air and faced the missiles. Without wasting another second. Mike fired his own missiles, immediately realizing that he didn't have enough to counter all of the enemy's missiles. "Damn it," he said and watched as the weapons exploded, then watched as the remaining missiles shot through the smoke.

Azagon's shield appeared in his hand and he held it in front of him. At the same time, he shut his rockets off. The knight fell through the sky, towards the sea. Before he hit the water, the missiles slammed into his shield and exploded. They projectiles were tiny, but their explosion and the resulting fire consumed his whole form. Azagon fell out of the flame and landed in the water. His shield was on fire, black and dented. His body was charred, but intact.

Mike was shaken and held the rail beside him for dear life. "Damage report?" Mike asked. "We're fine, the shield did its job this time. However, I don't believe we should try that again," Atador replied. "Yeah, I'll do my best to avoid being blown up," Mike replied and slowly started to stand up.

Grace avoided the missiles, however, she was on the receiving end of the yellow eye beams in the air. Her shield was withstanding the blast for now but it was slowly pushing her back. That wasn't the problem. Grace could have easily deflected the attack and got away, but behind her was Hadoth. If she moved out of the way, the beam would cut the city to ribbons and burn it to the ground.

The beam was likely going to do that anyway because she couldn't stop it despite putting all her power into pushing back. The others were busy with their own problems so she didn't bother asking them for help.

"Do we have any more power to fight this or are we just screwed? Grace asked. "If we put any more into the boosters we run the risk of disabling other systems, this is it," Thal replied and Grace, well, that wasn't what she wanted to hear.

"I'm coming, Grace," Mike said and she looked over. She thought of a million things to say that weren't appropriate to the situation. "Well hurry up. I can't last much longer and the city is going to be burned to the ground," she replied. It was a nice gesture, but she wasn't sure what Mike was going to do to help the situation. Maybe a little team work could push back the eye beams. She didn't know, but it seemed to make sense.

Then out of the water beside the giant machine. Anset rose out of the water beside Rabor. With no hesitation the beast opened its mouth and let loose its dark red fire into the Rabor's side. It was enough to shake the metal titan's attention and cause it to stop all of its energy attacks. The machine only stumbled one step to the side and quickly regained its balance.

Anset prepared to fire again but the machine swung its hand back and bashed the side of the monster's head. Knocking it off its feet, back into the ocean. Anset screeched in pain as it fell back into the sea. It was more than enough of a distraction to allow Nanic and Azagon to rush the thing.

Azagon fired its own yellow beams into Rabor's chest sending sparks in all directions, however the attack did no visible damage. Nanic was right behind him. Grace flew under the arm of the enemy knight, at the same time she ran the edge of her blade across the side. The friction of the attack caused sparks to fly in all directions, but her blade couldn't penetrate the armor. The second she was clear, she managed to stop by landing, sliding in the water behind it.

"Okay, this obviously isn't working, does anyone else have any better ideas because we need to come up with something and in a hurry," Grace said, looking at the edge of her sword was still glowing red. "My attacks did nothing, maybe we should just call it a day and go home," Mike said but no one entertained that idea. "Well, I had to try," Mike said to himself.

"Let's get her to chase us, we need to control the battleground here. Come on. Use your heads. Hit and run, lead her out to deeper water. She'll follow us," Jack said and flew overhead, out to sea. "I agree, come on," Jay said and followed Saphiel. At the same time firing beams at Rabor's head, every shot was a direct hit.

Grace and Mike followed their lead. "If you want us, come and get us," Grace said. Rabor turned in the direction they were flying. Meria knew they wanted her to follow but wasn't sure why. "Fine," she said to no one and took off into the sky. She was fine but Ryan wasn't used to any of this and held on for his life as the thing jolted to life.

Size didn't matter, Rabor blasted out of the water and took off after them, Meria didn't bother paying attention to Anset, but the green beast swam after them in the direction they flew.

The red titan was not only bigger than the four she was chasing, she was also faster. Her rockets blasted bright blue fire and made the machine look like a comet burning through the night sky. Azagon trailed behind the other four and Rabor quickly grabbed the machine by the back of its neck.

Mike clenched his teeth. "Guys this hunk of metal is faster than we thought, she's got me," he managed to say just before he was thrust into the sea face first, disappearing under the waves at once.

Grace looked behind her just in time to see this happen. "So, she's chasing us. Did we have more of a plan than just to be minor annoyances?" Grace asked. "Yes. Now that we are not close to the city we are trying to not get blown up. We can fight without worrying about wrecking anything. Let's take this thing apart," Jay replied. He wasn't sure how they were going to do that.

Saphiel was tired of running. He spun around in the air, never touching the water as he did. Then he rushed the titan. Jack had no idea what he was going to do so he did the first thing that came to his mind. "Aim for the eyes," he yelled and his knight did exactly that. Saphiel outstretched his hands and fired. His blue hand beams flew forward, making the water below it boiled as they did. The beams hit their targets.

Rabor was hit in the face and proceeded to fly straight through the attack. "Are you kidding me, what is this thing made out of?" Jack asked, even the flesh of the monsters would have been damaged. Jack was in shock as the giant machine closed the distance between them. Grabbed him by the upper torso and slammed him under the water. Jack was in pain as he felt the pressure baring down on his chest. "Damn it," he said, helpless against the power of the thing as it held him.

It was then he saw a shape above the water crash into Rabor, it was just enough to make it let go of him and stumble back but only two steps. Jack wasted no time and fired his beams into the chest of the machine again. The sparks flew in every direction. "Be careful, I'm up here too trying to save you so don't shoot me," Jay replied and Jack stopped his attack. "Sorry," he replied as he did his best to stand up.

Jack pushed himself up of the water just in time to see Valzin's shoulder getting blasted with bright yellow beam, and straight through him. "Jay!" Jack yelled in surprise. Nanic dived straight into the machine's back, left foot first. It was enough to knock it forward. It tossed Valzin in Jack's direction as it struggled to keep its balance.

Saphiel caught Valzin. "Jay, are you alive in there, speak to me man," Jack said in a hurry. "Yeah, I'm alive, but we need a better plan. Did you scan it, see if you can find a weakness?" Jack asked "I tried but the scanners aren't penetrating that metal. I don't know what that thing is made out of but I don't think we can beat it. Maybe if we hit it all at the same time?" Jay suggested.

Jack groaned. "That's so generic and typical it hurts. But I suppose we can give it a try," Jack said and helped Valzin back to his feet and the two knights looked at their enemy. "Grace, Mike. Group up. We're going to attack it all at once and see if we can put a dent in that armor," Jack said "Really, that's the most boring thing I've ever heard but alright," Mike replied, Jack couldn't help but laugh about that, at least to himself.

The four knights backed away from Rabon. Meria knew what was coming and made no attempt to get out of the way. "Knights. I've been playing with you up until now. I know you want to combine all of your power to try and beat me. So, fire away. Hit me with your best shot," she said and waited for the attack.

"Awesome, so four corners or all in one?" Jay asked. Concentrate on one point, it's our best bet to tear through the armor," Jack said and it was decided. The four of them lined up side by side in a few seconds. Then they wasted no time in opening fire. Multi colored beams flew at the red titan. Meria smiled, pushed a button just before the energy made contact. The beams never made contact with the metal. They burned against a purple forcefield of energy, scattering in all directions.

They watched as their attacks were about as harmful as a gentle breeze. "Okay there is lots about this that isn't fair," Jay said and he realized that there was only one way to win. "Break off the attack, keep her busy. If she could use the forcefield before now she would have and we're on to something, I'll be back. I'm no good in this fight anyway with my arm like it is," Jay said, Valzin cut off his attack and blasted off into the sky.

"Keep her busy, sure, no problem," Grace said as she watched him fly away. "You heard him boys, let's keep her busy," Mike said and shut his energy attack down. Azagon unleashed his chainsaw blades. The others stopped firing too and brandished their weapons. "Now we do it my way. Go for the joints, hit and run. Don't stay in one place," Mike said and rushed forward to attack.

"How long do we have to keep her busy, what is Jay going to do. Why is all of this happening?" Jack asked out of frustration. No one bothered answering him. Meria watched Jay fly off. "No one said you could leave," she said to herself and prepared to attack, but she was distracted as a chainsaw blade against her arm.

She looked down to see Azagon there, sparks flying as his blade tried to cut into her metal skin. "Are you serious right now?" she said in disbelief. Ryan let out a small yell of excitement as the chainsaw made contact. She ignored him.

Meria fired her yellow eye beams but Azagon jumped out of the way at the last second. Nanic came from behind and put her right shoulder into the titan's back thrusting her forward. Meria was shaken by the impact, spun around to attack, but Nanic was already gone.

"Okay so you're being pests now, wonderful," she said to herself and Saphiel's blue eye beams hit her in the back, this time they hit metal. Meria always thought the forcefields being active only when she was standing still was a bad idea, but it was better than none at all. The sparks flew around her and she was beginning to get frustrated.

"I've had enough of all of you," she said to herself and flew into the air, out of the water and turned to face the remaining three who were still standing there, looking up at her.

"Do you think this is good enough of a distraction?" Jack asked and watched their enemy fly into the sky. "The missiles, we need to get out of here," Grace said and didn't bother waiting around for the attack to come. Nanic took to the air. The other two followed her lead. Grace didn't know if the missiles were what had been coming or not, but it was better to be safe than sorry.

Meria prepared to fire her missiles when Anset's deep red ray exploded from the dark water and struck her in the face and blinded her. "Damn these lizards," she said as her screen turned black. Before she could see again something hit her in the chest. Her vision returned and Meria was face to face with Nanic's eyes.

The point of Nanic's blade was attempting to impale Rabor's heart. The metal was strong, but Grace could see that the repeated attacks were beginning to take their toll. The point of her blade had managed to cut through the metal, if only a little.

Meria wasn't blind to this. Neither were her internal sensors. The alarm started to blare as they detected the damage. "Shut those off, it's barely a scratch, we'll be fine," Meria said and the alarms shut off. "It's just a matter of time now before they kill us both," Ryan said. Meria ignored him again.

Rabor grabbed Nanic by the waist and didn't let go this time. She flew straight down into the ocean with her blasters at full power.

Grace admitted to herself silently that maybe this was a mistake as they fell. Grace felt the impact of the water, it was about the same as hitting the ground. Then they fell farther. Every alarm she had was going off, it wasn't anything she wasn't aware of right now. Everything was going wrong. To her horror, however, Rabor drew its free hand back and it took aim. It was taking aim right above the imaging chamber.

"Well, this was a fun ride," Grace said, realizing what was about to happen. She prepared to die but smiled. Even if it was all going to end right here. It was alright, she supposed. Rabor's giant metal hand thrust forward. Grace refused to close her eyes, she was going to face death with as much bravery a she could summon.

The hand never reached its target as a shadowy form came out of nowhere from the side. Anset had smashed into the side of Rabor and knocked It away from her. Grace flinched as she watched a tail pass over her vision. She never thought she would be thankful to see a monster, and she really didn't understand why it was helping them fight. If all the other beasts would fight this battle would have been over a long time ago. Grace took a breath and rose up through the water.

Chapter Fifty-One

Meria was going to end this right now. She regained her balance, twisted around to toss Anset off of her. Immediately after that she rushed in Azagon's and Saphiel's direction with all the speed she could manage. The two giants in the water had no time to react as she crashed into the both of them, knocking them off their feet. Mike put his chainsaw blades under the wrist of the machine and sent sparks flying in every direction.

Jack was faster. Before they Rabor's hand could grip his metal throat. Saphiel twisted away from the grip and blasted back through the water. He fired blue energy beams from his hands and they struck Rabor's chest, right where Grace had earlier. The energy found it's mark. The tiny crack let the power inside and the once untouchable armor began to break apart.

Mike saw the injury and reached for it. However, his arms were just too short to reach the target. Black smoke began to pour out of the small wound and Meria panicked. She tossed Azagon into the air and away with her one hand as she backed away from everyone. She put her right hand over the wound, protecting it.

The three knights knew that if that towering metal thing was anything like them, their advantage wasn't going to last very long. "She's hurt, I think she's just going to try to kill us and get it over with," Grace said and was trying to get ready for anything that might be coming their way.

"So much for being invincible," Meria said to herself. The damage wasn't much but it was enough to do the worst thing. It would give them hope, the one thing she couldn't allow them to have. She took to the air. "Lock on to them with everything we have," she said. "Didn't we try this before and it didn't work?" the computer asked her. She thought about it.

"Okay. Lock on to them and everything around them. Set the missiles to proximity status," she said with a smile. "Oh, excellent choice," the computer replied to her. "We should have done this the first time," Meria said as her weapon systems recharged and prepared to fire. "No, don't do that. We can still work this out," Ryan screamed but it was pointless, if he wasn't cuffed to the railing he would have attacked her already. Meria fired the missiles again.

"Guys, scatter," Mike said and took off into the air first. The other two followed him as they saw the missile batteries slide back out. The missiles fired again, just like last time and once again did their best to escape the barrage.

Nanic was going to fire at them, just like last time to avoid being hit but the second she did and the missiles got close. To her surprise, they exploded. The shockwaves of the countless projectiles and the fire caught her off guard. Nanic was consumed with fire and fell lifelessly to the sea. The others realized what happened and what was going to happen.

"Get to the water," Jack yelled the obvious. Mike was already heading that direction. The missiles intercepted them and exploded in their path sending bright yellow and red fire. The two knights flew right through it and splashed into the sea at the same time.

"Grace, are you alive?" Mike asked. The explosion shook him so hard that he lost his footing and was smashed against the far wall. All he could feel was pain right now and he was pretty sure he was bleeding from somewhere. There was a soft thud as Azagon hit the soft bottom of the ocean floor. Grace didn't answer all Mike got was static.

Jack was thrown too. He landed on his right arm and was pretty sure it was broken. "Well, that was a dumb plan," Jack said. "A really dumb plan," he finished as he tried to sat up. A shooting pain tore through his arm as he moved.

"Saphiel, what's the status?" Jack asked. "We are operational, the damage was external. You are moderately damaged. I suggest you get to the emergency med station before continuing the fight," the computer replied to him. "Thanks, do you think you could bring it to me?" Jack asked with a groan. "Yes, I can do that. Please stand by," it replied to him. Jack looked around but all the imaging chamber was showing was the inky black of the seawater.

Grace opened her eyes. Blood ran down her forehead between her eyes and she groaned in pain. "Jay, were in bad shape down here. I don't know what you plan to do but you should play your hand pretty soon. I don't think we can last much longer," she said and almost started coughing but managed to hold it off. She didn't expect an answer. "Don't worry. I got this," Jay replied much to her surprise.

Meria was going to kill all of them, she took aim with her energy beams. "Meria. That's a fancy machine you have there. However, it's over. Stand down," Jay said and she stopped. "You ran off like a coward, and now you are giving orders. Don't worry. I'll find you and kill you sooner or later," she replied.

"No, I didn't run away. I knew we couldn't beat you so I took a trip. I'm going to kill everyone on Seran station. I have my sword on the hull right now and If you don't surrender I am going to start cutting into it," he replied.

"You wouldn't do that. If you destroy the station you know what will happen," she replied to him in disbelief. "Besides, you don't kill innocent people. You won't dare do it, come back down and die like a man," she replied.

"Normally I wouldn't. But if you're willing to kill a whole world, I figure I can cross a few lines of my own. And destroy, I won't destroy the station. I'll keep the power intact. The people on the other hand, are as good as dead, stand down. Leave the earth and never return. You or any of your people. If we ever see an outlander on the surface again, I'll kill every one of you," Jay said and the anger in his voice made Meria know that he was serious.

"Okay, don't hurt them, I'll leave. But when your world dies a long, slow death, don't come running to me for help," she said. "Don't worry, we'll manage," Jay replied to her. Meria looked at the ocean. The enemies she had rising up out of the water and how easy it would have been to kill them all. She wasn't going to risk losing everyone. "Can you send me back?" Ryan asked with a smile. Meria pushed two buttons on her console and he disappeared, his cuffs hung on the rail.

Rabor's rockets blasted and the massive machine took off into the sky. "What do you suppose that's all about?" Mike asked as he watched it fly. "I don't know, but good riddance," Jack replied as he watched the thing fly away. Anset watched it fly to the beast grunted in what could only be satisfaction, then with a sigh of relief, the green beast looked at the knights, then it turned and walked into the sea. Disappearing under the waves.

"Let's go home," Mike said. The others weren't convinced that it was all over yet. "Jay, what did you do?" Grace asked, still sore from the events that took place. "I'll let you all know on Oriab station, get up here when you can do it," Jay replied to them.

The three knights blasted into the night sky towards their respective stations.

Three Weeks Later

Ryan woke up in his bed. The breaking sunlight of the morning was barely lighting up the night sky. He carefully stood up. "Are you up already?" Alexis asked him. "Yep, I think so," he replied with a stretch and a smile. "Living with you isn't so bad I guess," she said and he rolled his eyes. "It's been three weeks or so. Do you have to say that every day?" he asked her and she smiled. "Yes. Yes, I do," she replied.

"Well, do you want to get the water this time or should I?" he asked. "I went last time you can do it," she replied and he nodded. "Yeah, okay fine," he replied as he finished getting dressed. "See you later," Alexis replied as Ryan walked out. "You can count on it," he said and shut the door behind him.

Sticktown was rebuilt since the attack, not that there was much to rebuild anyway. Ryan walked to his hoverbike and attached the trailer. Even If it was full of plastic water jugs, blood on the trailer, the stain of it anyway, could still be seen. All of that happened and even if wasn't long ago it made him sigh. It was a lifetime ago when all of this started and that person didn't exist anymore.

He shook his head, got on his hoverbike and slowly pulled away from his house. The trip was short and soon he got to the gates. Joppo was there as he had been for the past few weeks. "Matt still isn't better yet?" Ryan asked and Joppo shook his head. "And enjoying every minute of it," he replied with a smile. Ryan nodded. "Alright, I'll be back soon," Ryan replied and Joppo opened the gates.

Ryan drove to the river, blaster at his side. This was a job that needed to be done, but lately, his heart wasn't in it anymore. He knew there was much more out there and for a brief moment in time he got to experience a much bigger world. Ryan missed all it all now that it was over and he was doing his best to put the past behind him. He started to get to work filling the jugs of water.

Jay sat at his desk in Narvoi. The kids started to file into the classroom and he smiled. The world was right again. He couldn't help but wonder if Meria was right. Was everything coming to an end anyway or was it all nonsense? None of that mattered right now. All that mattered now was that he had to do what he had done for the past five years and do his best to ensure the future. One kid near the front raised her hand.

"Yes," Jay said and she put her hand down. "Do you think we'll ever see the knights again?" she asked. Jay smiled. "I suspect if we need them, they'll be around," he replied to her and continued. "Alright, it's been three weeks. I think its high time we all move on, don't you?" Jay asked and prepared to start the day's lesson on basic survival in the wasteland.

Mike returned to his old ways. Drifting from town to town, spending every Zop he earned on getting his next meal and drink. But at night, when he had enough he returned to Syrgoth station to sleep. It was where he was now, just waking up. He didn't know what time it was and honestly, it didn't matter. It was always happy hour somewhere in the wasteland, all he had to do was find it.

But the truth was he didn't drink to forget or dull the pain. He realized that he did it just to not be alone. Even if he was alone, at a bar, it was usually crowded with other people. That is what he needed the most. This empty old station was threatening to drive him insane. However, an idea was forming in his mind. Something that was crazy enough that it just might work.

Jack had returned to his island and nothing had changed. The raiders there were not even aware that anything was at stake at all. He had restored order, as much as there was to restore. Now he was watching a captured ship crew fight for their lives and freedom against the barbaric people he ruled over.

He took no pleasure in it, but it was either this, or let the Nogra people spread unchecked to other island civilizations. Jack knew no one else would do the job, he just didn't know how long he would have to do it for.

Grace returned to Liberville. The cold air didn't make her feel any better and life had returned to normal. However, instead of keeping herself isolated. She took over the role as the town doctor. After learning what had to be done to save the world and how close they all came to death. She would never again stand by while people were suffering, and on this world, suffering was never in short supply.

She still visits the grave of her son, it's something she never would get over and now that the ordeal was over the painful memories would return. Especially at night.

The world moved forward. Most of the cities and all the people in them never knew just how close they came to being destroyed. However, high above it all Meria sat in Seran station. Defeated along with the rest of her people.

Nyogyth felt responsible for everything because she got captured. She was sitting in her chair on the station, thankful that they negotiated her release so she could come home. Then there was a curious beeping on her long-range scanners. At first, she was too lost in thought to notice it, but it's constant beep was unending and forced her to look.

"Oh my," she said once she took a good look at it. "Commander you might want to look at this," she said and Meria made she way over to the screen. At first, she didn't know what she was looking at. Then the outline became clear. It was the outline of a large ship.

"It'll be here in six months, if it continues its current speed," Nyogyth said. Meria narrowed her eyes. "Maybe the world is going to end sooner than I thought," she replied as the both of them watched the ship on their screen silently moved its way through the depths of space.

About the Author

My name is Jesse Wilson. I live in South Dakota and I am 36 years old.

I am also a lifelong Godzilla fan.

A long time ago, I realized that the world inside my head was more appealing than the world I lived in on a day to day basis most of the time and real life was something I was never particularly good at. There was always something missing and I never seemed to find it.

I had dabbled in the art of writing since as long as I can remember. Silly stories that never really amounted to anything, while most people give this up and move on, I just kept moving forward. Never stopping, by the time I was 13 years old I had managed to create my first Godzilla fan fiction stories. None of them were that great, but not too many people are at the beginning of anything.

At 15 had started to role play online, free form role playing, they called it. This is where I learned how to show things and not just tell them. This was way before the online games they have today. For fun I used to help other people create their character profiles, I got rather good at it, too. This is where I became addicted to writing.

I wrote my first "novel" when I was 16 years old in High school, it started out as something I just wanted to try, but the thing ended up saving me in English class when I told the teacher and she allowed me to turn the thing for extra credit. I still don't know how that ended up working, but it did. I managed to turn the thing into a trilogy before I graduated high school.

Unfortunately, the whole thing was lost when a storm rolled through, teaching me the importance of backing everything up.

After graduation I just got a job and committed myself to "real life" everything that wasn't needed took a back seat, writing included.

In 2006 I rejoined the online world of roleplaying and rediscovered why I liked to do it. From 2006 to 2010 I managed to create one of my favorite characters, Bob the Supervillain.

In the summer of 2010, I began the thing that would unknowingly become an epic. The Delta Squad series, inspired by the people I worked with at the time. It started out as two thousand word drop in the bucket. By the time 2013 came along, the series had evolved into a thirteen-book series! However, it was all a hobby. Something I wanted to see how far I could take it.

2013 was a major turning point in my life. I contracted a near lethal MRSA infection. I was in the hospital for three weeks and almost didn't make it. Up until then I had just decided to "do my best to get by," facing death in such a painful way and making it this time, made me want to try a little harder. I decided that I would do my best to get the Delta Squad books published. Not self-published, but actually done by a real company.

However, I wanted to do more. Delta Squad was my main project but writing offered so much more. So, I dived into the world as deeply as I could. I discovered NaNoWriMo in 2015 and gave it a shot. I've done it three times and won each time, I'm happy to say.

In 2016 I discovered Kaiju fiction was actually a thing. So, I wanted to try my hand at it. I created a monster called Narbosaurus! Everyone I told the name to, thought it was one of the worst names they had ever heard, and idea too, even though I never revealed very much.

So, I wrote it anyway, edited it the best I could and sent the thing in. My very first book I had ever sent in. I had no expectations. To my surprise they accepted it! My very first book was accepted, the thing everyone I had told in advance had said was a bad idea, it worked out way better than I hoped it would.

Now, in 2018 I hope to see my writing career go further than I ever thought possible, and with time I know this will just be the first steps into something truly amazing.

* * *

To learn more about Jesse Wilson and discover more Next Chapter authors, visit our website at www.nextchapter.pub.

Nuclear Knights
ISBN: 978-4-82412-099-1

Published by
Next Chapter
1-60-20 Minami-Otsuka
170-0005 Toshima-Ku, Tokyo
+818035793528
13th December 2021

Lightning Source UK Ltd.
Milton Keynes UK
UKHW012006020122
396528UK00002B/128

9 784824 120991